THE KERI CHRONICLES

JADE SECRETS

A.C. ARQUIN

GET YOUR FREE STORY!

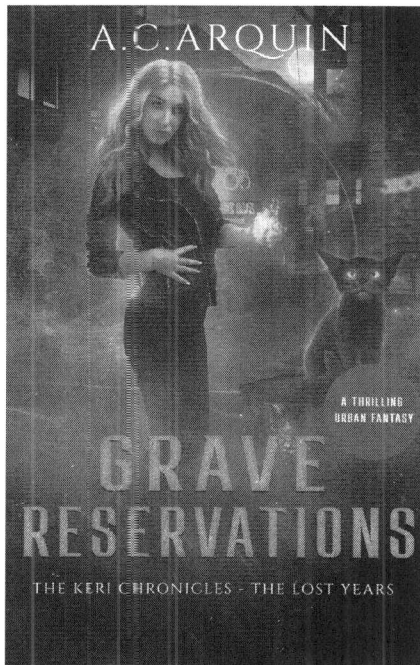

Join the Arquinworlds Reader Group to get your free story from The Keri Chronicles - The Lost Years! Go to www.arquinworlds.com.

1

The gray sky brooded low overhead, mist brushing the sinuous hills of the cemetery. White headstones spread out in neat rows, surrounding a small knot of black-clad mourners. Valora Keri lurked at the edge of the crowd, hunching her shoulders against the steady drizzle. The chill made the petrified fingers on her right hand ache, so she cupped them around the warmth of her butterscotch latte as she eyed the people gathered to pay their respects to the late crime boss, Andrei Vasilevski.

Val wasn't sure what she was doing here. Most of the mourners were strangers, and she and Vasilevski hadn't exactly been friends. She could see representatives from all of San Francisco's major crime organizations and families: the Wongs, the Anands, the O'Ceallaighs, the Yakuza, the Black Knights, as well as others whose names she didn't know.

But she'd been working behind the bar when Andrei was gunned down in the Alley Cat, and she'd been plagued by nightmare visions of his death ever since. The crime boss's niece and heir, Zoe Vasilevski, had explicitly invited her to the funeral, so Val felt obligated to show up. She definitely did not want to piss off someone who might end up being the next head of the Vasilevski clan.

Also, she kind of liked Zoe.

The girl in question stood beside the grave in a black raincoat, the fringes of her pink hair peeking out beneath a black head scarf. A stone-faced bodyguard held an umbrella over her head. As always, the petite girl looked like a porcelain doll. The last time she saw her, Val thought Zoe looked like a child. But there was nothing childlike about her today. Her eyes were dry, her expression hard as she stared at her uncle's casket.

Near her, Padraig O'Ceallaigh stood in a black suit and trench coat, looking as beautiful as ever with his tousled auburn hair and hazel eyes. His mouth tightened when he saw Val, and he pointedly averted his eyes.

Val sighed. She'd ruined that friendship when she was forced to fight Padraig for Pandora's Box in order to fulfill a deal she'd made with a Fae harbinger who, unbeknownst to Val, had wanted to use the box to open a portal and bring the armies of winter into San Francisco. Val had won the fight and the box, pounding Padraig's pretty face into pulp in the process. Even though she ultimately vanquished the harbinger and returned the box to him, Padraig showed no signs of forgiving her.

"He was too pretty, anyway, with his fae glamour," Mister E opined, following her gaze. The demon cat reclined on top of a white marble headstone beside her, puffing on his candy cigarette and blowing smoke rings into the air. *"You can never trust things in shiny boxes. They're usually meant to distract you from what's inside."*

"If you're trying to make me feel better, you can stop. Padraig was a good friend. He was kind and generous and helpful, and I messed it all up when I made that bargain to retrieve Pandora's Box. He's right to hate me now."

"Since you also hate yourself, perhaps the two of you can patch things up. You can form an 'I hate Valora Keri' club. You can invite Melinda Pearl and your former coven members from the Emerald City too. Membership would be booming."

Val opened her mouth to make a cutting reply, but another voice interrupted her.

"Not enough sense to bring an umbrella, Valora Keri?"

She turned to find Shen Wong standing beside her. The young man was swathed in black like everyone else, but his almond eyes sparkled.

"Would you like some umbrella? I've got plenty," he asked, offering her half of his oversized golf umbrella.

She hesitated, wondering what his intentions were. She'd only met Shen briefly, at a party where she'd been acting as Zoe Vasilevski's bodyguard. She knew he was Zoe's friend, and part of a Chinese organized crime family, but not much else.

He smiled at her hesitance. "No ulterior motives. You just look wet."

Val acknowledged this with a nod and gratefully stepped under the span. "In that case, I don't mind if I do. Thank you."

He raised an eyebrow as he noticed her gray fingers.

"Are those new?"

Val rubbed at the fingers with her thumb, feeling the rough surface. She sighed.

"It's a long story. The moral of it is: Don't lock eyes with a gorgon."

"Ah."

He let the matter drop, and they stood in companionable silence for a minute as the priest said a few words.

Shen leaned over and whispered, "Such a terrible thing. Did you know Andrei well?"

Val shook her damp curls. "Not really. He came into the Alley Cat a lot, but I mostly just served him vodka. I wouldn't say we were friends."

"The Alley Cat? Isn't that where he was killed?"

"Yeah. Some thugs came in with machine guns and opened fire. I tried to chase them down, but they got away."

"That must have been a memorable night."

"That's one way of looking at it."

Another way of looking at it was: Val had failed.

As the bartender on duty that night, the Alley Cat had been her responsibility. It was her job to keep everyone safe, from the girls on the stage to the customers. And she had failed. Andrei had died on her watch.

She could see the getaway car clearly in her mind. Unfortunately, remembering a black BMW with no license plates wasn't particularly helpful. Val had chased the gunmen for several blocks, but thanks to her lack of skill with her magic, they had gotten away.

Not only had she failed to prevent Vasilevski's death, but she'd also failed to catch the killers. A real red-letter day.

To top it all off, the Alley Cat had been closed down by SFPD, adding Val's livelihood to the list of casualties. She had no idea where next month's rent was coming from.

She looked at the sad faces gathered around the grave and tears started to well in her own eyes. She blinked them back furiously. She was not going to stand there and wallow in self-pity. Andrei Vasilevski was dead. She was still alive. She'd figure something out.

"Pride comes before the fall," Shen said.

Val glanced at him sideways. "What does that mean?"

"It means Andrei Vasilevski was rocking the boat. Expanding his operations. Stepping on toes. It's no surprise someone decided to take him out."

"Do you know who did it?"

"Not for certain. But I have my suspicions."

"Who do you suspect?"

"If you're looking for motive, any of the major families would have their reasons. But if I was a betting man, my money would be on Joumala's family. The Anands."

Val followed his gaze to the dark-haired young woman standing beside the grave. In contrast to most of the mourners, Joumala wore an expensive-looking white-wool trench coat over sleek black boots and a black headscarf. She looked tall and elegant beneath her yellow umbrella. Large dark sunglasses covered her eyes.

"I thought you were all friends?"

Shen laughed. "Whatever gave you that idea?"

"You helped me fight off the vampires together on the night of Padraig's party."

"Don't confuse temporary alliance with friendship. Just because we all hate vampires doesn't mean we like each other."

"What about the name they call you as a group? The Young Lions?"

"A marketing ploy," Shen scoffed. "Padraig's father came up with the name when we were children. A more apt name would be the Young Jackals. Here they come now."

The ceremony had ended, and the crowd was starting to disperse. Val straightened as Zoe Vasilevski strode towards her with Padraig O'Ceallaigh and Joumala Anand trailing at her heels. Padraig's eyes hardened when he saw Val.

"My condolences for your loss," Val said to Zoe.

"Fuck condolences." The Russian mafia princess's tiny doll face was hard. "I want the head of the bastard who did this."

Val couldn't stop her eyes from flicking toward Joumala. The tall woman's smooth expression gave nothing away. If Shen's suspicions were true, you would never know by looking at her.

To Zoe, Val said, "I'm sorry I let the assassins get away. I wish I could have done more."

"You still can."

"How is that?"

Zoe gave a jerk of her chin. "Walk with me." She glanced at the other Young Lions. "You can come too."

Joumala inclined her head coolly.

Shen said sardonically, "My eternal gratitude."

Padraig remained silent. He wouldn't meet Val's eyes.

When they'd moved down the path a bit, Zoe said, "I want you to find the murderers and bring them to me."

Val ran a hand through her wet hair. "Don't you have people for that kind of thing?"

"I do. I'm looking at one of them now."

"I don't mean any disrespect, but I'm not one of your people."

Zoe stopped and faced her.

"I know you're not. That's why I'm asking you. My usual information channels are coming up dry. I've heard the people who murdered my uncle may not have been entirely human. You have resources in that realm I do not."

Val raised an eyebrow. "You suspect the vampires?"

"Possibly. Or maybe something else. I don't know." The tiny mob princess locked eyes with her. "Help me get justice."

"By justice you mean revenge."

"It's the same thing."

"It's really not."

"You'll be well compensated for your time."

Val considered the girl for a long moment. On the one hand, Andrei Vasilevski had been killed on her watch, in her club, which made her feel responsible. And with the Alley Cat closed due to damages and the SFPD investigation, she also needed the money.

On the other hand, she didn't want to get any more mixed up with the Vasilevski family than she already was. Andrei Vasilevski had strong-armed her into working for him in the first place; if she'd been given the choice, she never would have.

"I'm sorry for your loss, but your world is not my world. Leave me out of it. The answer is no." Val turned to go.

She hadn't taken two steps before a scream of pain split the air. Val whirled to find a black-shafted arrow lodged in Zoe Vasilevski's chest.

2

"Get down!" Val shoved Zoe behind a headstone and slammed up a shield of wind. Padraig, Shen, and Joumala dove for cover.

Val's eyes widened as she watched the flight of the next arrow curve towards where Zoe was hiding. Gray chips filled the air as it ricocheted off the granite.

"Enchanted arrows. Not good," she muttered.

Val searched for the attacker. The mourners had their backs to her as they walked away from Vasilevski's grave. She swept her gaze across the graveyard… and screamed as the next arrow sliced her shoulder, spinning her to the ground.

The razor-sharp arrowhead had cut through her leather jacket and shirt and left a finger-long gash in her skin. Blood ran down her arm.

"Flying toads," she cursed as she reached for the wound, her head thick with pain and shock.

"Leave it. You have more pressing things to worry about," Mister E hissed.

"More pressing than a huge slice in my shoulder?"

"Yes. Such as, who shot the arrow? Where are they now? Are they going to shoot you again?"

"Right."

Val cursed once more. One little arrow wound, and her common sense went out the window.

Pressing her back against a headstone, Val squinted into the steady drizzle, trying to figure out where the shaft had come from. The cemetery was empty and quiet. The shots had stopped as quickly as they started.

Where was the assassin? Were they trying to line up a better shot?

"Lend me your eyes," she hissed.

Mister E complied, and the graveyard exploded with color as the magical currents became visible. Mostly the magic drifted in green and gold clouds, like the fog San Francisco was so famous for. Ambient magic that was being put to no particular use at the moment.

As Val had suspected, the shaft of the arrow lying on the ground nearby shone neon red. Definitely enchanted.

She thought about which direction the arrow had come from and followed the flight path with her eyes… then threw herself to the side as the next glowing arrow whistled through the space where her head had just been. Val scuttled around the tombstone, getting solid granite between her and the archer.

"This is insane," she muttered. "Who uses arrows?"

"Presumably someone who doesn't want the sound of gunfire to draw the police," Mister E answered.

She groaned. "In other words, a professional killer. Thank you for the theory; I hate it."

Val peered around the stone. There. A figure with a curved bow slung across their back was throwing one leg over a sleek black motorcycle. Gravel flew as they accelerated down the path. The assassin was dressed all in black, with a black mask covering the lower half of their face.

"Was I just shot by a ninja?"

She cursed as the attacker raced toward the cemetery gate. Val's own motorcycle, an ancient Ural with a sidecar, was parked in the other direction. Even if it had been parked closer, the Ural wasn't exactly built for speed. She'd never catch the assassin.

She struggled to her feet and called out. "They're gone. Is Zoe OK?"

"She's not great. We need to get her to my car," Padraig said tightly.

Val came around the headstone and found Zoe lying on the ground, her face pale, a glowing shaft protruding just below her collarbone. A purple stain spread over her black funeral dress. Shen held Zoe's hand while Padraig used his scarf to put pressure on the wound. Joumala stood off to the side, still wearing sunglasses in the rain, her expressionless face peering after the assassin.

Shen's eyes went wide when he saw Val's shoulder. "You've been shot too!"

"It's only a flesh wound." Val tried to smile, but it came out as a grimace. "Don't worry about me. We need to get that thing out of Zoe's chest so Padraig can put proper pressure on the wound."

The arrow had gone completely through the mafia princess, and the wicked-looking triangular head glinted just beside her shoulder blade. The aluminum shaft was slick with blood. Until they got that thing out, they were fighting a losing battle.

"We need to cut the head off," Padraig said. "But I'm afraid I forgot to pack metal shears in my funeral suit."

"Not a problem," Val said. "I can cut it off. Hold her still."

She dropped Mister E's magical sight — she could only concentrate on one thing at a time — and scooped up a handful of fine gravel. Val spun it into a tightly focused whirlwind the size of a grinder blade, then carefully applied the edge of the tiny storm to the aluminum shaft just below the head.

Zoe screamed and thrashed as the force of the wind twisted the shaft inside her. Val lost her concentration and the dissolving whirlwind flung tiny rocks in all directions.

"Watch it!" Padraig growled, ducking away as gravel peppered his face. "You almost put my eye out with that."

"That's why I'm wearing sunglasses." Joumala stood off to the side with a fashion model's studied nonchalance. She showed no inclination to help.

"Flaming ships," Val cursed. "One of you needs to hold that shaft still while I cut it. If it moves inside the wound, I'll never get through it."

"I'll hold it." Shen gripped the shaft, one hand on each side of Zoe's shoulder. "Just don't cut my fingers off. I'm rather attached to them."

"No promises." Val took a deep breath and resummoned her little whirlwind.

Zoe sucked in a sharp breath as the vibrations traveled through the metal, but Shen held the arrow steady this time and Val was able to maintain her focus and shear through the shaft in seconds.

She puffed in relief as she released the whirlwind.

"All right." Shen held Zoe's gaze. "I'll pull the shaft out on the count of three. Ready?"

The girl nodded.

"One…" Shen ripped out the shaft.

Zoe screamed and bucked in Padraig's arms, but the young fae held her tight, refusing to let her hurt herself further.

"What happened to two and three?" Zoe finally gasped.

Shen grinned. "I didn't want you to tense up."

"Can you sit up against this headstone?" Padraig asked gently.

When Zoe nodded, he released her and stripped off his black coat and jacket. He started to unbutton his shirt, and Val averted her eyes, heat rising to her face.

"What are you doing?" she asked.

"We've got to bandage the wound. Can't have her bleeding out before we get her stitched up."

Cloth ripped. Sneaking a peek out of the corner of her eye, she saw Padraig ripping his black button-down shirt into strips. To her relief, he was still wearing a tight tank top that he'd had on underneath. While the tank covered his skin, it did nothing to hide his lean muscle.

She averted her gaze as her cheeks flamed again. For his part, Padraig steadfastly refused to meet her eyes.

Val dug her nails into her palm and told herself to let it go. She'd burned that bridge. There was no sense crying over spilled milk.

As Padraig tended to Zoe's wound, Shen bound a strip of cloth around Val's shoulder.

Zoe called out, her voice thin with pain, "Now will you help me track those assholes down? Or are we going to wait and see who dies next?"

Val winced as Shen pulled the bandage tight. The assholes in question had just shot her friend. And they'd shot Val, too, which made it personal.

She met the mafia princess's gaze.

"I'll find them. These scumbags just pissed off the wrong witch."

3

Val searched the graveyard for more clues but came up empty. She did have the head of the arrow she'd cut out of Zoe, however. Hopefully she'd be able to track that back to the assassin. She carefully placed the wicked thing in the lockbox on the back of the Ural, along with a manila folder Zoe had given her containing all the information the mafia princess's people had about her uncle's suspected killers.

Before Val could embark on her quest for justice, she needed to get her shoulder stitched up. Fortunately, her housemate, Hillary, was a former nurse. Hilary was also a vampire, but Val tried not to hold that against her.

Riding the Ural home one-handed was a challenge, but the sidecar helped her balance and she eventually made it home in one piece. As she was backing the old motorcycle into her usual parking spot, right behind the stripped frame of a long-abandoned car now held together primarily by rust, the hair on the back of her neck stood up. She was being watched.

Val did her best not to show her alarm as she shut off the Ural and swung her boots onto the sidewalk. She pretended to straighten the sleeve of her leather jacket while carefully scanning the street. A tomcat with a half-chewed ear watched from the stoop across from her. Halfway down the block, a donkey was slowly pulling a scrap metal cart away. Otherwise, the street was deserted.

Still, the feeling remained.

"Lend me your eyes," she whispered.

"We really need to put this on our lesson plan," Mister E complained. *"You should be able to see magic on your own by now."*

Despite his whining, Val's vision shifted as the demon cat lay his magical sight over hers. As she scanned the street, a few objects stood out from the drifting clouds of ambient magic, shining with a light of their own.

One of them was the rusty car behind the Ural. It shone with a white light Val had put there herself. The car had an alarm spell that would send Val an invisible pulse if a magical creature came within fifty feet of it. Since it was parked right outside the door to her building, this was especially handy for guarding against sneak attacks or the witch hunters from the coven who'd been chasing her.

She'd needed to tweak the spell a bit when Hillary moved in so it didn't alert her every time her housemate entered or left the building. Which would have been annoying, and more than a little stalker-like. She'd had to adjust it again when Sandra became a gorgon and started living in the basement.

Unfortunately, thanks to her tweaks the alarm spell was now practically useless at guarding against vampires. Which was problematic, considering the queen of Hillary's former coven, Melinda Pearl, still wanted Hillary dead. Pearl would be more than happy to rip Val's throat out in the process.

But magic wasn't science. Sometimes it would not do precisely what you wanted it to, and you had to make the best of it. Also, casting spells that stuck around when you weren't actively pouring power into them wasn't Val's strong suit.

She'd learned a little bit of ritual magic from a witch named Paula when she'd lived with a coven in the abandoned warehouse they called the Emerald City in New York, but Val's knowledge on the subject was very limited.

She hoped to one day find some other witches she could learn from here in San Francisco, but until then her only teacher was Mister E. And while the demon cat living inside her had a lot of power — which meant Val had a lot of energy to draw on — his magic was a blunt force, old and primeval. If Val wanted a door blown off its hinges, Mister E's magic was perfect for the task. If she wanted that same door warded against intruders? Not so much.

She continued her scan of the street. The door to her building shone a dull orange, as did the windows of their apartment on the third floor. She didn't fool herself into thinking the imperfect warding kept them safe, though. If the vampires really wanted to get into the flat, her wards would barely slow them down.

Val had milked straightening her jacket as long as she could. She turned, ready to give up and go inside, when a cold, malevolent energy signature caught her attention. It was only a flicker in the corner of her eye, there and gone so quickly Val wasn't sure she'd really seen it at all.

Mister E's low growl confirmed that she hadn't imagined it. His back arched, his gray-striped fur standing on end.

Val's breath caught in her throat.

She knelt to fix the laces on her boot, stalling to buy herself more time to search the street. But the energy signature did not reappear. Whatever it was, it had gone.

Reluctantly, Val got up and ran her finger over the warding rune she'd carved into the doorframe before unlocking the front door and stepping into the building.

Her mouth pinched into a worried frown as she discovered another notice from the landlord tacked to the mailbox. Rent was past due, and she still didn't have her share. Her financial situation was becoming precarious, to say the least. One more reason to find Vasilevski's killers as quickly as possible.

Climbing the dilapidated staircase, she whispered, "Maybe it was just a random monster passing by on the street and not a hunter. Maybe they didn't see us."

"And maybe pigs have wings," Mister E retorted.

Val sighed.

"Yeah. That's what I thought too."

4

The smoke alarm screamed as Val stepped into the apartment. Choking black smoke boiled across the ceiling.

She dove into an instinctive roll, coming up with her knife in her hand, cursing as her injured shoulder shrieked in protest. She cursed again when the knife slipped out of her half-handed grip and bounced on the carpet. Val was training herself to use her left hand instead, but it took time to break a lifetime of habits. When instinct took over, she still defaulted to her right.

Smoke filled her lungs and she coughed. First things first: breathing.

Val spun up a small whirlwind, drawing fresh air in through the door and blowing the smoke up and away from her. She scrambled on her knees toward the living room window. Before she could do anything else, she had to clear out this smoke.

She'd just thrown the top window open when Malcolm's voice came from behind her.

"It's only burnt quiche, Val. You don't have to be so dramatic."

Her housemate stood on a chair in the hallway, waving a kitchen towel at the smoke detector. Malcolm wore green jeans and a chef's hat over a fledgling afro. His baby-blue apron featured a picture of a flying Pegasus that read, "Piss rainbows and fart glitter."

"You did this?" Val asked. "What happened? Did you forget to set a timer?"

Malcolm coughed and pulled the neck of his shirt over his mouth, yelling through the material.

"I was pooping, if you must know. I thought it would be OK if it cooked for a few minutes extra."

"Looks like you need some laxatives."

Val angled her whirlwind to act as a high-powered exhaust fan, sucking the smoke out the open window. Soon the air was breathable again, though the apartment still stank of burnt quiche.

"It's going to reek in here for a week," Val complained.

"Says the woman who never cleans," Malcolm shot back.

"I clean. I never leave dishes in the sink."

"You clean up after yourself. You do not clean. There's a big difference."

"You're making enough noise out here to wake the dead," Hillary complained as she wandered out of her room in a short red kimono. "And I would know."

Her black bangs were pillow-smashed to one side of her pale forehead. She yawned as she headed for the kitchen, exposing long white incisors.

"Hillary, back me up here," Val implored her vampire housemate. "I clean, right?"

Hillary made a vague warding motion with her hand. "Leave me out of it. I need coffee."

"I dusted the living room just the other day," Val insisted.

"The other day?" Malcolm cocked an eyebrow at her. "Which day was that, exactly?"

"Um… It was… last week? No, the week before."

"It was four weeks ago," Malcolm corrected. "And if you think dusting once every three months is cleaning, you've made my point for me."

Val huffed. "Fine, I'll make an effort to clean more."

"Thank you. That's all I ask. Now get out of the way while I spray everything down with essential oils."

"What? Why?"

"Would you rather the apartment smell like smoke or lemongrass?"

"When you put it that way…"

"Shoo. Hillary is making fresh coffee in the kitchen. I hear it calling your name."

Twenty minutes later, the three of them were settled in the living room, drinking coffee. They'd eaten the quiche with the blackened crust scraped off, which wasn't as bad as Val expected. The flat now smelled like smoked lemongrass, which wasn't entirely terrible.

Hillary cleaned Val's wound, examining the puncture with a practiced eye.

"Not too bad, all things considered. At least it's small. A few stitches on each side and you'll be as good as new."

"I can't believe you got shot by a ninja," Malcolm said. "I was sitting home, making quiche, and you were fighting with a ninja. Why do you get to have all the fun?"

"If you think getting shot with an arrow is fun, I can arrange for you to have that experience." Val brandished the razor-sharp arrowhead she'd recovered at him.

"Touchy, touchy."

"So you're going to be working for the Vasilevskis again?" Hillary asked. "I thought you weren't comfortable with that."

"I'm not," Val said. "But working for Zoe feels different than working for Andrei. She's just a kid, you know? Also, the assassin was using magic. And did you notice there's a hole in my shoulder? I'd hunt that goat-licker down even if Zoe wasn't paying me to do it. Nobody takes pot shots at me and gets away with it."

"You're so sexy when you get all aggressive." Malcolm sighed. "I wish I could find a guy like you."

Color crept up Val's cheeks. She tried to hide it by burying her face in her coffee.

"Awww, you're embarrassing her, Malcolm," Hillary smirked. "I think you've discovered Val's Achilles Heel — talking about feelings."

"She just needs to get laid," Malcolm said cheerfully. "Whatever happened to Alain? He was cute. I thought you two were hitting it off."

"Alain is just a friend," Val muttered.

"Too bad you screwed things up with Padraig," he lamented. "Now there was some tasty Irish cream."

Val's flush deepened as an image of Padraig taking off his shirt in the cemetery flashed through her mind.

"Can we not talk about my love life?" she squeaked.

"Or lack thereof," Hillary said.

"Or lack thereof," Val agreed. She cleared her throat. "Anyway, I don't have time for that stuff. Too many ninjas to track down. Speaking of which…" She dumped the manila folder on the coffee table. "This is the information Zoe gave me. It's all that they know so far about who may have killed Andrei."

"Your distraction tactics are transparent, Val. But I'll allow it." Malcolm leaned in and started leafing through the stack of papers and photographs. "Wow, there are a lot of suspects in here. I didn't know the city had so many criminals."

"Your naiveté is adorable," Hillary said. "I can name half a dozen organizations off the top of my head."

"But you used to be Melinda Pearl's secretary," Malcolm pointed out. "That gives you a bit more contact with the city's sordid under-belly than most."

Hillary inclined her head, acknowledging the point.

Val chewed her lip as she scanned the documents.

"Shen said he suspects the Anands, but this file has information on every crime family in the city. I don't even know where to start."

"You could start with the Anands and go from there," Hillary suggested.

"Or you could use deductive reasoning and take into account the fact that you got shot by a ninja," Malcolm said. "Doesn't that suggest anything to you?"

"Um. Japan?"

"Japan," he confirmed. "The Yakuza. Give the girl a prize."

"They were at the funeral." Val's tone was thoughtful.

"Isn't that racial profiling?" Hillary asked.

"Yes, but you've got to start somewhere, and in this case it seems warranted. I mean, you can hunt for ninja assassins among the O'Ceallaighs if you want, but you'll probably have better results looking in a culture that's known for actually having ninjas," Malcolm pointed out.

Val winced at his mention of the O'Ceallaighs. Yet another reason she wished she hadn't messed things up with Padraig. The Irish fae had a lot of connections, and would have been an excellent resource for finding Andrei's killer. If Val hadn't alienated him with the whole Pandora's Box incident, that is.

She sighed. Malcolm may have thought she had chemistry with Alain, but there had never been anything like that between them. Malcolm was the one who found Alain attractive; the greyhound shifter was too gaunt for Val's tastes.

Padraig, on the other hand...

She pushed the thought firmly aside. She didn't have time for romantic entanglements. And even if she did, she'd messed that one up irrevocably. That door was firmly closed.

She leaned forward and plucked at one of the papers.

"OK," she said. "Let's start with those two. Pull everything out of here that has to do with either the Anands or the Yakuza."

5

Two hours later, Val leaned back and stretched, her spine popping like balloons at a carnival. She groaned and ground her knuckles into her eyes.

"I don't know how you do this for hours on end, Malcolm," she said. "I feel like my eyeballs are about to fall out of my head."

Hillary grunted in agreement. She wasn't even trying to help anymore, and sat in the armchair knitting what looked like either a scarf or a very long red sock.

"We all have our superpowers." Malcolm beamed. "You know all that action hero stuff isn't for me. Fighting vampires once was enough for this lifetime."

"Oh yeah, about that…" Val took a sip of her coffee and turned to peer out the window. The street was empty. "I think I saw something out front on my way in."

Hillary froze in the middle of her knitting, needles poised in her hand. "Something?"

"I can't be sure what it was. I only saw a flash out of the corner of my eye, and it was gone when I looked again. But whatever it was, it gave me bad vibes."

"The vampire coven has found me." Hillary's face turned paler than usual.

"Maybe, maybe not. It could have been anything. Or I could have been mistaken."

"You know that's not true. They've found me."

"Perhaps." Val held up a hand to forestall Hillary's next protest. "But just to be safe, we should act like they have."

"What does that mean?" Malcolm clutched his coffee cup to his chest like a shield. "What do we do?"

"Don't worry Malcolm, you're the safest of all of us," Hillary said.

"I am?"

"It's the Renfield effect," she explained. "Other vampires will be able to smell that I've been feeding on you. Because of that, they probably won't hurt you. We like human feeders. We try to be nice to them."

"That's not as reassuring as you think it is."

"It's better than worrying about having your throat ripped out, isn't it?"

"Let's all calm down," Val said. "The sky is not falling. We don't know if I even saw a vampire. Everything is probably fine. But to be extra cautious, we'll implement the safety protocols we put in place when Hillary first moved in. Malcolm, keep your portable disco light with you at all times. Both of you should always have a buddy with you when you go outside. At the very least, don't leave the apartment without telling someone where you're going."

She directed this last towards Hillary. The woman had secrets and often disappeared on mysterious errands. Val had never investigated the matter because she understood that people needed a certain amount of privacy. But if vampires were hanging around outside the apartment, they could all be in danger. That changed things.

"Understood?"

Hillary scowled. "My business is my own."

"We can't protect you if we don't know where you are."

"I never asked you to protect me."

"Didn't you? Wasn't it you who came to me, asking me to help you escape from Melinda Pearl's coven?"

"I asked you to help me escape," Hillary growled. "Not to protect me."

"That's a pretty fine distinction."

"Ladies!" Malcolm held out his hands to separate them like a boxing referee. "Can we be civil? We're all on the same side here. I know you're both tough bitches. You don't have to prove anything."

"She started it," Hillary said.

"I did not. You…"

"Hey!" Malcolm said. "The next person who attacks the other gets no fresh bread for a week."

Their mouths dropped open.

"That's not fair!" Hillary whined.

"Don't you think that's a little harsh?" Val agreed.

"I have spoken. I'm making bread tomorrow and you'll both have to smell it and suffer. Now be nice."

"Fine," Hillary said.

Val folded her arms over her chest. "You don't have to be so aggro."

"Says the woman who pulled a knife on a burnt quiche." Malcolm laughed.

"Wait a minute." Val narrowed her eyes at them. "How would other vampires know that you've been feeding on Malcolm? I thought you were using a syringe to extract his blood."

Malcolm looked sheepish. "Well… we kind of stopped doing that."

"Hillary has been biting you?"

"Only a little bit. It's OK, Val, really."

"No. It is not OK." Val whirled on Hillary. "Why did you stop using the syringe?"

"I asked her to stop," Malcolm said. "The syringe hurt. It doesn't hurt when she bites me. It feels good."

"That's because her vampire chemicals are infecting your system. You could become addicted to them."

"That's not…" Hillary began.

Val cut her off. "How could you be so irresponsible?"

"It was my choice, Val," Malcolm said. "I told you…"

"He doesn't know what the dangers are." Val remained focused on Hillary. "You were supposed to keep him safe. I trusted you."

"He is safe," Hillary said.

"No, he's not. Any of your chemicals entering his bloodstream puts him in danger. Maybe there's no chance of him becoming a vampire, but there's a very real chance of addiction." She stepped toward Hillary and the vampire rose to her feet to meet her. "You've broken our deal. You've been feeding on Malcolm. On top of that…"

"It was my choice, Val," Malcolm insisted.

"On top of that," Val repeated, overriding him, "there are vampires lurking in the street outside. I think you need to leave."

"Val, stop." Malcolm tried to push his way between them, but the two women wouldn't budge. "You're overreacting."

"Fine. I'll go." Hillary's icy tone was the opposite of Val's fiery one. "This was always a temporary arrangement."

"Hillary, no." Malcolm finally succeeded in separating them as the vampire turned away. He grabbed her arm. "This is my home too, and I say you can stay."

"You don't get an opinion," Val said. "You've got her chemicals in your bloodstream. Your judgement has been compromised."

"It all right, Malcolm," Hillary said. "My being here puts you in danger. If Melinda Pearl's Coven has found me, it's better that I leave."

Malcolm turned on Val. "You have to at least give her time to find another place. You can't kick her out on the street. Especially if the Coven is out there. They'll tear her to pieces."

Val's mouth pressed into a hard line.

"You have one week. Then I want you gone."

"Don't worry," Hillary spat. "I'll be out of your hair before that."

The vampire stalked off down the hall. She slammed the door to her bedroom so hard the apartment shook.

6

Val was still fuming as she swung the Ural into the Richmond District. She couldn't believe Hillary had been feeding on Malcolm directly. It was like having sex without a condom. If you were careful, maybe you could avoid consequences for a while. But one slipup and you were screwed.

She was angry at both of them, but Malcolm she could sort of understand. Hillary's saliva was a narcotic. Of course being bitten felt better than being jabbed with a needle. Malcolm didn't understand the danger.

But Val had expected better of Hillary. She'd been a nurse in her former life. She knew better.

Val had trusted her. Opened her home to her. And Hillary had betrayed that trust.

Val was too worked up to stay in the apartment after the showdown with her vampire housemate. She needed to move. To do something.

So she'd grabbed all the notes on the Anands and the Yakuza they'd separated from the pile and shoved them into the pocket of her leather jacket. Then she wrapped the arrowhead in an old sock and took it as well.

The Anand residence wasn't the palace Val had expected. Sitting on an unassuming street in the inner Richmond District, the house looked like all the other well-cared-for Victorians on the block. The sunset orange paint and gold trim were shiny and new, the hedges in the tiny front garden perfectly trimmed

Val's heels rang over hardwood floors as a housekeeper with a severe bun and a white apron escorted her through the house to a sunroom in the back. The interior was immaculate, with printed wallpaper and matching furniture. The Anand house might not be a mansion, but they were clearly making the most of their money.

The windows of the sunroom overlooked a walled back garden every bit as tidy as the front. The woman deposited Val in a rattan chair and went to fetch chai. As Val gazed out at the sun-streaked garden, she reviewed what she knew about the Anand family.

Which was not much, as it turned out. Val rarely came out to the Inner Richmond, instead moving between the Mission and Polk Gulch most of her time, so she had no personal experience with the Anands other than her brief interactions with Joumala at Padraig's party and Andrei's funeral.

According to the dossier Zoe had provided, the Anand family's territory was sandwiched between Golden Gate Park and the Presidio, and stretched from Stanyan Street out past the old Highway One. The family imported a lot of spices and other things from India and other parts of southern Asia, which seemed like a legitimate business to Val and made her wonder where the criminal part of their enterprise came in. The dossier was not enlightening in that regard. It only contained a single page.

"I guess Zoe was more interested in giving me a quick sketch to help me identify the assassin, not a history lesson on the Anand family business," she muttered, turning the page over to find it blank on the back. "I'll have to use my own eyes and ears."

"Don't forget about my eyes and ears," Mister E added. *"My perspective is always enlightening."* He waggled his eyebrows at her from where he floated upside down near the ceiling.

Val suppressed a laugh.

"Your perspective is definitely… something. Do you see any magic around?"

"As a matter of fact, I do. That altar, for instance."

She followed his pointing tail to a small, colorful shrine on a table by the wall. Two candles burned on silver plates beneath a painting of the four-armed goddess Kali, brandishing a pair of swords and wearing a necklace of demon skulls.

"The altar is magic?"

"It has magical energy swirling about it, yes."

"Does that mean it's actually connected to the gods?"

"Perhaps. Or perhaps there is other magic at play here."

"Thank you for clearing that up," Val said dryly.

Mister E grinned his crescent moon smile down at her.

"Anytime."

Joumala Anand appeared in the entranceway, dressed in an expensive-looking pink dress. She had a white silk scarf draped around her neck, white heels, and a string of pearls. A chunky bracelet set with jade encircled her left wrist. As she entered the sunroom, Val noticed her nails were French-tipped with white as well. Her eyes were once again hidden behind large black sunglasses.

"Ms. Keri." Joumala lowered herself into the chair opposite Val, her scarf and shoes perfectly matching the white cushion. Her tone was frosty. "To what do I owe this visit?"

Val noted the formality and lack of pleasantries. Joumala was not in the mood for small talk. That suited Val just fine.

"I'm investigating Andrei Vasilevski's murder and the recent attempt on Zoe's life at his funeral."

Val's words hung in the air, as the housekeeper chose that moment to return with a silver tray. They waited in silence while she poured chai into delicate china cups. The spices smelled heavenly.

When she left, Joumala said, "What does this have to do with me?"

"You're one of Zoe's friends. Do you have any insight on who could be behind these attacks?"

"I'm sure you know more than I do, Ms. Keri." Joumala stretched a long-fingered hand and lifted her teacup and saucer. Her expression never changed.

Val scooped up her teacup as well, though she didn't bother with the saucer. The chai tasted as good as it smelled. She wished she could see Joumala's eyes. The woman was so good at controlling her facial features, Val was getting nothing from her. She decided to stir the pot and see what happened.

"Is it me you don't like, or are you a frigid bitch to everyone?"

Joumala's mouth dropped open, and despite the sunglasses Val saw the muscles at the corners of her eyes tighten.

"I didn't allow you into my home so you could insult me."

"You've made it clear we're not on the same side, Ms. Anand," Val returned the formality with a vengeance. "Is it because I rub you the wrong way? Or because I'm working for Zoe? Do I make you nervous?"

Lips pressed into a thin line, nostrils flaring as she fought to get her features under control, Joumala stared at her for a long moment. Val could feel her glare through the sunglasses.

"I do not think of you at all, Ms. Keri. You are beneath my notice."

"Why let me in then?" Val pressed, trying to keep the cracks in Joumala's facade from smoothing over.

"I let you in as a courtesy to Zoe Vasilevski. I assumed you were here as a courier of some sort. I did not expect to be interrogated."

"So you assumed I was working for Zoe. And I am, just not in the way you thought. You didn't seem very upset at the funeral or surprised at the attack on Zoe. Is that because you knew it was coming?"

Joumala's mouth opened to retort, then she grimaced and closed it with a visible effort of will. She deliberately sipped her tea before answering.

"I am a very reserved person. I find public displays of emotion to be unbearably gauche. I do not cry at funerals. My grieving occurs in private."

"So you grieved Andrei Vasilevski?"

"I did not say that. I didn't know Mr. Vasilevski well enough to feel any particular way about his death."

"His murder," Val corrected.

Joumala took it in stride. "Yes, his murder."

"What about the attack after the funeral? Shen and Padraig seemed pretty shook up after Zoe got shot, but you just stood there. Were you glad she was attacked?"

"I was not glad. I did not feel any way about it at all."

Val cursed silently. Joumala's expressionless mask was back in place.

"So you weren't sorry your friend got shot?"

"Zoe Vasilevski is not my friend."

"What is she then?"

Her pinky finger extended, Joumala took a careful sip of her tea. In other circumstances, Val might have found it funny. Now she was just annoyed and impatient with the woman's stalling tactics.

"Is she a rival? An obstacle on your path to the throne like some kind of medieval period drama?"

"Of course she's a rival," Joumala admitted calmly. "We live in a world of limited resources. Everyone's a rival."

"Is that why you tried to have her killed?"

The woman's lips curled ever so slightly in what might have almost been a smile.

"Assassinating someone is like attacking a problem with a meat cleaver. I prefer more elegant solutions."

"That's not what Shen said."

Joumala's smile soured.

"Shen. He's the real reason you're here, isn't he? That vengeful little shit."

Val leaned forward in her chair. She'd finally struck a nerve.

"Vengeful in what way?"

"In the boring jilted-lover way. Shen and I used to be an item. I broke it off. He's never forgiven me."

"When was this?"

"About six months ago."

"Why would he think you'd try to have Zoe killed?"

"Because he's been hanging around her, trying to make me jealous."

"And has he?"

"Please. I broke it off with him."

Despite her dismissive words, there was tension in Joumala's tone. Val turned this over in her mind. Cliché though it may be, it was not uncommon for jilted lovers to resort to violence. She would know, having been down that road herself.

"So you have no feelings about someone you know well getting shot, and no feelings about your ex-lover hanging around this person. Either you really are a frigid bitch, or you're lying. Which is it?"

Joumala put down her cup and saucer with a clink.

"I think I've allowed you to insult me quite enough for one day. The housekeeper will see you out."

7

Hillary slipped out the bathroom window and scurried onto the roof. It was a tight squeeze, but she made it through by reaching out and wrapping her fingertips around the overhang above the window. A normal person couldn't have pulled themselves up like that, but ridiculous strength was one of the advantages of being a vampire.

She slunk across the roof and knelt in the shadow of a chimney, fixing her eyes on the street below. For a full five minutes, she stayed there, motionless as the ancient brick, watching bicycles and the occasional car move past the rusted-out junker in front of the building's entrance. She saw no sign of the creature Val had mentioned, but she stayed motionless for another five minutes just in case. After all, if a vampire was watching the apartment, they could stay still and silent as easily as she could.

Finally satisfied nothing was out there, she moved away from the chimney and leapt lightly onto the roof of the building next door. In this way she crossed to the end of the block, where she clambered down a fire escape and dropped into an alley. Again she froze, taking stock of her surroundings, looking, listening, and, most importantly, smelling.

That had been one of the biggest surprises when Melinda Pearl first made Hillary into a monster. How incredible her new sense of smell was. Whereas before the world was full of muted human smells, now every stray breeze told a story. She could smell the rotting sausage inside a garbage can a hundred feet away. She could tell how many people had pissed in the alley, and how recently. And she could smell human emotions.

People had no idea how many biological signals their bodies put out that their conscious minds missed entirely. Every time two people came into contact, pheromones were released. Hillary could smell if a person in the next room was sad or happy, angry or aroused.

She also knew how those emotions affected their blood chemistry, and that in turn affected the way their blood tasted.

Hillary grimaced. That little tidbit was something she'd rather not know. But drinking blood was part of the package, and she'd accepted the dark price of her immortality when she'd agreed to become part of Pearl's Coven. That was the most important lesson life had taught her: There was always give and take, and you had to take the bad with the good.

Her vampirism was the most extreme example of this, but there had been plenty of others. Her alcoholic mother. Her ex-husband, Hank. Her little brother. The list went on, but those were the big three. The inflection points around which her entire life pivoted.

When she'd come down with stage-four terminal cancer, her decision to become a vampire to prolong her life was due to those three factors. Her mother and Hank were long gone, but her brother still needed her. She hadn't wanted to keep living for herself. She'd needed to keep living for him.

Hillary slipped out onto the sidewalk and started walking. She didn't slink, or hide her face, or act in any way that would make her stand out from the other people moving around in the early evening gloom. Melinda Pearl had taught her that the secret to surviving as a vampire was blending in with the crowd. Act like everyone else and people will assume you are one of them.

As she passed the open door to a busy pizza shop, her heightened senses were assaulted. Bright lights. Music blaring. People chattering away.

There were so many scents. Smoke from the wood-fired oven. Baking crust. Melting cheese and sauce. Dozens of toppings.

But strongest of all was the scent of humanity. She could smell every person in the crowded shop. The overpowering reek of their perfumes and colognes. The musk of underarms and breath. One couple who couldn't keep their hands off each other were putting out pheromones so thick she felt like she was passing through a fog bank.

Her stomach rumbled and she felt her canines push out from her gums, poking the inside of her lips. Her instincts screamed at her to stop and eat. The shop was full of food, and it wasn't pizza.

Hillary set her jaw and clamped down on her impulses. Her body quivered as she turned down a deserted alley and focused on walking, putting one foot in front of the other until the pizza shop was a distant memory.

After several minutes, she was finally able to unclench her jaw. The intensity of her hunger had surprised her. It was a good thing she'd gotten off the busy street. She had been feeding off Malcolm as little as possible, trying to spare her roommate as much as she could. But obviously she wasn't feeding often enough. She hadn't felt that close to losing control in a long time.

Perhaps she'd fooled herself with all of the delicious food that Malcolm had made lately. A stomach full of quiche made her conscious mind think she didn't need to eat anymore.

That wasn't true, though. For her, regular food was empty calories. It was like a normal human trying to live off nothing but french fries. She might feel full, but she would slowly starve to death if she didn't drink blood.

Hillary crossed Cesar Chavez Street and approached an abandoned school building. Inside, the classrooms had been converted into apartments and the open space of the gymnasium divided into dozens of small cubicles. As she approached the cubicle that was her destination, she was unsurprised to hear the hum of the exercise bike and video-game sound effects.

She checked the door handle, grimacing as she found it unlocked.

No matter how many times she told Benji to keep it locked, he always forgot. Locking doors simply wasn't in his nature.

Her little brother was in the living room, furiously pedaling the exercise bike that generated his electricity. His childlike face was focused on his ancient monitor and the 8-bit Space Invaders marching down his screen.

Benji had found the old Atari console in the garbage and spent two weeks taking it apart and fixing it. Now all his free time was spent either playing Space Invaders or searching for other game cartridges in the drifting rubbish heaps of the electronic recycling yards.

Space Invaders was the only game he'd found so far, but that didn't dampen his enthusiasm. That was the thing about Benji, he was a font of boundless joy and energy. He loved life more than anyone Hillary had ever known. Her primary goal in life was to nurture that spark. The world needed it. She needed it. And Benji needed her.

"Hilly!" Benji finally noticed her standing there. He came hurtling into her arms, squeezing her in a tight embrace.

"Hi Bungee." She called him by his nickname, as always, and ruffled his hair. "How are you today?"

"I got to level twelve!" Benji crowed, his eyes shining.

"That's fantastic. Have you eaten anything?"

"I don't remember."

That meant no, so Hillary headed for Benji's tiny refrigerator to make him a sandwich. The doctors had predicted Benji wouldn't live past ten due to heart abnormalities. But he was twelve now, and still going strong.

He wasn't very good at taking care of himself, but that was all right. That was what Hillary was for. Benji was all the family she had left, and she would never stop taking care of him.

Even if she'd had to become a vampire to do it.

8

Outside the Anands' home, Val sat on the Ural and consulted her notes.

"That was a waste of time," she groused.

"Was it? I found the whole exercise fascinating." Mister E perched on the sidecar. He'd taken to wearing leather goggles while riding, and he had them jauntily pushed up on his forehead.

"What was so fascinating about it? That woman is infuriating. Her calm upper-crust reserve makes me want to punch her in the face."

"Cracking her facade is part of the fun. It's like shelling an oyster. You never know if the gooey insides will contain a pearl."

"Did you get a pearl out of that?"

"Perhaps. The bit about Joumala and Shen was certainly juicy."

"That was the one interesting part. It definitely gives Joumala a motive for trying to kill Zoe," Val conceded. "Anything else?"

"Her bracelet oozed magic."

"That chunky piece with the jade? I was wondering why she was wearing that. It was the only thing that didn't color coordinate with her outfit. Did you get a read on it? What does it do?"

"I have no idea. It didn't do anything while you were talking to her. I'd have to see it in action to even hazard a guess."

"Still. Just the fact that she has it is interesting." Val drummed her fingers on the handlebars as she thought. "Between that and the altar, it at least establishes that the Anand family are no strangers to magic."

Mister E started cleaning himself. *"What's our next step?"*

"I think we've wasted enough time on the Anands for now. I'm going to focus on what we probably should have been chasing from the beginning. The assassin."

Val drove a few blocks and parked behind the boarded-up shell of the old Geary Theater building. In the small side alley where the building's trash cans were stored, she pulled the arrowhead from her pocket and carefully unwrapped it. Back here, her tracking ritual would be hidden from curious eyes.

The arrowhead couldn't be burned like hair or blood, but the weapon was enchanted, so she didn't need to do that anyway. She just needed to get properly tuned in to the arrowhead's frequency. Hopefully that would lead her back to the other arrows, or the bow that shot them.

Val drew a quick chalk circle and sat in the center with the arrowhead in her hand. After a few minutes of focusing, the metal began to pull in one direction like a compass needle.

She erased the chalk circle with a quick wind-broom and returned to the Ural, keeping the arrowhead cupped in her hand. The enchanted metal pulled her back toward the center of town.

San Francisco's Japantown squatted in a valley across from the Fillmore District. Whereas the Fillmore District was famous for jazz and music in general, Japantown wasn't famous for much of anything, as far as Val knew. Unlike Chinatown, with its fancy arches and statuary, Japantown's clean lines were bland and modern.

She parked the Ural on Fillmore Street and sat for a moment, feeling the pull of the arrowhead. It started to tug in the direction of Post Street, but then it changed directions. It did this several times.

"What's making it do that?"

"The spell is getting too much information," Mister E replied. *"That arrowhead must have circulated in this neighborhood extensively."*

"So, what? There are too many traces for the spell to hone in on one?"

"Precisely."

"That's not very useful."

"I swear, this younger generation wants everything handed to them on a platter." Mister E rolled first his eyes, then his whole body. *"The spell got you to the right neighborhood, didn't it? You'll just have to get off your pretty little bottom and do the rest the old-fashioned way."*

"Fine."

She wrapped the arrowhead back in the sock and shoved it into her pocket, before walking into the heart of Japantown.

The sidewalks were mostly empty, and the district felt barren and sterile. She passed a cluster of sushi restaurants, a sake bar, and a handful of Japanese shops and bathhouses, but there was none of the everyday hustle and bustle of Chinatown. No street vendors or local residents going about their lives. Japantown was a shopping district long past its prime, dominated by the ancient and crumbling Japan Center mall. The mall had been condemned but not torn down, and it now sulked behind rotten fencing, its abandoned shops home to squatters and vagrants.

Val quickly covered the six blocks of the district and felt no more enlightened than when she'd arrived. She ended up in a short pedestrian mall lined with shops — little more than an alley, really. On her left, an arcade blinked flashing lights and explosions at her; to her right hunched the low red doorway of a teahouse. She chose the latter, sitting at a table by the front window so she could keep an eye on the street. What she was keeping an eye out for, exactly, she had no idea.

She slid onto a dark wooden bench, ordered a mug of green tea, and pulled out her notes.

"Is there anything in there about how to make vampire housemates bend to your will?" Mister E appeared on top of the table, lounging on the dark wood.

"Not funny." Val bent forward over the stack of papers, trying to ignore the demon cat. Unfortunately, Mister E was feeling chatty.

"I never said it was. I've always thought you were letting your soft heart interfere with your logic when it came to Hillary. I have no idea why you agreed to help her in the first place."

"Because she asked me to."

"*Just because someone requests your help, does not mean they are worthy of it.*"

"You should have told me that when you asked for my help to get out of that mountain you were trapped in. It would have saved me a lot of trouble."

"*That's hardly the same thing. I offered you power in exchange for your help. What did Hillary offer you? Nothing but danger and the enmity of Melinda Pearl.*" The cat puffed on his candy cigarette, which was mounted on the end of a long cigarette holder made of bone. He blew a pair of smoke rings at the ceiling.

"Melinda Pearl already hated me. Helping Hillary escape the Coven didn't change that."

"*No, but it certainly cemented that status.*"

Val scowled at him over her teacup. "Everything doesn't have to be a transaction, you know. There are reasons to help people that don't involve payment or reward."

"*So you don't plan to collect that paycheck from Zoe Vasilevski after you track down her uncle's murderer?*"

"Of course I'll collect it. I need that money to pay my rent."

"*That doesn't sound very altruistic to me.*"

"I never said it was."

"*Then you're admitting you have a price.*"

Val clenched her hands into fists. The effect was spoiled by the petrified fingers on her right hand refusing to cooperate.

"Do you see the wound in my shoulder? The rip in my jacket? That toad-licker shot me. That's why I'm tracking him down. The money is just a bonus."

"*Ah, so your true motivation is revenge. That doesn't sound very altruistic either.*"

"Go kiss a dog," Val snapped. "And shut up. I'm trying to work here."

Mister E laughed and blew another smoke ring, but mercifully did as she asked.

Malcolm had helpfully jotted down some historical notes about Japantown for her. Val figured she'd better start with those.

Japantown had been a thriving community of Japanese at one time, much the way Chinatown still was for the Chinese. In the early 1900s, San Francisco had been the primary point of entry into the country for Japanese immigrants and home to the largest Japanese community in the United States. But during World War Two, the US government scooped up the citizens of Japantown, along with all the other Japanese on the West Coast, and locked them up in internment camps. After the war, many chose not to return to the city, and most of those who did return found homes in other neighborhoods.

Since then, Japantown had been through several ups and downs. The city had struggled to keep it alive as a cultural center, but without a true community of Japanese living in it, the district had first become a soulless shopping area, and then fallen into disrepair.

Despite all that, Japantown retained a thread of Japanese culture. Many businesses were still Japanese owned, and some had been in operation for many decades. Many of these old standard bearers were run by the Yakuza.

The Yakuza were Japan's version of the mafia and, according to Malcolm's notes, they had been around for hundreds of years. That fact astounded Val. Entire countries hadn't lasted that long, including the United States. Sure, some of the states were still around, but they now were far from united. Yet this Japanese criminal organization was still going strong.

Her reading was interrupted by a pair of Japanese men with slick hair and sharp suits walking past the tea shop window. They had athletic builds, colorful tattoos on their hands and necks, and the aggressive stride of dangerous men. She watched them swagger into an arcade across the street.

"What are the odds those guys are exactly what we're looking for?" she murmured.

"*Better than average,*" Mister Eagreed. "*The way those two carry themselves screams that they're up to no good.*"

Val sat watching the arcade for ten minutes, but the men did not come back out.

"Well." She slid off the bench and got to her feet. "I guess we've got to go in after them."

9

The interior of the arcade was long and narrow, and it went a lot further back than Val was expecting. It was a maze of machines, a riot of flashing lights, color, and sound. It was also strangely deserted. Other than a handful of teenagers clustered around a machine near the front, there wasn't a soul in sight.

She threaded her way deeper into the maze until the back wall finally loomed up in front of her. There was no sign of the sharp-suited men.

"Toad-spit," she muttered. "Where did they go?"

"Maybe they're magicians. Vanished into thin air," Mister E suggested.

"I doubt it. They looked like muscle, not magic."

"Why can't they be both? You certainly are."

Val bit back a sharp retort. The demon cat had a point.

"Let me borrow your eyes for a minute."

The world shifted as Mister E's vision overlaid her own. She waited for the shop to explode into magical colors, but other than the flashing lights of the machines, there was nothing.

"That's disappointing."

Val made her way back through the shop, scrutinizing the

machines for traces of magic. She still found nothing. It seemed to be no more than a normal arcade.

Furtively glancing around, she pulled the arrowhead out of her pocket. She let it pull her behind a set of old skee-ball machines, where she discovered a small door she hadn't noticed before. On the surface, the door was unremarkable — plain wood with a silver handle. The interesting thing was that the door had a small security camera mounted above it, which meant something back there was worth protecting.

The glowing wards carved into the doorframe were even more interesting.

Val put the arrowhead back in the sock and slid behind the skee-ball machines, out of the security camera's field of view. She peered around the corner, examining the runes.

"Do you recognize those?" she whispered.

"No, they're written in a language I don't know."

"Presumably Japanese."

"Doubtful. Magical languages are separate from mundane ones. Though guessing that it is a language native to that part of that world seems reasonable."

"So you can't tell me what the runes are for."

"Not with any certainty. Given the location, I'd guess they serve the same function as most wards around a threshold."

"Protection or an alarm."

"Likely both."

"Odds are that's where those two guys disappeared to. What do you think is back there? It's got to be more than just an office with those wards."

"I don't know. But something tells me you are determined to find out."

"Do you have a better idea? We're trying to find the Yakuza, and two guys that fit the description just disappeared through a warded door. The arrowhead wants me to go that way. I'd say we're on the right track."

"I disagree," said a male voice behind her. Val whirled to find one of the guys in suits standing there. A green dragon tattoo wrapped around his neck, the tail disappearing under the crisp collar of his gray shirt. "You are poking your nose where it doesn't belong. That is definitely the wrong track."

A decision flashed through Val's head. She could confront the guy, or she could play dumb. Confrontation was more her style, but it might be better to learn more before she stirred up the Yakuza like a hive. Also, Val didn't know how much the guy had heard.

She tried on a smile.

"Sorry, I'm looking for the restroom. Can you point me in the right direction?"

The gangster's hard expression didn't waver. "There is no restroom."

"Oh, sorry to waste your time." Val edged past him. "I'll just be going then."

The man made no move to stop her, but his flat eyes remained fixed on her as she made her way out of the arcade.

It wasn't until she was out the door and half a block away that her hammering heart came down out of her throat and she started to breathe more easily.

"Well, we've definitely found some shady characters," she whispered, glancing around to make sure no one was tailing her.

"Yes, but are they the correct shady characters?" Mister E drifted lazily on his back at shoulder height, his golden eyes contemplative.

"I don't know. But I intend to find out."

"And how will you do that?"

"We'll have to come back and try that door later, when no one is around."

"Breaking and entering into someplace the Yakuza don't want you to go? If you were going to do that, why didn't you simply kick down the door while we were there and be done with it?"

"There's being bold and being stupid."

"And here I always thought you didn't know the difference." The demon cat blotted imaginary tears with his tail. *"Look at our little girl. She's all grown up."*

"Keep it up, fuzzbutt. We'll see if you still have that sense of humor after I shave you like a poodle."

They retraced their steps through Japantown. They were almost back to where they'd started, when the rumble of a familiar engine came from around the corner.

Val looked at Mister E, her eyes widening as she broke into a run.

"The Ural!"

She pounded around the corner just in time to see the old motorcycle's taillights disappearing up the street.

10

illary spent the next couple of hours hanging out in Benji's cubicle and making sure he ate something. She read him a chapter from *The Hitchhiker's Guide to the Galaxy* and played a couple of games of Space Invaders with him — getting roundly trounced by her brother despite her enhanced vampire reflexes.

She was pushing her luck. The more time she spent with Benji, the more danger she put him in. Melinda Pearl's vampire hunters were looking for her. If they found out about Benji, they wouldn't hesitate to use him against her

Yet she couldn't help herself. Benji was the reason she'd accepted Melinda Pearl's dark offer of immortality. Their mother had drifted away on a sea of alcohol when Hillary was twelve and Benji was hardly more than a baby. From that point on, she had been forced to be the practical one. The caretaker. Friendless and serious, focused on ensuring that they both survived in a hostile world.

By contrast, Benji was a shining star, full of boundless enthusiasm and joy. His laughter gave her hope for a better tomorrow. He was the bright spark in her otherwise dark existence.

But Benji couldn't take care of himself. He was a genius with machines, but he didn't understand people at all. His enthusiasm and joy were impractical. The world would eat him up in a heartbeat. He needed her.

And she needed him.

She sighed as she put down the controller. She'd stayed too long. Every minute she spent with Benji put him at risk.

Maybe Val was doing her a favor by kicking her out of the apartment. Truth be told, Hillary should have fled the city weeks ago.

But wherever she went, she would have to take Benji with her. And that presented a whole host of problems.

So she'd ignored the danger and allowed herself to be lulled into a false sense of security. She'd let inertia win. Benji was hidden away in his little cubicle, and she'd felt safe in the flat with Val and Malcolm. She'd refused to think about the future and buried her head in the sand.

Maybe it was Val's influence. The witch didn't seem to be afraid of anything. She had faced down Melinda Pearl more than once, and each time she'd walked away unscathed. Living with Val made Hillary feel invincible too.

But that was all over now. Val had kicked her out of the apartment. There was no avoiding reality any longer.

She and Benji would have to make their own future. That meant getting out of San Francisco. Out of the Bay Area entirely. Abandoning their comfortable existence for dangers unknown.

She tucked Benji into bed and hugged him goodbye.

"Stay, Hilly, stay!" he begged, as he did every time she left.

"You know I can't, Bungee," she said, her heart aching. "It's bedtime for Bonzo. But I'll be back before you know it."

"What's wrong, Hilly?" he asked, touching her cheek with his soft fingertips.

"Nothing's wrong. Everything's fine." She cursed the empathic connection she and her brother shared. No matter how hard she tried to hide her emotions, he always knew. "It's nothing you need to worry about." She put on a smile and ruffled his hair. "Now go shoot some space invaders in your dreams. If you're good, maybe I'll bring you a Pan Galactic Gargle Blaster tomorrow."

Benji's eyes lit up and he laughed with his whole heart. Hillary's heart throbbed in response. It was almost scary how much she loved the kid.

Stepping onto the street, she turned her mind to the subject she'd been avoiding: How could she get Benji out of the city safely? And where would they go after that?

Since the United States had collapsed, most of the country had become a lawless wasteland. There were lots of wide-open spaces between San Francisco and anywhere else that could be considered civilized, spaces where a lone woman with a kid would be considered easy prey.

She thought about simply moving across the bay. The big quake had made the top level of the Bay Bridge unsafe for automobile traffic, and a shanty town had spread across it like fungus. They could walk across the bridge and try to hide in Berkeley or Oakland.

Hillary rejected that thought as quickly as it came. That was her laziness talking, looking for the easy solution. The East Bay wasn't far enough away from Melinda Pearl's Coven. The vampires would find her, and she and Benji would be back in the same pickle all over again.

No, she had to dream bigger.

Sacramento was the closest city outside of the Bay Area, but she got a bad taste in her mouth just thinking about it. Stockton or Modesto were even worse. California's central valley had been a shit show even before the collapse. Now it had been overrun by ghouls on motorcycles and survivalists with semi-automatic weapons who shot anyone that approached their gated enclaves on sight.

No, their best bet was to stick to the coast. Maybe head north into redwood country, or keep going further up into what used to be Oregon or Washington.

Alternately, they could go south to Los Angeles, or even all the way down to San Diego. Though she had heard that Southern California had its own vampire problems.

Hillary was so wrapped up in her deliberations that she didn't notice the shadowy figure who watched her emerge from the old school and stalk away into the night. Nor did she notice the figure step out of the shadows once Hillary was well past.

The black-clad figure crossed the street with smooth, gliding strides, almost as if they were skating on ice. Their dark eyes glinted as they paused to glance up and down the street.

Unobserved, they followed Hillary into the night.

11

Val sprinted after the Ural, shouting and waving her arms. No one paid her any attention. Apparently, thefts were common around here. Or maybe it was people running down the street yelling and screaming that was common.

Either way, the thief was getting away.

The good news was that the Ural wasn't very fast, and the rider was weaving down the street. The thief was either drunk or not a very good rider.

The bad news was that even taking those things into account, the old motorcycle was still faster than she was. And it was daylight and there were people around, so Val didn't want to use her powers to fly after the thief.

So she pounded down the block on foot, racking her brain, trying to come up with a way to stop them that wouldn't immediately expose her as a witch.

"You can knock their head off with a cross wind," Mister E advised.

She considered this, but quickly rejected it.

"If I did that, the Ural would crash, and instead of a stolen motor-cycle, I'd end up with a totaled motorcycle. Also, blood all over the frame. Not ideal."

"Spoilsport."

She grinned as another idea came to her. "But maybe I could slow him down with a headwind."

She reached her arm forward and yanked back, as if tugging on a rope. A wind sprang up and howled down the street towards her, snatching up dust and debris as it came.

Val was surprised by the instant ferocity of the wind. Mister E had been teaching her to use her body to help focus her energy when casting spells, kind of the same way that martial artists used sound. She was still getting the hang of it, but in this case it seemed the rope-yanking motion had really helped get things moving.

As the gust hit the rider, they coughed and flung up an arm to protect their face. The Ural slowed as the thief's wobbling ride became even more unsteady.

Val sprinted forward, keeping her path clear by bending the wind around herself. She even curled part of the air so that a gust was pushing against her back, giving her a boost that nearly doubled her speed.

The thief had given up trying to ride into the howling storm, and the Ural nosed to a stop against the curb. The rider crawled out from behind the handlebars, coughing and choking.

As Val got closer, she could see that the would-be-thief was just a scrawny Japanese kid. Maybe seventeen. He wore tight fitting clothes with lots of zippers and fingerless leather gloves. His eyes widened as he saw Val coming up the block towards him.

The kid bolted, slipping through a cut in a chain link fence before Val could hit him with another blast of air.

She cursed and charged through the fence after him.

Val found herself in a vacant lot full of high grass and rusting appliances. To her left, the kid danced along a winding foot trail. She chopped a side wind at him, but he was too fast, disappearing into a dark crevice between a pair of old refrigerators.

"Seriously?" Val peered into the tight space. The narrow passage wound through a stack of old appliances.

She considered just letting him go. After all, she'd stopped the theft in progress and gotten the Ural back. He was only a punk kid.

"*Locals have knowledge outsiders don't,*" Mister E said.

"You're probably right. Good thing I'm not very large." Val sighed and slipped into the maze after the kid.

The rusting metal closed around her. Bright shafts of light pierced the gloom, lancing down through the scraps. She heard scrabbling ahead of her and moved that way, hoping it was the kid and not one of those gigantic city rats.

The scrap heap leaned against the concrete wall of a huge building. Val turned a corner in time to see the kid's foot disappear through a gap in the wall.

"This is getting ridiculous," she mumbled.

She ducked through the gap and found herself in a musty passage inside the building. Dim light filtered in through cracks in the wall. Old machinery lined the walls, along with wheeled carts full of moldy fabric. Val covered her mouth with her hand to avoid breathing in the spores.

"*This looks like a service corridor,*" Mister E mused. "*I believe we are now inside the old Japan Center.*"

"An abandoned mall? Lovely. Just where I wanted to spend my time."

She turned to the right, following the sounds of hurrying feet.

The service corridor curved around the outside of the mall, and Val hurried past dozens of doors. Most were closed, but a glance inside one standing ajar showed her an abandoned clothing store. Most of the racks had been emptied long ago, but a few items still hung here and there.

The sound of something falling made her hurry forward.

She emerged in an abandoned food court beneath a high atrium ceiling. Rusted metal shutters covered the faces of several restaurants, and stacks of abandoned tables and chairs teetered like anthills.

The kid was halfway across, running for the other side. But the food court was a large open space with little cover. A perfect environment for a wind witch.

Val repeated her yanking motion, pulling the wind towards her. A hurricane gust roared up out of nowhere, catching the boy full in the face. Only this time, he didn't have the weight of the Ural to anchor him.

The wind lifted the thief off his feet, sending him sprawling and rolling across the food court until he finally slid to a halt beside Val's boots.

She put one of them on his chest and gave him a smile.

"Glad you could drop by. We're going to have a little chat."

12

The young thief slouched in his plastic food-court chair, skinny arms crossed defiantly over his chest. He was a good-looking kid, with blond tips on straight black hair that slanted down across his forehead. Val sat facing him, their knees almost touching, close enough that she could grab him if he tried to make a run for it.

"What's your name?" she asked.

"What's it matter to you?" he answered sullenly.

"I'd prefer to keep this friendly. It's easier to be civil if we know each other's names. I'm Val."

"Friendly?" He scowled at her. "You chased me down and stepped on my chest. Is that how you treat your friends?"

"The ones who try to steal my motorcycle, yes." She pulled out her knife and started cleaning her nails with the tip. The boy's eyes widened. "Now, let's start with your name."

"My name is Obi."

"Like the Jedi?"

"No, not like the Jedi," he snapped. "Obi is a traditional Japanese name. It's not my fault George Lucas thought it sounded cool."

Val held up her hand for peace.

"OK. Sorry I asked. You obviously get that question a lot."

"Every day of my life," he grumbled.

"Let's start with the basics. Why did you try to steal my motorcycle?"

"To sell it. Obviously."

"Sell it to who? The Yakuza?"

Obi's face twisted in disgust.

"No. I'd never sell to those idiots."

"Really?" Val raised an eyebrow. "Why not?"

"They try to control everything around here. Working for them is as bad as working for some soulless corporation. I'm a freelancer. Emphasis on the 'free' part."

"I'm surprised the Yakuza let you get away with that. Isn't it dangerous to be a freelancer on their turf?"

"Not if you're smart." Obi grinned.

"And you are?"

"Obviously."

"I caught you," Val pointed out.

"You cheated. You never would have caught me if you weren't a witch."

"But I did catch you."

"Because you cheated," he insisted.

Val chuckled. "Fine, I cheated. But it's the result that matters. Nobody cares how you win the game. They only care if you win."

Obi didn't have anything to say to that, he just scowled at her from under his bleached bangs.

Val eyed him speculatively.

"You really don't have any fear of the Yakuza?"

The boy made a rude noise through his lips.

"The Yakuza are like an elephant. They're big and slow. And they only pay attention to other elephants. I can walk in and out of any of their joints I want. They don't notice small fry like me. I'm invisible."

"Invisible, huh?" Val mused. "What do you know about the arcade?"

The boy's face grew crafty.

"I know a lot. Information isn't free, though. What do I get out of it?"

Val leaned forward, knife in hand.

"For starters, you get to keep all of your fingers and toes."

Obi leaned away from her. "Take it easy. Relax. What do you want to know?"

"Is the arcade run by the Yakuza?"

"Obviously."

"What do they do there?"

"Everything. It's one of their primary joints. It's mostly gambling, but they run protection and drugs too. Stolen goods." The boy shrugged. "All kinds of stuff."

"Do you know what's in the back room?"

"It's not a room," he said. "It's an underground fight club. The whole arcade is a front."

"Fight club? What kind of fights?"

"All kinds. Some nights it's roosters or other animals. Sometimes they have bare-knuckle boxing or no-holds-barred MMA. It depends on the night."

"How do you find out what's happening on any given night?"

"Word gets around. It's not hard."

"Do you ever go to the fights?"

"Sometimes."

"You just walk in the front door? I thought the Yakuza didn't like you."

"No, I go in through the back. There's a service entrance. I've got friends who work inside."

"Do you bet on the fights?"

"No." Obi made another rude noise with his lips.

"So why do you go? Seems awfully risky."

"There's lots of people that go. Fight nights get pretty packed. Once I'm in, I disappear into the crowd. Lots of pockets hanging open, if you know what I mean."

"Is there a fight tonight?"

"Yeah, a big one. Some shifter fight."

"They have shifter fights?" Val wondered if Alain knew about this. He wouldn't be pleased if he did.

"Not very often. That's why it's a big deal."

She thought for a moment.

"If it's a big deal, I imagine the Yakuza bosses will be there?"

"Of course," he said scornfully. "Everybody who's anybody will be there."

Val made up her mind.

"Can you get me into the fight tonight?"

Obi's expression became crafty.

"Maybe. If the price is right. And don't give me that shit about my fingers and toes. I gave you plenty of information for my fingers and toes. This type of risk costs credits."

Seventeen years old, staring at the blade of a hunting knife, and Obi had the gall to demand payment. Val smirked. The kid had confidence, she had to give him that.

"Payment once I get out safely," she said.

The kid shook his head.

"You pay me to get you in. Once you're in, you're on your own."

"I'll double your fee if you get me back out again."

Obi tried to hide his excitement, but his eyes lit up like lamps.

"Half up front, half after."

Val thought about it. She was operating on Zoe Vasilevski's expense account, so for once she had money to burn.

She grinned. "You've got a deal."

13

The alley Obi led Val through was remarkably clean. The garbage cans were lined up neatly behind the shops, and she didn't see so much as a stray scrap of paper on the ground.

"This might be the first alley I've ever walked down that doesn't smell like piss," she observed. "Do they wash the pavement or what?"

"Of course," Obi said. "We Japanese respect our environment. We don't piss all over it. Who would want a stinking alley when they could have a clean one?"

Val chuckled.

"Weren't you the one arguing against the Yakuza's rules? Telling me how free you are?"

"I don't have to piss all over the planet to demonstrate my freedom. That's disrespectful. We live in a big city. Millions of people rubbing against each other. Sharing space. Breathing the same air. If we don't respect the city and help keep it clean, we'll end up in the filth like animals."

Val gave him the side eye.

"You're the most polite thief I've ever heard of."

"Some rules are basic human rules. Those rules we don't break."

They reached the back door to the arcade building, and Obi bowed to the woman standing guard. The petite woman was dressed all in black, with the handle of a long blade sticking up over her shoulder. She also had a pistol strapped to her hip.

Obi leaned toward her and whispered something Val couldn't hear. The security guard's dark eyes went to Val. The witch's fingers went to the handle of her knife and she carefully drew in her power, ready to defend herself if Obi betrayed her.

After an interminable moment, the guard gave a small bow and stepped smoothly aside. She held the back door open for them as Obi led Val into the building.

They entered a world of steam and banging pots and pans. Meat and vegetables sizzled, and the aromas of seaweed and salt filled the air. Cooks in spotless white coats performed their tasks with the precision of long practice, well-honed knives snicking against cutting boards.

"There's a kitchen in an arcade?" Val whispered.

"I told you, the arcade is just a front. The real action happens down below," Obi hissed back.

The staff paid Obi and Val no attention as the thief led her around the periphery of the kitchen to an unassuming door at the back of a pantry. Inside the door, another guard stood at the top of a set of wooden stairs leading down. Again, Obi leaned forward and whispered something, and again the guard let them pass without incident.

Val was grateful she'd hired the young thief to act as her guide. Walking politely past the guards was much better than whatever messy gambit she'd have devised on her own.

The stairs led down into a passage hewn from reddish stone. Oil lanterns on hooks hung on the polished walls, creating little pools of light that waxed and waned as they moved forward. Perfectly level paving stones formed a mosaic under their feet. An ancient hush filled the air.

Then they rounded a bend, and everything changed again.

The passage opened into a wide bowl of a room. Stone benches had been carved directly into the bedrock, forming a sunken amphitheater. The walls and benches were a dark slate, streaked with veins of red and polished to a meticulous shine. But whereas the entrance passage had contained the silence of the ages, the amphitheater hummed with noise and life.

At the center of the space was a circular fighting ring. A throng of people pressed close to the ropes, faces upturned and expectant. Hundreds more sat on the carved benches or moved about the amphitheater, talking or drinking. Money exchanged hands as people placed bets on the upcoming fight.

To her surprise, the people waiting for the fight weren't all Japanese. The crowd contained people from several other Asian nations, as well as a healthy contingent of African and European descendants.

Obi read her expression. "People come from all over to see the fights. Not just the city."

Val slipped the arrowhead into her palm and focused. It gently tugged toward the far side of the room.

She nodded at a platform on the far side of the ring that was roped off from the other spectators. It contained a handful of well-dressed Japanese sitting on thickly cushioned chairs. It reminded her of the box the emperor would occupy at gladiator fights.

"Who is that?"

"Those are our hosts for the evening. The ruling hand of the Yakuza. The man in the golden robe is the dragon."

"I need to get a closer look."

"Follow me."

Obi led her down into the crowded bowl.

Their progress slowed as they moved down the stairs. Once they reached the floor, people were packed so close together they had to push to squeeze past. Val smirked as she remembered Obi's usual reason for coming to these things. A crowd like this was definitely a pickpocket's paradise.

Down here, the scents weren't nearly as nice as in the kitchen. A lot of these people needed more deodorant or less garlic in their diets. It reminded Val of trying to get to the front row at a big concert.

Before they'd even made it halfway across the bowl, the lights dimmed and a bright spotlight came on over the ring. The crowd pressed towards the ropes, swelling together like wet planks in a ship's hull.

Caught in the crush and immobilized, Val cursed. It didn't look like she'd be making any more progress toward the dragon until after the fight.

An announcer in a shiny suit took the stage, his voice booming over the quieting amphitheater.

"Ladies and gentlemen! Let's get ready to rumble!"

The crowd roared.

14

A nother spotlight came on, bringing the dark mouth of a tunnel across the arena into focus. Velvet ropes delineated a corridor from the tunnel to the fighting ring.

The announcer was whipping the crowd into a frenzy.

"Coming to the ring first is our challenger. Standing eight feet tall and weighing in at over six hundred pounds, please welcome Grizzly Grant!"

An enormous brown bear emerged from the tunnel, standing on its hind legs and roaring, spreading its arms wide. The bear's paws were as big as dinner plates, topped with wickedly curved claws.

Val shuddered. "That thing looks like it could tear your face off with one swipe."

"Oh, it definitely could," Mister E confirmed. The demon cat was floating above her head so that he could get a clear view over the crowd. *"Bears are very underrated predators."*

"Underrated by who? I certainly wouldn't want to meet that thing alone in the woods."

"I only mean they are underrated on the list of predators that humans are frightened of. Everyone is terrified of sharks, for instance, but sharks only kill

four people per year on average. Bears kill many times that number, with griz-zlies accounting for the largest percentage of attacks."

"Remind me never to leave the city again."

The grizzly had reached the ring, and he strode around the apron roaring at the crowd. The crowd roared back their approval.

The announcer took the microphone once again.

"And now, please welcome to the ring our champion. The Tower of Power, the Totem of Terror: Takashi Titan!"

The roar that went up from the crowd this time was twice as loud as the one for Grizzly Grant. Takashi Titan came sauntering out of the tunnel, his dark purple skin shining in the light. Golden dragons glinted in the light, chasing each other across the surface of his black silk kimono. He was an Oni, and stood a head taller than the bear, while his muscled torso was just as thick. The Oni bellowed and waved at the crowd, yellow tusks curving down the corners of his mouth, his grin exposing a mouth full of very sharp teeth. Long black claws tipped his fingers.

Val swallowed. She wouldn't want to be in the ring with either of the fighters, but at that moment, she almost pitied the grizzly shifter. Oni were very, very bad news.

Mister E echoed her thoughts.

"This doesn't look like much of a fight to me. The only question is how long will the Oni toy with his opponent before he finishes him off?"

As the fighters entered the ring, the crowd pressed in toward the ropes. By drifting backwards, Val was able to find some space to move. She began to slip toward the raised box containing the leaders of the Yakuza.

"Hopefully they'll distract the crowd long enough for us to learn something useful."

"Such as?"

"I don't know." Val focused on the arrowhead, letting it guide her through the crowd. "I'm going to follow this and see where it takes us. If we're lucky it'll lead me to the assassin."

Obi noticed her slipping away and raised an eyebrow at her.

"Stay here," she whispered. "I'll be back."

Curiosity lit his eyes, but the thief shrugged and tried to look nonchalant.

When Val was halfway across the room, the fight started.

The grizzly shifter roared and charged in, swiping with his massive paws. Dark blood splattered across the ring, but the Oni appeared unfazed, retreating with measured steps while keeping the grizzly at arm's length with swift jabs. As Val watched, the Oni's wounds began to close, the long gashes sealing as if by magic.

And it was magic.

The Oni's powers of regeneration were legendary. It was the main reason they were such feared fighters. Sure they were fast and strong, but so were a lot of things. What set them apart was their regenerative powers. They could heal from just about anything, and with remarkable speed. The only way to keep them from regenerating was to cauterize the wounds with fire.

But Grizzly Grant didn't have any fire. If Takashi's strategy was to keep his distance until Grant wore himself out, Val was afraid the bear shifter was in for a long night.

On the plus side, that meant the fight could drag on for quite a while. Which was exactly what Val needed.

As she got closer to the Yakuza leadership, Val frowned. The arrowhead had started to pull her away from the platform. She took a moment to get oriented, concentrating on the sharp metal in her hand and turning slowly until she could be certain.

"It's not the box," she whispered. "It's in the tunnel the fighters came out of."

"That's unfortunate." Mister E pouted. *"I was looking forward to seeing you challenge the Yakuza's entire leadership council."*

Val rolled her eyes and started moving toward the tunnel.

"I thought you didn't want me to die."

"I don't. But I'm a sucker for dramatic confrontations."

"Well, don't be too sad. If I don't find anything in the tunnel, that could still happen."

She paused just outside the mouth of the tunnel and looked around. The fighters were both covered in blood, savagely going toe to toe. The crowd was in a frenzy, every eye glued to the carnage. No one was watching her.

Val ducked her head and slipped inside the tunnel.

15

The tunnel was like the one Obi had followed with Val from the kitchens: smooth stone walls about twenty feet high, dark slate in color, threaded with reddish veins. The air was cool and she could feel the weight of the stone pressing down on her. This tunnel, too, was lit by oil lamps on hooks, which struck Val as odd, considering she'd just come from an amphitheater with giant spotlights.

"Do you think they're low on electricity? Or do they just prefer oil lamps?" she wondered.

"It could be either," Mister E replied. "Those giant spotlights draw so much current, they could make it difficult to run a lot of other lights at the same time. But there's something to be said for the sedate glow of oil lamps. I prefer them myself."

The tunnel curved and curved again, and Val was struck by how quickly it became silent. The thick stone swallowed the roar of the amphitheater like a pebble dropped into a well.

She moved cautiously but saw no one. Everyone was out watching the fight. Perfect.

An intersection loomed and Val stopped at the crossroads, turning slowly to let the arrowhead lead the way. The metal led her down the left-hand corridor.

The first door she came to opened on empty showers, the second a small dressing room. A pair of warm-up pants and a hooded sweatshirt lay draped over a wooden bench. She wondered which fighter they belonged to.

The arrowhead tugged her deeper down the hall, past a second dressing room. She poked her head in the door and saw a hand-wrap kit sitting on the table. She stepped in to examine it, smiling fondly. Her own hands had been wrapped countless times for sparring sessions at the gym. Val balled her fists in remembrance of the adrenaline and the tingle of anticipation. The split-second thrill of impact.

Her smile wilted as her petrified fingers refused to curl. She hadn't been able to spar properly since Sandra turned her fingers to stone. She could hardly get a glove on that hand. Old George, the trainer, had been modifying her fighting style, adding more chops and forearm strikes, helping her find things that didn't require her to make a fist.

It all felt awkward and unnatural. Mastering a fighting style required a lot of repetition. The moves had to be so ingrained they became instinctive. The time you took to think during a fight was time your opponent was using to strike. By the time you decided what to do, you'd already lost.

She sighed.

She didn't blame Sandra, though.

Well, if she was being honest, she did blame her a little.

Perhaps blame wasn't the right word. Resented maybe. But not in a personal way. Sandra was as much a victim as Val. More, really. Sandra had to live with snakes for hair and a gaze that would turn you to stone if she looked you in the eye.

Val couldn't imagine how difficult that would be. Never being able to look anyone in the eye?

She shuddered. No, thank you. She'd gotten off easy with petrified fingers.

Voices in the hall broke her from her reverie.

She peeked out and immediately pulled her head back in. Several people were approaching.

"Flaming toads, the fight must be over," she hissed. "Do you see anywhere to hide?"

"That door leads to the showers," Mister E pointed out. *"You could wait in there."*

"Because a fighter coming back from a fight would never take a shower. Brilliant idea."

"I didn't say you could hide in there. I said you could wait for the naked fighter. Big difference."

"Funny. I'm not that desperate."

"Maybe you aren't, but I am. Do you know how long it's been since I got to watch sexy times?"

Val screwed up her face in disgust.

"I'm well aware of how long it's been. And thanks to that image of you watching me get it on, it's now going to be a lot longer before it happens again. I may just become a nun."

Mister E pouted. *"Modern humans are so ridiculously self-conscious when it comes to sex. In the old days people flopped down in a field and went at it whenever they felt the urge. You'd be picking grapes in the vineyard while your sister had an orgasm in the next row. All perfectly natural."*

"Gross. And not helpful."

The voices were right outside the door now. Any second the door was going to open, and they'd discover Val standing in the middle of the dressing room.

She grabbed the nearest door handle, yanked it open, and ducked into the space within. The voices entered the room just as the door clicked shut behind her.

She stood frozen, adrenaline rushing through her veins, waiting to hear someone shout.

All she heard was the pounding of her own heart.

Whoever was speaking continued in the same tone of voice. They hadn't seen her.

Val blew out a shaky breath and examined her surroundings. She was in a supply closet full of towels. Perfect.

Then she remembered the showers and gulped. Maybe not so perfect.

She put her eye to the door and saw slices of the room through the slats. Three people were in the room. Grizzly Grant sat on a bench, forearms on his knees, head down. He was still huge, though he'd shifted back to human, and his thick, hairy torso was covered in blood. He was obviously in a great deal of pain, despite the shifters' accelerated healing ability. His breath was bubbling in his lungs.

The other two men moved with crisp professionalism, talking in low, consoling voices as they cleaned and stitched his wounds. Val guessed the old bald guy was his trainer and the thin one was his cut man.

Finally, the trainer stepped back and said, "Hit the showers, kid."

Grizzly Grant nodded and slowly levered himself to his feet. As he stepped toward the closet, Val's breath caught in her throat.

A towel. He needed a towel.

She squeezed back, but there was nowhere to go in the small closet. As soon as he opened the door, he would see her.

Desperately, Val tried to decide what to do.

Should she push past him and try to run? Even if she made it out of the room, they were bound to raise an alarm. And the only way out was through the amphitheater. She'd have the whole Yakuza down on her head.

What if she tried to talk her way out of it? Make up some excuse?

But what possible reason could she have for crouching in the towel closet inside the fighters' dressing room?

The bulky fighter's shadow blocked the light coming in through the slats. Grizzly Grant extended a meaty paw.

16

Hillary went hunting.

She hunted not for blood but for human connection. For life. For laughter and flirtation and that quick spark that makes your breath catch in your throat when you turn and find your reflection dancing in someone else's eyes.

She might be a vampire, but she wasn't dead.

The underground bar in the outer Mission District was loud, the lighting dim. Hillary slipped into the crowd as if stepping into a pool of dark water. Human smells filled her nostrils: sweat and excitement and desire. The last two might not have a scent to a normal human, at least not to the conscious part of their brains, but to Hillary human emotions contained scents richer than any bouquet. She breathed in the aroma of the dancers, the drinkers, the desperate and the desirable.

It was intoxicating.

Hillary glided to the bar and ordered a gin and tonic, then turned to survey the crowd.

This wasn't one of her usual haunts — those were all closed to her now, as they were frequented by members of her former coven. If the vampires caught her out in public, they'd tear her apart. Or worse, capture her and take her back to Melinda Pearl for judgement.

Even coming here was a risk, but it was one she had to take. Hillary was a social creature, and she couldn't hide herself away forever.

She needed human connection — physical connection.

A couple of guys at the end of the bar eyed her. She let them, pretending she didn't notice. A female standing alone at a bar always attracted attention, and Hillary knew she looked good. Her black bangs were sleek across her forehead, and her pale skin and ruby lips were striking, even in the dim light of the bar. She wore a little black dress with fishnet stockings and red heels that matched her lipstick and nails.

It was a cliché for vampires to dress goth, but Hillary didn't care. She had been goth long before Melinda Pearl turned her into a creature of the night, and she wasn't going to change her style simply to avoid cliché.

Besides, goth girls attracted a certain type. Guys who weren't afraid of a little danger. Hillary appreciated that. That way she could be sure they knew what they were getting into.

The two guys at the bar were working up the courage to approach her. The blond-haired one was egging his dark-skinned friend on. Even with the throbbing noise pumping out of the sound system, she could still hear their words clearly. Which wasn't as impressive a feat as it sounded; they were shouting to each other to be heard over the music.

She could tell she wasn't really their cup of tea — which was the reason it was taking them so long to make a pass at her — but they were the type of guys who saw a female alone as an opportunity they couldn't neglect. No matter who she was or what she looked like, these guys would take their shot. They were just looking for a warm body they could explore for the night. Any warm body would do.

Hillary didn't necessarily have a problem with that. She was seeking the same thing. Her situation dictated that she keep everyone at an emotional distance. Love, or even a relationship, was firmly off the table.

But physical warmth? Human touch? Two bodies alone in the dark?

These were things she desperately needed.

The two guys had finally screwed their courage to the sticking point. The dark-skinned guy gulped down the last of his drink and set the glass on the bar. He took a tentative step towards Hillary.

Too late.

A shirtless guy with glowing tattoos curling around his ribcage slithered out of the crowd, took Hillary by the hand, and pulled her out onto the dance floor. As she went, she gave the dark-skinned guy a tiny shrug. You snooze, you lose.

The energy on the dance floor was electric. Hillary closed her eyes and let her other senses drink it in: the warm bodies inches from her skin, the heartbeat thump of the bass, the scent of sweat and desire, the bitter taste of gin on her tongue. The shirtless guy was dancing close but wasn't getting handsy, which Hillary appreciated. The dance repertoire of too many jerks started and ended with grinding their pelvis against strangers.

If the shirtless guy had been one of those, she would have been forced to show him the error of his ways. Just because she was looking to get laid didn't mean she wanted some dude rubbing his genitals against her on the dance floor.

At least not right away. There was a natural progression to these things.

But the guy clearly understood that. He was taking his time, enjoying the music, and — more importantly — letting her enjoy the music too. In Hillary's experience this was a good omen. Men who took their time on the dance floor usually took their time in other places as well.

She checked him out as they danced, enjoying the glimpses afforded by the strobing lights, the play of shadows and planes across his features. Sweat glistened on his shaven scalp and several piercings glinted in his ears. She enjoyed the way his lean muscles flexed and bent as he moved with the music. He had a strong jawline and full lips lurking beneath tear-shaped eyes.

She leaned in and shouted over the music, "You're very graceful. Are you a dancer?"

His lips curled into a smile, but he said nothing, letting his eyes and his movements do the talking for him. Which they did quite eloquently.

Hillary returned the smile. She could work with that.

Hours later, when the club closed and he led her back to his apartment, she was happy to discover that he did, indeed, take his time.

17

The big shifter reached for Val. She could smell his sweat and the copper tang of blood through the slats of the closet door. His bulky shadow blocked the light.

She closed her eyes. This was it. There was nowhere she could go. She was busted.

Val held her breath, waiting for the door to swing open. The light to fall on her face. The big fighter's cry of surprise.

Nothing happened.

Cautiously, she cracked one eye open.

Grizzly Grant was gone.

Astonished, she peered out through the slats. The bald trainer and the cut man were silently packing things up, going about their business in the solemn way of professionals who have lost a fight. The big fighter himself was nowhere to be seen.

She heard the hiss of the shower in the next room. Steam billowed out of the open doorway. Grant had gone to the showers, as his trainer had instructed. Had he gone without a towel?

As she peered through the slats, Val could see the edge of something white, low and to the left of the door. Awkwardly squatting down in the cramped space, she peered through the slats at that level…

And breathed a sigh of relief. Beside the door was a small table piled with fresh towels.

Thank the almighty Bob.

She leaned back against the wall as her hammering heartbeat slowly returned to normal.

"That was entirely too close for comfort," she said under her breath.

"I knew you should have waited in the shower. Just think of all the fun you could be having right now." Mister E laughed.

The image of the bloodied fighter's well-muscled torso flashed through her mind. She pushed it firmly away.

"No, thank you. Besides, as beat up as he is, I'm sure sex is the last thing on his mind."

"You'd be surprised. Sex and violence are well-connected in the human psyche. Why do you think conquering armies rape so much?"

"Because they're disgusting animals," Val spat.

"Exactly my point. People are animals. They get all overstimulated on violence, and when they run out of enemies to kill, they stab each other with their naughty bits instead."

Val wanted to argue with him, but what could she say? She might not like it, but she knew that on a fundamental level, he was right. Sex and violence were a recipe as old as the human race. How many people bit or scratched or bruised each other during sex? Or were into consensual BDSM? There was some weird wiring in the back of the human brain, and the conduits for sex and violence definitely ran in close parallel.

Not that anything ever excused rape. Those assholes deserved to be castrated and left holding their severed dicks in their hands.

Her musing was interrupted by Grizzly Grant's return from the shower. Thick dark hair covered his arms and torso, and his muscles stood out in slabs. The blood had all been washed away, leaving his skin crisscrossed with raw pink gashes. The larger ones had been stitched up by the cut man, but most were still open wounds.

The big man sighed as he sat back down on the bench for more treatment. They'd throw bandages over the smaller cuts and leave the rest to the shifter's natural healing powers.

She watched the process with fascination. The cut man and trainer moved over Grant's body like worker bees over a hive, doing their jobs quietly and efficiently. The fighter just sat there, brooding over his loss, paying no attention to them at all.

Val couldn't imagine letting people work on her body like that, let alone ignoring them while they did so.

"It's eerie," she hissed.

"Hillary stitches you up at home."

"Yeah, but not like that. He looks like he doesn't even know they're there. Like he's a sculpture or something. It's inhuman."

"Athletes are horses bred for racing. They are used to people constantly grooming their bodies. Do dancers find it strange when their partners touch them? This is no different."

"Yeah, but…" Her words trailed off as Grant's head jerked up. His eyes narrowed, fixing on the door to the closet.

Val pressed her lips together and shrank back, willing herself invisible. She'd only been whispering to Mister E, but she'd forgotten to factor in the shifter's unnaturally sharp ears. She held her breath, listening to her heart thump in her ears.

The cut man continued stitching Grant's wounds, unaware of the fighter's sudden tension. Grant watched the door of the closet for a dozen long heartbeats before he finally shook his head and muttered something under his breath.

Val sagged against the shelves and wiped beads of sweat from her forehead.

"You should let him find you already," Mister E advised. *"He is only wearing a towel after all."*

Val bit back a sharp retort. Muttering to the demon cat had almost gotten her caught. She wasn't going to make that mistake again.

The cat laughed, and Val's scowl deepened. The little toad-licker knew exactly what he was doing.

Mister E continued to taunt her with inappropriate comments as she watched the cut man finish stitching up Grizzly Grant. Val averted her eyes as the big fighter got dressed, which prompted a renewed round of mirth from her invisible companion.

Finally, the trainer and cut man were all packed and Grizzly Grant was dressed in a baggy blue track suit.

The fighter crossed the room and tossed his towel in a hamper beside the shower door. Then he turned…

And yanked open the closet door.

18

Val stood frozen, pinned like a butterfly to a specimen board. Grizzly Grant's mouth dropped open. He stared at her, crouched there in the closet among the clean towels. Val stared back.

The big fighter opened his mouth, but before he could speak Val's emergency improvisation muscles kicked into gear. She leaped out of the closet as nervous words poured out of her.

"Grizzly Grant! I'm a huge fan. I'm so sorry, you probably think I'm a creepy stalker. I wasn't stalking you, I swear. I was just, uh… using the bathroom. You came back and I knew I wasn't supposed to be in here and I panicked and hid in the closet." She started to edge past him. "I'm sorry. I'll be going now."

Val lunged for the door, but the bear shifter was faster. His fist clamped around her bicep like a manacle.

"Valora Keri?" His rough voice was soft with surprise.

She tried to jerk her arm free, but his grip was steel. Then his words registered.

"You know me?"

His face stretched into a big, goofy grin.

"Don't you remember me?"

"Should I?"

"We met in the alley outside the Metropolis. I told you about the weather."

The weather? Val thought back to the night she'd gone to the Metropolis, hunting the Puca. A lot of supernaturals were there that night, with nearly half the bar wearing glamours to mask their appearance. She hadn't found the Puca, but she had run into a red cap in the alley out back who would have carved her up if it wasn't for...

Realization dawned on her.

"You're the bear shifter from the alley?"

"That's me." His grin got wider and he puffed up with pride. "I didn't know you were a fan."

"Oh. Yeah. Big fan," Val stammered.

"What did you think of the fight tonight?" Grant asked.

"Um..." Val groped for words. "Well, obviously an Oni is a tough opponent. I didn't think that was fair to you, to be honest."

"I know, right?" Grant shrugged his thick shoulders. "But that's life on the supernatural circuit. There's no such thing as a fair fight, you know what I mean?" His face became solemn as if he'd said something profound.

"Oh, yeah. Absolutely." Val nodded along. "Would you mind letting go of my arm? You're squeezing a little too tight."

Grant jerked his hand back as if she were electrified.

"Oh! Sorry! Sometimes I don't know my own strength."

Val's laugh echoed his.

"No worries. It happens to all of us."

They both smiled and stood staring awkwardly at each other. The cut man and trainer hovered just behind Grant, flexing their hands, unsure what they should be doing.

Val cleared her throat.

"Anyway. Good fight tonight. I've got to get going, but it was great seeing you again."

She was almost out the door when Grant said, "Wait a minute."

Val half turned with one hand on the door frame. "Yes?"

"Why were you all the way down here looking for a restroom? We're nowhere near the amphitheater."

"Oh... I got lost. I've got a really terrible sense of direction."

His brows scrunched up as he thought about that. Then he nodded his big head.

"That makes sense."

"Right. Well, it was really lovely seeing you again. Better luck in the next fight!"

With that, Val ducked out of the doorway and fled down the hall before the fighter could try to stop her.

She dashed around a corner and kept right on going. It wasn't until she'd put several passageways between her and Grizzly Grant's dressing room that she finally allowed herself to slow.

"That was smooth," Mister E purred. *"Who knew you were such a fast talker?"*

"Necessity is the mother of invention," Val shot back. "I guess I've never been in the right situation before."

"It seems it's never too late to teach an old dog new tricks. What will you be doing for an encore?"

"I'm going to find the pot of gold at the end of this arrowhead." Val stopped at the next intersection and held the arrowhead in her palm. It pointed straight down the hall in front of her.

She followed it another hundred yards before stopping and examining one of the lamps. The metal was scorched and tarnished with age.

"This complex is huge and seems ancient. What do you think it's for?"

"Smuggling, probably. That's what most tunnels that aren't sewage or utilities are used for."

"Aren't you forgetting mining tunnels? And the old BART and MUNI tunnels?"

"BART and MUNI fall under utilities. Public transportation is a utility," he said archly. *"And mining tunnels are so obvious they do not need to be discussed."*

"Uh-huh. I don't know. These tunnels seem awfully well finished for smuggling tunnels. Why would they polish the walls of mining tunnels? Or hang fancy oil lamps on the walls?"

"Well, obviously they aren't smuggling tunnels any longer. At least not in

the traditional sense. The Yakuza are far too large an organization for that now."

"Just admit that you don't know."

"Ridiculous. I'm offended you would even think that." Mister E flicked his tail in agitation and slowly faded away, his gray stripes the last visible part of him before he disappeared completely.

Val rolled her eyes and kept walking.

The arrowhead tugged to the left and Val let it lead her toward a closed door set in the wall. Like the other doors in the complex, this one was made of dark lacquered wood inlaid with traditional Japanese carvings. Val ran her fingers over a stylized mountain she assumed was Mount Fuji, looming over a pastoral forest and lake.

"It's carved in the style of the Edo period." Mister E's voice came to her ear, though he refused to reappear.

"Thanks, but I'm more interested in what's behind it," Val said. The arrowhead was definitely leading her to something behind the door. She pressed her ear to the wood but heard nothing. "Do you see any alarm runes on this door?"

"No. The wood is not enchanted."

She pocketed the arrowhead and put her hand on the hilt of her knife instead. She gripped the door handle with her other hand.

Taking a deep breath, she slowly pushed the door open a crack. She heard nothing. No one called out an alarm. Nothing moved.

Swiftly she stepped inside and shut the door behind her.

The room was dimly lit, and it took her eyes a few seconds to adjust. When they did, she cursed.

"It looks like we found the rest of the arrows."

Lying on the floor of the room was a man. His mouth was frozen in a grimace, his face contorted with pain. Blood stained his shirt around the black shafts that pin-cushioned his body.

Val sighed. "Just what I need. Another dead body."

19

As she moved toward the man on the floor, Val quickly scanned the rest of the room. The walls were covered in dark wood paneling and the oil lamps on the wall were turned down so low they emitted only a faint glow. The air smelled of old incense.

The room seemed to be a museum of sorts, with ancient objects sealed in glass display cases. The lid of the nearest one was hinged slightly open and a glance inside revealed tiny jade figurines and an intricately carved set of jade earrings. Something was missing from a space beside the earrings. The slight discoloration of the velvet it had sat on told her it was something round. Maybe a pendant.

None of the objects appeared immediately dangerous, so she put them aside. A man was lying in a puddle of blood on the floor with several arrows buried in his chest. Everything else could wait.

She knelt and put her fingers to the man's neck. There was no pulse. His skin was not yet cold.

"He hasn't been dead long," Val muttered.

She checked the room again, looking for closet doors or other places the murderer could be hiding. Finding nothing, she returned to the body.

"Who killed you? And why?"

Val gnawed her bottom lip. The arrowhead had been her only lead, and it had brought her here. To this man full of black-shafted arrows. She guessed he was in his forties, with Japanese features and an expensive-looking suit. She needed to know who he was and, more importantly, who had killed him. She had a feeling it would be the same archer who had attacked Zoe Vasilevski in the graveyard.

She needed to make a decision. The arrowhead had brought her back to the other arrows from the quiver, which were currently embedded in the dead man's chest. It would lead her no further.

Quite a lot of blood, however, lay on the smooth stone floor. Blood was a very powerful tracker. Even if none of it belonged to the assassin, casting a spell using the victim's blood might give her a glimpse of the assassin, or even a connection with the assassin that she could track. This was especially true now, while the victim was still warm. The lingering traces of his spirit would be bound to his killer.

The longer she waited, the more that connection would dissipate. In a few hours the victim's soul would be gone and his blood would tell her nothing. She had to act now if she wanted to catch the assassin.

But could she risk casting a tracking spell here? It was ritual blood magic, and rituals took time. How long would she be alone in this room before someone discovered her?

"You're certainly not doing yourself any favors by standing here being indecisive," Mister E observed.

The demon cat was right. She needed to get to work.

First Val dipped her finger in the victim's blood and traced a quick ward on the doorframe. It wouldn't keep anyone out, but it would give her a few seconds' warning if someone came to open the door. Not ideal, but it was the best she could do.

Next she used the cooling blood to trace a circle around the corpse, with a quick pentagram inside it. She pulled candle stubs from her pocket and lit them at the corners, then settled down cross-legged.

Val closed her eyes and began a slow chant, focusing on her breathing and the beating of her heart. The words were mostly nonsense syllables; the important thing was the rhythm and cadence. Focusing on these things helped put her in the right state of mind for this type of magic.

As she sank into her trance, Val forgot about the chant. Forgot about her breath and the slow beat of her heart. Her awareness began to drift back in time, following the path of the cooling blood to the lingering spirit of the dead man.

She breathed in his spirit and entered the dead man's memory. Opening her eyes, she found herself inside the man's body, standing in the center of the room. He was leaning over one of the glass display cases, holding something in his hands. Lockpicks. He was trying to open the case.

Suddenly the door swung open and a dark figure stepped into the room. He raised a bow of polished wood, drawing the string back to his cheek in one fluid motion. The black-shafted arrow flew.

Pain stabbed through Val as the arrow sank into the would-be thief's flesh. His breath caught in his throat. Before the man had time to do more than stagger a single step sideways, another arrow hit him.

The man started to fall.

Val fought past the pain. Past the shock. She pushed her awareness into the man's eyes, trying to get a good look at the assassin.

There.

The archer was wrapped in black cloth, like the man in the grave-yard who had shot Zoe Vaslevski. The difference was that this man's face was uncovered. His eyes were as cold and flat as those of a dead fish. Val didn't recognize him, but she stared hard, engraving his features into her memory.

Perhaps this was the same man who had sliced open her shoulder.

Or perhaps there was a whole clan of ninjas running around shooting people with black arrows.

Either way, she had a new lead. She now had a face.

The ward on the door pulsed, pulling her attention from the vision. Someone was approaching the door.

She only had seconds to act.

Val flung herself to the side, rolling across the floor. She slid to a stop behind one of the display cases just as the intricately carved door swung open.

For three heartbeats she lay there, barely breathing, wondering how the unknown intruder would react to discovering a dead body lying inside a bloody pentagram.

She didn't have to wait long. A deep voice rang out.

"Come out slowly. Keep your hands where I can see them, and I won't have to break every bone in your body."

20

Val lay frozen, her options flashing through her mind. She could play innocent. She could fight. She could try to flee.

Before she could decide, the deep voice called out again.

"You have until the count of three to come out. If I have to drag you out, it will not be pleasant. One."

Val's face scrunched up. The voice was familiar. Where had she heard it before?

"It's the fighter from the ring upstairs," Mister E said.

Val's heart sank. She knew the voice didn't belong to Grizzly Grant. Which only left…

"Two."

She peeked around the edge of the case she was crouching behind. Sure enough, the purple-skinned Oni, Takashi Titan, stood in the doorway, yellowed tusks curling down from the corners of his mouth. Or rather, the Oni stood in front of the doorway, not inside it. He was much too large to stand inside it, in both height and width. The creature must have crouched and turned sideways to even get in the room.

"Thr—"

"OK, I'm coming out." Val stood up and raised her hands. She'd seen what the Oni had done to Grizzly Grant in the ring. She had no desire to tangle with the monster, especially in such an enclosed space.

"Turn around. Kneel down. Hands on top of your head." A flat-faced woman in a black security kit stepped around the Oni, barking orders. Her black hair was pulled back in a no-nonsense braid, and she steadied her handgun with both hands.

"Take it easy," Val said. "This is all a misunderstanding."

"You're going to tell me you didn't draw that pentagram or light those candles?" the woman asked, cocking her head at the still flickering tapers.

"Well, no. I did do that, but—"

"Now you're going to tell me you didn't kill this man either? You just happened upon his dead body and thought it would be fun to start fingerpainting with his blood?"

When the security woman put it like that, Val had to admit it did sound pretty bad. She noticed the dried blood flaking off the fingers of her raised hands. OK, make that very bad.

"I didn't kill him. If you'll let me explain…"

"On your knees. Hands on your head. Now!" The woman raised her gun so that the snub nose of the ugly thing was pointed directly at Val.

"OK. Fine. Relax." Val reluctantly followed instructions.

The woman stepped up, cuffed her wrists behind her back, and marched Val down the hall. The Oni followed, looming like some gigantic gargoyle.

After passing through several stone hallways, they entered an audience chamber with a vaulted ceiling. Huge carved pillars rose on either side, white marble wound around with intricate scenes of landscapes and people. Oil lanterns hung on the walls, but the main illumination came from a pair of gigantic jade chandeliers, each supporting dozens of candles.

A beautiful curved throne on a raised dais dominated one side of the room. A man in a black robe trimmed with gold sat upon the throne. The hair on his upper lip and chin were silver, but his skin was unlined, giving him an unsettling ageless quality. His eyes were bright, with irises shading from brown to gold at the center.

The woman kicked the back of her legs and pushed Val to her knees.

"Kneel before Daisuke Sada, the Dragon of San Francisco."

"What is your name?" the Dragon asked. His voice was quiet but powerful, resonating around the chamber.

"Valora Keri." She raised her chin and met his eyes, struggling not to look away. There was immense power in the Yakuza leader's golden orbs, and holding his gaze took every bit of Val's willpower. Her heart leapt with sudden fear.

"Do not trifle with this one," Mister E hissed. *"Unless you want to end up very dead, very fast."*

Val wanted to ask him what he meant, but she couldn't. She felt with certainty that if she muttered to him under her breath, the man on the throne would hear her. So she bit down on her questions and concentrated on holding the robed man's gaze — no small feat in itself.

"Why do you not grovel before me?" the man asked.

Val was happy to note that his tone was more amused and curious than angry. Something told her she did not want to see this man angry.

"Should I?" Val worked to keep her voice calm and level, despite the panicked battering of her heart. "Groveling isn't really my thing."

Daisuke Sada narrowed his eyes at that, and sudden sweat ran down the back of Val's neck.

"Who sent you to kill me?" he asked.

"Kill you?" A surprised laugh burst from her lips. "I'm not here to kill you."

"Do not lie to me." His golden eyes burned. "You are an assassin. What other reason could you have for being here? I ask again: Who sent you?"

"Nobody sent me. I sent myself." This was technically true. Zoe Vasilevski might have tasked Val with finding the assassin, but she had tracked the man to Japantown all on her own.

The Dragon cocked an immaculately sculpted eyebrow.

"You came here to kill me on your own? Do you seek to steal my treasure?" As he leaned forward, his eyes shone. Val felt her bowels turn to liquid.

"Your treasure?" she breathed. "I don't know what you're talking about."

"Do not lie to me!" He sprang to his feet and the candles flared overhead in unison. "You are after my gold. My ivory. My jade."

Immense pressure pushed down on Val, as if she were being crushed by a giant hand. She gasped when her forehead was forced to the floor.

"I ask one final time." The weight of Daisuke Sada's voice was like a mountain on her back. "Who sent you?"

"You should think very carefully about your answer," Mister E sounded scared. Val wondered what could possibly make the demon cat frightened.

His next words answered that question.

"The Dragon of San Francisco isn't just a title. The Dragon is exactly that. You are talking to a centuries-old dragon in human form."

21

Val squinted up at the man in the robe. Daisuke Sada, the Dragon of San Francisco, was an actual dragon? How was that possible? "Dragons are real?" she hissed at Mister E under her breath.

The Dragon heard her. But instead of squashing her head like a grape, the man laughed.

"Of course I am real. Did you think you came to assassinate a myth?"

"I told you," Val growled. "I didn't come here to kill you."

"You could not kill me." Daisuke Sada smoothed the golden dragons down his black robe before settling once again upon his throne. He had regained his composure, and now looked at her with a face as placid as the desert sands. "But that does not stop fools from making the attempt. For the final time: Who sent you, and why are you here?"

Val struggled to get up, fighting against the man's power. It was like trying to deadlift the Ural. She knew the Dragon could slam her back into a posture of obeisance if he wanted to. He could squash her like an insect.

Fortunately for her, he seemed more amused by her struggle than anything, and waited patiently until she had strained and sweated her way back to her feet.

"For the final time"—she ground her words between her teeth—"nobody sent me. I'm tracking an assassin. The trail led me here."

"An assassin?" The Dragon quirked his manicured eyebrow once again. "Another assassin is hunting me? Are assassins sprouting like mushrooms these days?"

Val didn't know how much she could trust the Dragon, but she saw no reason not to tell him the truth.

"This assassin tried to kill a friend of mine. I tracked him across the city and his trail led here. To the dead man in that room."

The Dragon narrowed his eyes at her.

"Yet my people saw no sign of this person. The supposed existence of this assassin seems awfully convenient for you. No man could infiltrate this complex and escape without my knowledge."

"Really? I got in, didn't I?"

"But you did not escape," the Dragon said smugly.

"Think for a minute. The man was killed with arrows. Do I have a bow? How could I have shot him?"

"An interesting point. Aneka?" The Dragon directed his gaze at the security woman who had brought Val in.

"We did not find a bow," Aneka admitted. "But that does not mean she isn't the killer. She may have hidden it. Or disposed of it through other means."

"What other means?" the Dragon asked.

"She is a witch. We caught her performing a ritual with the victim's blood."

The Dragon turned his luminous eyes back to Val.

"You were performing a blood ritual. With the victim's blood. Yet you still wish me to believe you had nothing to do with the murder?" He snorted. "Concoct a better story next time. Take her away."

"But..."

Val sputtered, but what could she say? The Dragon was right. She'd been caught playing with the blood of a recently murdered man. It looked bad. Even a friend might doubt her word under those circumstances.

Aneka dragged her away and put her in a stone cell. The walls and floor of the cell were polished slate, as spotless as the rest of the complex. The silver bars of the cell gleamed.

"Who waxes your floors?" Val asked as the woman pulled the barred door shut behind her. "They deserve a raise. This is the cleanest cell I've ever seen."

Aneka regarded her coldly through the bars.

"You have seen many cells?"

"More than I like to admit." Val spread her hands in a what-are-you-going-to-do gesture.

"I do not expect you will be walking out of this one." The woman turned her back and strode away, the heels of her boots clicking against the polished floor.

"Well, it was nice to meet you too," Val muttered. She ran her hand over the smooth walls, her fingertips tracing red veins in the gray stone. "Seriously though, who puts this much effort into a cell? I've seen penthouses less luxurious."

"Dragons value riches above all else." Mister E floated on his back at Val's eye level, his head pillowed on one arm. *"Not just currency, either. Riches in every sense of the word. Rich fabrics, rich furnishings, rich food, rich building materials."* He gestured at the polished walls and bars of the cell. *"Dragons want to have the best in all things. Apparently, that extends to the tiniest detail of their domain."*

"If I'm going to be a prisoner, there are certainly worse places to be." Val settled on the gleaming stone of the bed and put her back to the wall, crossing her legs at the ankle. "Do you see a bell pull anywhere? I'm kind of peckish. I could use some room service."

"You are awfully calm for the captive of a dragon."

"I'm innocent. We both know I didn't kill that guy. Besides, if the Dragon wanted me dead, I'd be dead already. That means he has other plans for me. I just have to wait and see what they are."

"So you are not going to try to escape?" Mister E cocked his head and gave her an upside-down look of surprise. *"That doesn't sound like the Val Keri I know."*

Val made a rude noise with her lips.

"Of course I'm going to try to escape. Don't be ridiculous. But first, we need to examine the pieces of this puzzle."

Mister E gave her a Cheshire Cat smile that stretched past the edges of his face. His ears puffed up to twice their normal size.

"In that case, I'm all ears."

22

Hillary kissed her lover on the cheek and slipped out of bed. She was careful not to wake him — moving with a silence that only a vampire could muster. They'd had a long night together, and he had earned his rest.

She felt rejuvenated by the tryst. For the safety of all involved, she avoided emotional attachments, but she still craved human contact. Flesh on flesh. Hearts racing. Breath hissing in the dark.

A night of fun with a sexy man had been just what the doctor ordered. It was almost enough to make her feel human again.

Almost.

Silver fog enveloped her as Hillary stepped out into the predawn chill. The street was silent and empty. No cars. No people. It was as if the entire city had been abandoned overnight and she strode through a post-apocalyptic wasteland.

This was her favorite time of night. The interstitial space between the realm of the night owls and the kingdom of the early birds. Lost hours slipping between the cracks.

She stalked through heavy fog and silence, a ghost in the mist. A pair of gleaming cat eyes watched her pass from a windowsill. A rat scurried away at the fall of her shadow.

Her body felt good. Powerful. Her nerve endings still tingled in the afterglow.

Sex was the only way she ever felt alive anymore. The only thing that got the blood moving through her cold vampiric body.

Most of the time she felt detached. A spectator of life. Never a part of it.

That was something no one had warned her about. The alienation. How being a monster pushed you away from the rest of humanity. As if life were a performance she was watching through a dirty window.

She didn't know if all vampires felt this way, but for her it had been nearly instantaneous. The moment she'd opened her eyes after Melinda Pearl turned her into a vampire, Hillary knew she had been irrevocably removed from other humans. Like a specimen pressed under glass, the world around her bright but distant.

It was an odd dichotomy. With her heightened senses, the world was closer in many ways. She was aware of so much more nuance, so many shades and textures she'd never known existed.

And yet.

None of it ever truly touched her. She was a stranger walking in a garden. She could admire the flowers, touch them, smell them. But she was not a flower, and never would be again.

Hillary shook herself from the melancholic turn of her thoughts. She'd been so deliciously warm and content when she'd rolled out of bed, and now she'd gone and spoiled it all within a few blocks.

It was this city. The stress of being hunted all the time.

She hated to admit it, but it really was time to leave. Stop procrastinating and move on. Val kicking her out of the apartment was the motivation she needed. She sighed and buried her hands in the pockets of her long jacket, hair growing damp as she strode through the fog.

Four blocks from the apartment, she felt a change in the air. She cocked her head, her senses sharpening. Something was wrong.

She heard movement behind her. A kicked rock skittered across the sidewalk.

Hillary didn't hesitate. She slipped off her heels and dashed forward on bare feet. Better cut feet than getting caught by whatever was stalking her.

Footsteps ran behind her. Her stalker trying to chase her down. Her blood froze as she realized her pursuer's steps were as unnaturally fast as hers.

The blocks blurred by in seconds. Four blocks became three.

Then two.

Then one.

If she could get inside the building, she would be safe. Val's wards would protect her.

She almost made it.

A hulking figure stepped out of the shadows ahead of her. Hillary tried to dodge, but a meaty hand closed on her hair, jerking her to a painful halt.

She cried out as Jonathan Gray lifted her and twisted her body to face him. She kicked at him, but the massive vampire didn't even flinch. Nearly seven feet tall and built like a truck, Gray was Melinda Pearl's most trusted enforcer.

"Hello, Hillary," he rumbled. Then he punched her in the face.

The man hit like a jackhammer. Hillary thought it was a wonder the blow didn't snap her spine. He hit her again, twice more in quick succession.

All the fight went out of her. Her head swam as the world became soft and fuzzy. She hung limp in the vampire enforcer's grip.

Rodrigo came sauntering up behind her. He had been the one chasing her.

Melinda Pearl's top lieutenant wore a red silk button-up shirt. The sleeves were rolled to expose his muscular brown arms despite the nighttime chill. His black hair was slicked back from a sharp widow's peak above his forehead.

"Little Hillary," he mocked. "You've been a bad girl."

"Fuck you." Hillary spat at him, the white glob landing on red silk over his navel.

Rodrigo blurred forward, slashing open her chest with his long nails. Bright red lines bloomed above the neckline of her dress. Hillary cried out and thrashed, but Jonathan Gray easily held her suspended from the ground.

"You've wasted a lot of my time," Rodrigo growled. Another slash. "You and that witch made me look like a fool."

Multiple slashes punctuated his words, until Hillary's flesh hung in strips. Blood soaked her dress. She kicked out at Jonathan Gray, trying to get free. Her toes found his shins, his knees, his groin, but she might have been blowing him kisses for all the reaction she got from the gigantic man.

Rodrigo laughed.

"Oh no, you're not going anywhere this time. We're delivering you back to the queen. But first I'm going to take my pound of flesh."

23

"Point one: Someone is killing people with arrows."

Val ticked off one finger on her left hand. She sat with her back against the wall, feet propped up on the smooth bed before her. Her head rested against the stone, eyes turned up to the ceiling as she cast her mind back over recent events.

"Your insight is astounding. Watch out Sherlock Holmes," Mister E said.

Val ignored him.

"Point two: The assassin is targeting people within the city's mafia organizations. I would say 'leaders,' but I have no idea what position that dead man held within the Yakuza."

"Point of order," Mister E interjected. *"Mafia is an Italian word which traditionally refers to Italian organizations, either in Italy or abroad. I don't know if you can use mafia as a blanket term for all large criminal organizations."*

Val gave him the side-eye.

"Your objection is noted, Professor Pedant. If you want to get technical, every language has its own name for their local criminal organizations. Rather than list each of them individually, I'm appropriating the Italian word 'mafia' as a general term which I will use to refer to large, organized criminal organizations, regardless of their origin, ethnic, or national identity. Is that all right with you, Professor?"

The demon cat smirked. *"I only wanted to make sure we defined our terms before we started throwing them around willy-nilly. Words are important, you know."*

"Uh-huh. Anyway, this brings me to point three: There are factors at play we don't know about."

"Brilliant! Bravo, Sherlock!"

Val spoke over her floating heckler, "The dead man was trying to break into that glass case. Maybe he was trying to steal something out of it. There was definitely something missing. Judging by the discoloration it left in the case, my best guess is the object was a pendant. Probably made of jade since everything else in the case was.

"By the time we arrived, the man was dead, the case was open, and the pendant was gone. Which means the assassin must have taken the thing the man was after. Which begs the question: Was the assassin's primary goal to kill the man? Or was the assassin there to steal the pendant, and our victim was simply in the wrong place at the wrong time?"

They pondered that for a moment.

Mister E said, *"How does that fit with the attack on Zoe? That assassin wasn't trying to steal anything in the graveyard. He was just there to shoot people."*

"Not 'people.' Zoe." Val said. "The new head of one of the most powerful *mafia*" — she glared at Mister E as she said the word — "organizations in the city. An attack like that couldn't be random, especially following on the heels of her uncle's assassination." She laced her hands behind her head. "So where does that leave us?"

"In a cell. Obviously."

Val ignored her companion's quip and ticked the points off on her fingers again. "We have two murders, one attempted murder, and one theft. A theft, I should add, from one of the city's most powerful organizations, headed by a literal dragon. Not someone you want to steal from unless you have a really, really good reason. We have one suspect, Joumala Anand, who definitely has a motive for the killing." She snapped her fingers as a realization hit her. "Joumala was wearing a magical jade bracelet! Do you think it's connected to the jade pendant the assassin stole from here?'

Mister E floated upside down near the ceiling, revolving slowly on his back as he thought.

"It certainly could be."

"We need more information. We need to question that assassin."

"If we can find him."

She gnawed on her lip.

"True. But I got a good look at his face when I performed the ritual. That might be enough to track him."

Mister E looked skeptical.

"Without his hair or blood, he would have to be very close for that to work. Tracking without a physical component is unreliable at best."

"Do you have a better idea?"

"No, I'm just pointing out the flaws in your plan."

"Very helpful. Thank you so much."

"Anytime." The demon cat's smile was large and luminous.

"I wish I had a piece of paper, though," Val's mouth twisted. "I need to get his face down while it's still fresh in my memory. The ritual vision will fade with time."

"You could use your whirling-gravel trick to carve a relief sculpture of his face into the stone wall."

"Yeah, because that wouldn't make noise or draw the attention of the guards at all." Val rolled her eyes. "Also, it would take all day. And have you seen how pristine this place is? This isn't some crumbling SFPD cell that has plenty of little pebbles lying around. I haven't even seen any dust in this place, let alone tiny pieces of gravel I could use as a carving tool."

"What about your knife?"

"That security woman took it. Aneka. Though if she thinks that's my only weapon, she's in for a big surprise."

"Except you are, in fact, groping for a plan and failing without your knife. So perhaps the surprise won't be as big as you think."

"Are you going to make any helpful suggestions? Or are you just going to sit there and poke holes in everything I say? Because I could do that fine without you," Val snapped.

A voice interrupted from outside the cell.

"I'm not sure who you're talking to, but I've got a suggestion."

Val whirled to find a familiar figure standing outside the cell. "Obi!"

The young thief held her knife in one hand and a ring of keys in the other. He jingled the keys and gave a lopsided grin.

"I can get you out of here. For a price, of course."

24

"Obi!" Val exclaimed. "How did you get the keys?"

The young thief winked at her.

"Don't worry about the how. Worry about the why."

"OK... so why did you get the keys?"

"To rescue you, of course. But more importantly, to get paid."

Val folded her arms over her chest.

"What's your price?"

"Double what we agreed."

"I'm already paying you double to get me out, remember?"

"I mean double that."

"So quadruple what we agreed."

"Look at you with your big words." The thief grinned. "Call it whatever you like. I'm only concerned with the number of zeros that will be transferred to my account."

Val glared at him.

"And if I don't agree, you'll leave me here to rot?"

"Not to rot, no. The Yakuza would never keep you here that long. I imagine they'll come up with something much more creative to do with you. Maybe they'll put you in the ring with Takashi Titan."

Val swallowed. She could more than handle herself in a fight. As a general rule, she wasn't afraid to mix it up with anyone. If she could stay out of the Oni's reach, she had a chance of defeating him with her wind powers.

But if she got tossed into the ring with him? She'd be hard pressed to stay out of his grasp in such a confined space. And she couldn't hope to match his strength. If the Oni got his enormous hands on her, the fight would be over quickly.

"Time's wasting." Obi cast an exaggerated glance down the hall. "The guards might show up any minute."

Val's scowl darkened. It wasn't that she couldn't pay Obi's price — Zoe's expense account would cover it easily — it was the principle of the thing. The little shit was extorting her.

"What else did you expect from a mercenary? The boy's a thief. From the start, he was only in it for the money. Frankly, I'm impressed with his resourcefulness. Showing up here with both your knife and the keys so shortly after you were locked up shows uncommon initiative and skill. Swallow your pride, agree to his price, and let's get out of here."

Val sighed. She hated to admit it, but the demon cat was right.

"Fine," she ground out between her teeth. "I'll quadruple your fee. Now get me out of here."

Obi beamed and gave her a courtly bow, his hand sweeping the polished floor.

"Your wish is my command." Seconds later, the cell door swung open.

As Val joined him in the hall, Obi flipped her knife in the air. She caught it by the hilt and tucked it into the top of her boot.

"Thank you. Before we get out of here, do you have a piece of paper?"

"Paper?" Obi's forehead scrunched in confusion.

"Yes, paper. You know, thin material used for writing on. Made from trees?"

"Not just trees," Obi shot back. "Paper can be made from bamboo. Also rice, hemp, and all kinds of things."

"Whatever you make it out of, the question is still the same. Do you have any?"

"Sure, yeah." He pulled a thin notebook out of his belt pouch. "Will this do?"

"That's perfect." She flipped it open to a blank page. "Do you have a pencil?"

"The notebook would be pretty useless without one," Obi said, producing a worn nub of a pencil.

Val took it and rubbed the tip back and forth against the bars of the cell, creating a drifting cascade of graphite shavings.

"That's not how you use that," Obi pointed out.

"Thank you, Captain Obvious. Relax. I've got this under control."

When she'd created enough shavings, Val closed her eyes and recalled the face of the assassin. With every detail of the memory clear, she gently reached out and scooped up the graphite shavings with her magic. She let the shavings drift down over the paper, filling in the image of the assassin she held in her mind's eye. When the graphite had done its job, she gently blew away the shavings and opened her eyes.

The face of the assassin stared back at her from the top page of the notebook.

"All right, I'll admit it. That was pretty sharp," Obi said. "Do you do caricatures too?"

"Sure. First I beat your face into a caricature. Then I make a portrait to match."

"I was only asking." Obi backed out of reach. "You're awfully touchy."

"In case you forgot, I've been locked in a cell. That tends to put me on edge." Val peered up and down the hall. She saw nothing to differentiate one direction from another. "How do we get out of here?"

"This way." As Obi led her down the hall, he asked over his shoulder, "Did you at least find what you were looking for before you got caught?"

"Yes and no. The trail I was following led me to another corpse, but I got the assassin's face this time. I think he might have stolen something too, which gives me a possible motive for the murders I didn't have before. Maybe. Trying to solve a mystery is like unraveling a ball of yarn. You follow the thread from one knot to another, untangling as you go. If you're lucky, each knot leaves you with another thread to follow."

"And if you're not lucky?"

"You run out of yarn."

A shadow fell over the hall as the hulking figure of Takashi Titan stepped out in front of them, blocking the passage.

"Aptly put, Val Keri." Aneka said from behind the Oni. Her eyes sparked with anger. "And you have just run out of yarn."

25

"I think we've seen this movie before," Mister E said. "I didn't like the ending."

Val glared at the two figures blocking their path. She might be able to handle the Oni. Maybe. If she got lucky.

But Aneka was a wild card. Val didn't know what the head of Yakuza security could do. The woman looked more than capable. If Aneka was giving orders to an Oni, she would be no push over, that much was certain.

Val clenched a fist and drew in her power. She was tired of playing nice. She'd let the Yakuza put her in a cell once. She wasn't doing that again.

Obi spun around, his eyes wide.

"Run!" The young thief suited action to words, darting around Val and sprinting back the way they'd just come.

Mister E chuckled. "Or you could do that."

Running was never Val's first instinct. Fighting was.

She glanced from Obi's receding form to Aneka and back again.

Why not try something different for a change?

She turned and sprinted after her young guide.

"Stop thief!" Aneka's shout and the bellow of the Oni came right behind her. Val heard their feet pounding against the stone.

She followed her young guide around a corner. Another featureless hall stretched out in front of them.

"I hope you know where you're going," she called.

"Who do you think you're talking to?" Obi snapped over this shoulder. "I'm the best thief in San Francisco. I've always got a plan."

"Well, your plan didn't turn out so well when you tried to steal my motorcycle."

"That's because you cheated. If you hadn't thrown your magic around, I would have sold that piece of junk already."

Val's face darkened.

"Call my motorcycle a piece of junk again. I dare you."

The thief threw up his hands.

"Relax. Don't be so touchy."

"The world doesn't play by rules, you know. Cheating happens more often than you'd expect."

The Oni's bellow echoed down the hall, underscoring her statement. A glance over Val's shoulder showed that their pursuers were gaining on them. The hulking creature's long legs ate up the ground with every stride, while Aneka effortlessly kept pace.

"Point taken." Obi ran faster.

Val tried to throw a gale down the hall behind them to slow their pursuers, but sprinting and casting spells was like rubbing your head and patting your stomach at the same time. She could do it if she really focused, but the bellows of the Oni and the frequent turns taken by her guide kept breaking her concentration.

Finally, she gave up and worked on simply putting one foot in front of the other as fast as she could.

After two more turns, Obi pivoted and yanked open a nondescript door.

"Through here."

Val ducked into the dimly lit space as he slammed the door shut behind them. The closing door took the light with it, plunging them into darkness. She heard the lock click into place.

"That won't stop the Oni," she pointed out.

"No kidding." Val could hear the young thief's eye roll. "This way."

A ball of blue light appeared in his hand as he led her across a cavernous storage room. Stacks of dusty furniture stretched up to the ceiling, creating a maze of passages whose walls leaned precariously. Val couldn't see what made the light, but the illumination was enough to keep her from barking her shins on the jutting corners of end tables and dressers.

Val and Obi both ducked instinctively as a boom like a shotgun blast echoed through the room. Peering between the stacks, Val saw that the door had exploded into kindling.

"What the flock was that?" she asked.

"That was the Oni putting his shoulder into it," Mister E said.

"We need to hurry," Obi hissed, quickening his steps.

They rushed down a corridor between the tightly stacked furniture — some covered in dust cloths, some not. The walls zigzagged crazily in and out with the irregular shapes of the furniture. In places, the topmost pieces leaned so far out they almost formed a low ceiling.

Behind them, the Oni bellowed. Val saw a flash of purple skin through a tangle of ladder-backed chairs.

Obi led her down one dusty and cramped passage after another. The room seemed to go on forever.

From what Val could tell, the furniture came from every era, and had been stored without rhyme or reason. She passed a funky avocado-green set of chairs, clearly from the 1970s, stacked next to an intricately carved and stained armoire that looked like it belonged in a museum.

"Where did they get all this?" she breathed.

"Dragons are the original hoarders," Obi said. "They never throw anything away. The longer they live, the more things they accumulate."

"And you have a back door into this hoard? Why are you wasting your time stealing old motorcycles? Sell a few of these antiques and you'd be set for life."

"A very short life," Obi replied. "Dragons are extremely possessive, and every piece of this hoard is cursed. Those who have tried to steal from it have all met very unpleasant ends."

The tinkle of breaking glass somewhere nearby punctuated his statement, as the Oni's wide shoulders sent a stack of chandeliers crashing to the ground.

"Oh, here we are." Obi stopped before a large, antique wardrobe.

"A wardrobe? Really?" Val's face twisted in disbelief. "I'm not going to find a snowy forest and a faun inside, am I?"

"Do you want to make snarky comments, or do you want to get out of here?"

"Both, ideally."

They hit the ground as a pair of throwing knives whistled past their heads and thudded into the stained wood.

Val whirled. Aneka was standing less than fifty feet away, another set of knives already in her hands. The Oni loomed behind her, all yellow tusks and red eyes.

"Those were just a warning," the black-clad woman called out. "The next two will not miss."

"Shit, I need fifteen seconds to get the door open," Obi hissed. Val could see the whites of his eyes. "Can you distract them?"

Val set her jaw. "Do what you need to do. I've got this."

With a snarl, she flung her power down the passage.

To her credit, Aneka was ready for it. A flick of her wrist sent the knives spinning one after another, the blades flashing silver-blue in Obi's light as they tumbled toward Val's face.

Unfortunately for the Yakuza security head, she wasn't quite fast enough.

The gale that Val had been holding since their sprint down the hallway exploded in the tight space between the stacks, sweeping the blades aside like autumn leaves. Aneka was knocked off her feet, crashing into a tangle of ancient lamps.

The Oni, however, just stood there, leaning into the wind. His tusks gleamed as he snarled and took a step forward.

Val poured more power into the gale, but the giant just hunched his shoulders and took another step.

"You'd better get that door open fast," Val snarled. "The Oni's too strong. I can't hold him."

"Just a second," the thief said.

Sweat trickled down the back of Val's neck as Takashi Titan continued placing one giant foot in front of the other. He was less than twenty feet away now. She was throwing so much power at him, her body felt like a wide-open conduit. A raging river of magic was flowing straight through her.

Still the monster advanced.

Obi yanked open the wardrobe door. "Get inside. Quickly!"

"You don't have to tell me twice."

Val dove into the wardrobe, which was predictably filled with old fur coats on hangers. The thief's light winked out as he slipped in behind her, yanking the door closed just ahead of the Oni's grasping fingers.

"Don't stop," he croaked. "Go! Go!"

The door of the wardrobe rattled on its hinges as she pushed forward into the darkness, the silky feel of fur coats sliding over her skin. Her questing fingers did not encounter the back of the wardrobe.

After several seconds of complete darkness, Obi's fingers flared with blue light. A moment later, Val's eyes detected an answering light creeping around the edges on the furs ahead.

"Walk toward the light." Obi pushed against Val's back. "Go!"

With a final plunge, Val parted the furs and stepped out into the light.

26

To her relief, Val did not emerge into a snow-covered forest near a lamppost. Instead, she stood in what appeared to be a junkyard. Rotting furniture and decaying cars lay strewn about a vacant lot. She thought it might be the same lot she had chased Obi across that afternoon. An overcast night sky brooded above them, and she pulled her jacket close against the chill evening wind.

She whirled to find Obi closing the portal behind them, his fingers lined with blue light once again. She narrowed her eyes.

"That looks an awful lot like magic. Care to explain?"

The young thief grinned at her.

"Didn't I tell you? I'm part kitsune."

Val raised an eyebrow.

"A kitsune," Mister E said. *"That explains a lot. Those tricky little foxes make excellent thieves."*

"No kidding," Val murmured back under her breath. Aloud, she said, "No, you didn't mention it. That might have been an important thing to bring up earlier."

"Why? Do you reveal all your secrets on the first date?"

"No, but…" But what? The kid was well within his rights to guard his secrets. Especially one that big. Honestly, Val was surprised he'd told her at all. "It just would have been nice to know," she finished grumpily.

"Well now you know. Happy?"

"Not particularly."

"I'm not surprised. From your RBF, I can tell you're a sourpuss by default."

It took Val a few seconds to decipher that. When she did, she exclaimed, "I do not have resting bitch face."

"You keep telling yourself that."

Val glared at him. "Say that again and you'll meet my resting bitch fist."

The thief sprawled in a ragged leather armchair, stretching his legs out and crossing them at the ankles. "So, where are my credits? As agreed, I got you out safely."

Val ran her hand over the wall where the portal had been. Only a faint outline remained on the painted cinder blocks.

"Can they track us?"

"Nope. The portal is gone. There's nothing to follow."

"You've clearly done this before."

"Clearly." Obi's cocky smile was infuriating.

Val pursed her lips.

"So if you don't steal from the dragon, why break into his hoard? Isn't that asking for trouble?"

Obi's smile grew wider.

"That's half the fun, isn't it? Breaking into someplace where you're not supposed to be isn't any fun if there's no risk of consequences."

"You think getting eaten by a dragon is a fun consequence?" Val puffed her disapproval. "The folly of youth. I hope I was never that dumb."

"No, you were even dumber," Mister E said.

"That's what youth is all about," Obi agreed, ignoring her point. "Taking risks. No risk, no reward. Speaking of reward, I want my money. Now."

"Fine." Val pulled four bills from a hidden pocket in the lining of her leather jacket and tossed them down onto the thief's outstretched legs. "Thanks for your help. I'll see you around."

As she turned away, Obi's voice stopped her in her tracks.

"I know the man you're looking for."

Val raised an eyebrow at him over her shoulder.

"What man?"

"The man in the sketch."

Now she spun her whole body around.

"You know who he is? Why didn't you tell me earlier?"

Obi laughed. "We were kind of busy running for our lives. Besides" —he held up the bills between his fingers—"I needed to make sure you were going to pay me before I offered you any more services."

"Who is he? Where can I find him?"

"How much is it worth to you?" The young thief's grin widened.

Val scowled. Obi's cat-that-ate-the-canary smile reminded her of Mister E. Just what she needed: more insufferable smugness in her life.

"Payment for services rendered, remember?" Obi continued. "You show me the money, and I'll show you the man behind the curtain."

Val ground her teeth. She'd already given the kid a significant portion of the advance Zoe had paid her. The Russian mafia princess would probably reimburse her if she had to dip into her personal account, but Val's financial reserve was currently as shallow as the Great Salt Lake. She would rather not go there unless she had no other choice.

Also, the ease with which he kept fishing money out of her pocket grated. He had been helpful, but she couldn't deny the feeling that she was being played.

And yet.

She glared at the kid for a full minute, hoping he would crack. He didn't. His smile remained insufferable.

"Maybe I should just beat it out of you." She stepped forward and hauled him up by the front of his shirt.

"You could try. And I'd talk." Despite dangling from Val's fists, Obi seemed unfazed by the suggestion. "But there's no guarantee what I told you would be the truth. In fact, there's a high probability I'd send you into some kind of nasty trap. You know what they say: Violence only begets more violence."

Val knew he was right. And beating up kids wasn't her preferred method of dealing with things.

That didn't stop her from wanting to knock his smug teeth down his throat.

She tossed the boy into the armchair in disgust.

"What I'll pay depends on the information. Do you have a name?"

Obi put his hands behind his head. His grin stretched from ear to ear.

"I can do better than that. I can take you to him."

27

Hillary dangled in the grip of Jonathan Gray. Her little black dress was soaked with blood. The skin of her chest hung in strips. Her breath came out in pained gasps. Despair filled her mind. The vampires had caught her. She had foolishly thought that living with Val Keri would keep her safe. She had put off leaving the city too long.

Now she was paying the price for her lack of caution. And Benji would pay the price along with her.

"What do you want, Rodrigo?" she said desperately. "Let's make a deal. I'll give you anything you want."

"Anything I want? Didn't anyone teach you not to make promises you can't keep?" He slashed her again. Blood spattered the sidewalk. "All I want is your blood. I'm going to take that myself."

More slashes. Too many for Hillary to count.

She'd lost a lot of blood now. Maybe too much. Even vampires had their limits.

Would Melinda Pearl be angry if Rodrigo accidentally killed her? She hoped so. It would serve her right. Serve both of them right.

She was so weak she could hardly twitch. The pain of her injuries was receding as her mind sank toward the darkness.

I'm sorry, Benji, she thought. *I'm sorry I couldn't take care of you better.* Then the lights came on.

Blazing sunlight flooded the street, sizzling her skin and forcing her eyes shut. Rodrigo hissed and Jonathan Gray dropped her. Her limp body hit the sidewalk like a sack of potatoes. She barely felt the impact.

Along with the light came... music? It sounded like some kind of dance music, all thumping bass and upbeat melody.

Hillary lay under the glare, her skin sizzling. She didn't know what had happened to her attackers. They'd probably slunk into the cool safety of the shadows.

Then there were hands under her arms, lifting her to her feet. A familiar voice in her ear.

"Come on, Hillary. Work with me here. Use your legs. I can't carry you up the stairs all by myself."

Malcolm.

Now the light and music made sense. They were part of the new defenses. Malcolm had installed giant sunlight floodlights and speakers on the front of the building. He called it the no-vamp dance zone.

She tried to make her legs work. Did her best to stumble up the front steps and through the door. The stairwell leading to the apartment was daunting. She didn't think she had the strength to scale the steps, and there was no way Malcolm could carry her up.

Then another pair of hands helped to lift her. She turned her head and saw her own mangled face reflected in Sandra's mirrored sunglasses.

Somehow, the three of them made it up the stairs and into the apartment. Sandra and Malcolm laid her on the couch.

Malcolm stood wringing his hands. "There's so much blood. What do we do?"

"Blood," Hillary whispered. "All I need is blood." She was so weak she wasn't sure if she was even forming words.

But Malcolm understood.

He knelt beside her and pressed his wrist to her lips. "Here. Take whatever you need."

As the smell of his blood filled her nostrils, a raging hunger seized Hillary. Conscious thought disappeared and instinct took over.

She latched onto Malcolm's wrist, sharp fangs easily parting his soft flesh. Glorious warmth filled her mouth.

The room went away. The pain, the burns on her skin, her housemates. All of it. There was only the blood pulsing down her throat. She could feel power flooding outward through her veins. Her wounds knitting. Her burnt flesh healing. The strength returning to her body with every swallow.

Yes. This was what she was meant to do. Blood. It all came down to blood.

Distantly, she became aware of something hitting her. Fists pounding against her, accompanied by noises.

Hillary resurfaced from the depths of her hunger to find Sandra hitting and pushing against her. There were noises coming from the gorgon's mouth.

Words. The noises were words.

"Let him go. You're killing him. Let go!"

Hillary realized she was still latched onto Malcolm's wrist. Her housemate was limp and pale. Unconscious from blood loss.

With an effort of will, she tore her mouth away from his flesh. The hunger cried out in protest. She needed more blood. Needed to heal.

Hillary ignored it. She had fed enough. She was strong enough to heal the rest on her own time.

"Malcolm," she gasped. "Shit. I'm sorry."

She put her ear to his lips. The barest whisper of breath fluttered against her skin. His pulse was weak and erratic.

"No, no, no, no, no… What have I done?"

A rattling exhalation came from Malcolm's mouth. All the hair stood on the back of Hillary's neck. She knew that sound. She had heard it several times during her years as a nurse.

That was a death rattle.

She had taken too much blood. She had killed Malcolm.

"No!"

There was only one chance. One way to save his life.

Hillary slashed open her wrist and pressed it to Malcolm's mouth.

28

Val didn't want to follow the young kitsune. She had spent most of the day tracking the assassin, and a large portion of the night infiltrating and escaping from the Dragon's lair. She was tired and hungry and all she really wanted to do was go home and collapse into bed.

But she had to strike while the iron was hot. If she went home, the trail could go cold, and she might never get another chance this good again. The assassin was close, she was sure of it. She just had to keep pushing.

"OK," she agreed. "Take me to him and you'll get your money. But I need some food first. Trying to stop that Oni took a lot out of me. If I don't eat something, I'm going to pass out."

"No problem," Obi said. "There's a ramen place right around the corner."

"I don't care what it is. I could eat pickled herring right now and not even mind."

"Good, because that happens to be the house specialty. Follow me."

They ducked through a gap in the fence and out onto the sidewalk. The bustling afternoon shoppers were gone, replaced by blazing neon and drunk carousers wandering from bar to bar.

Val stopped, blinking in the sudden light. After skulking around for hours, trying not to be noticed, being thrust onto such a lively street made her feel as if all eyes were on her.

She knew the feeling was ridiculous. The drunks were intent on having fun, each the star of their own internal movie. No one spared her more than a passing glance.

Squaring her shoulders, Val buried her hands in her pockets and fixed her eyes forward. She flipped her attitude from "skulk" to "don't fuck with me." Eyes forward. A slight frown fixed on her lips. Every inch of her screaming that she was on a mission, and not someone to be trifled with.

"RBF," Obi muttered out of the corner of his mouth.

Val backhanded him without breaking stride.

"Ow!" Obi rubbed his chest.

Val smirked. She had warned him. That would definitely leave a bruise.

The ramen shop had a wooden counter facing the street with a handful of low stools in front of it. They ordered two bowls of noodle soup and spoke very little as they slurped down the salty broth.

"That was just what the doctor ordered," Val sighed as she finally pushed the empty bowl away.

"Ramen makes the world go around," Obi agreed. "I ate ramen every day when I was a kid."

"Did you grow up here?" Val turned a curious eye on him.

Obi shook a finger at her.

"No personal questions. This is strictly business."

"You're the one who brought it up."

"I was just making conversation. And I regret it already." He pushed himself up from the bar. "Come on. The place we're going is only a couple of blocks away."

To Val's surprise, the kitsune led her across Geary Street into the Fillmore District. In its glory days, the Fillmore had been a mecca for world class jazz musicians. All the greats had played there. Later, it had become a must-play venue for musicians of all stripes. The list of virtuosos and bands who had played the Fillmore was legendary.

The concert hall had fallen on hard times though, and now the little gulch had a dangerous reputation.

"This isn't Japantown anymore," Val pointed out.

Obi rolled his eyes.

"Not everything happens in Japantown. It's a big city. Broaden your horizons."

Val supposed it made sense. They were looking for a thief. Criminals didn't generally congregate in high-rent districts.

Well, this level of criminal, anyway. Zoe Vasilevski, Padraig O' Ceallaigh, and the rest of the mafia royalty enjoyed their high-rent lifestyles just fine.

Obi led her down a flight of cement stairs and flashed a big bouncer some hand signal that Val didn't catch. The man nodded and motioned them inside.

The basement bar was dark and crowded, reeking of smoke, sweat, and desperation. The walls and floor were painted black, and the ceiling was so low Val could reach up and touch it with her fingertips. Rough-looking people on wooden stools surrounded round tables, the lighting so dim it hid their faces in shadow. Voices rose and fell, waves of conversation breaking and receding, making it impossible to catch more than a word here or there.

Val leaned into Obi. "How are we supposed to find anyone in here?"

He looked indignant. "These are my people. Trust me."

The moment the words left his mouth, a thickly muscled man stepped into Obi's space. He wore a powder blue tracksuit, and his dark skin drank the light like the paint on the walls. The man's chest was as big around as a table. He seized the kitsune's lapels with one meaty fist.

"Obi. You'd better have my money."

"Kwame!" Obi tried to back away from the man, but Kwame's grip was solid stone. "How fortunate, running into you!"

"Fortunate because you have my money?" The tracksuited man shook the young thief so hard his teeth rattled.

"Maybe if you stop shaking him and let the kid talk; you'll get better answers," Val snapped.

Kwame sneered at her. "Shut up, bitch. Men are talking here."

Val saw red. Before her mind was even conscious of it, her fist had smashed into the man's nose. Bright blood burst across his face as he went down in a heap.

She whirled, her heart thudding, hands up, ready for the rest of the man's posse to leap to his defense.

But the other people in the bar barely glanced in her direction. She caught a few smirks, but no voices rose. No one moved.

Obi rolled his eyes and pulled her on through the crowd.

"I had that under control, you know," he said. "You don't have to leap to my defense like Lancelot."

"I don't like bullies." Val's eyes were scanning the crowd, adrenaline hammering through her veins. She couldn't believe that was the end of the incident. "And he called me a bitch."

"Touché. It was a poor choice of words on his part." He offered her a lopsided grin. "And I'll admit, it was nice seeing someone put that creep down."

"You're welcome." She surveyed the crowd as Obi steered her toward a small side room at the back of the bar. "Any sign of this guy we're looking for?"

The kitsune's grin widened.

"As a matter of fact, he is exactly where I thought he'd be."

29

In a small side room, Val and Obi found several men hunched over a green-felt-topped table. A long tube light fixture hung over it, casting the surface in crisp relief against the shadows surrounding it. The men's faces were studies in contrast. Bright planes and shadowed valleys. Their feverish attention focused on the cards dealt out on the table. Hearts and diamonds danced in their eyes.

The man they were looking for perched on a stool at the far end of the oval table. He looked just like the sketch Val had created of him: a middle-aged white man with dark pouches under his eyes, an alcoholic's nose, and sagging jowls. A battered Greek fisherman's cap covered his thinning brown hair. His skin was an unhealthy gray in the harsh light.

"That's the assassin?" Val muttered incredulously.

"The best assassins are the ones you never suspect," Mister E said.

"Yeah, but… that guy?"

"If one may judge his effectiveness by how easily you would be inclined to overlook him, perhaps he is a very good assassin."

"I guess that's one interpretation."

Val was unconvinced. This guy looked like he spent twelve hours a day in his current pose. Hunched over cards in a back room. Slowly drinking himself into oblivion. He looked like he might have a heart attack if he ran to the bathroom. There was no way this was the same guy who had shot at them in the graveyard. She doubted he was strong enough to even draw a bow, let alone wield one with deadly accuracy.

"I guess there's only one way to find out." She started to step towards the man, but Obi put a hand on her arm.

"Wait," he told her in a low voice. "It's not a good idea to interrupt the game. Not unless you want even more trouble." He nodded toward the bouncer standing discreetly in the corner of the room.

The black-suited woman stood in a relaxed parade rest, her hands clasped behind her back. Her blond ponytail was pulled through the back of her baseball cap. From her stance, Val knew she was either ex-military or a moonlighting cop, and in excellent shape. Her eyes were hidden behind mirrored sunglasses, but Val had the feeling the woman was watching her.

"I could take her," she said.

Obi rolled his eyes.

"I'm sure you could. And the other six security guards in this place. But while you were busy doing that, our man would rabbit in all the confusion, and we'd lose him. Also, I'd get eighty-sixed from this place. Which I'd rather not. Have some patience. I'll sidle over there and have a discreet word with him between hands. Relax."

"I don't have a lot of patience," Val muttered.

"Then learn some. They say it's a virtue. A little delayed gratification is good for you."

Val scowled. "What's this guy's story, anyway?"

"How should I know?"

"I thought you said you knew him."

"No, I said I knew where we could find him," Obi corrected. "I've never spoken to him in my life."

"Great. Very helpful." Val crossed her arms over her chest.

There were six players at the table in addition to the dealer, four men and two women. Two of the men were young and cocky, and the women were both wrapped in sharp designer clothes. They made quite the contrast beside to the weathered old man they'd come to see.

The final player was a middle-aged Japanese man in a practical gray suit. There was nothing flashy about him, but as Val watched the cards go around and around, her eyes kept returning to his efficient movements. Everything about him screamed quiet competence.

She leaned close to Obi and lowered her voice. "Who is that guy?"

The thief shrugged. "No idea. Why?"

"Something about him makes my spider-sense tingle. Lend me your eyes." This last was directed at Mister E, who obligingly slid his magical sight over hers.

The Japanese card player flared as the magical spectrum came into focus. His entire body was limned with a low orange glow. Her instincts had been correct. The man was definitely a practitioner of some sort. Or a monster.

But his wasn't the only magic in the small room. The gambler in the fisherman's cap shone too. Something beneath his shirt gave off a brilliant green light.

Val gasped and one of the women at the table glared at her.

"Keep it down," Obi hissed.

"There's something magic under our guy's shirt. Something powerful."

The kitsune snorted. "Did you just figure that out? You're a little behind the game."

"Not all of us are secretly magical creatures. I don't see magic all around me, all the time."

"Sounds like a personal problem. You might want to get that looked at."

Val's retort died on her lips as a round of curses went up from the table. One of the immaculately dressed young women smiled a shark's smile and raked in the pot. The guy they were there to see didn't react. His expression remained unreadable as he tossed in his cards, giving nothing away. A true professional gambler.

As the dealer shuffled the cards for the next hand, Obi circled the table and bent to whisper something in the man's ear. A flicker of surprise passed over the gambler's face as his eyes ticked up to meet Val's. He frowned and looked skeptical, then nodded at something Obi said and pushed his chair back from the table.

"I'm out." His voice was sandpaper on hardwood.

Val watched him circle the table. He walked with a shuffling hunch; nothing in his movements suggested that he could be a fighter.

"Curiouser and curiouser," she muttered.

The other players watched but said nothing. The middle-aged Japanese man's gaze lingered.

As the old guy reached her, Val said, "Hi, I'm Val Keri. I've got a few questions I was hoping you could answer."

The man regarded her silently for a moment, his steady eyes betraying nothing.

Then he punched her in the throat.

30

Val gagged and crumpled against the wall. Panic shot through her as she fought to breathe. Tears sprang to her eyes.

The gambler hadn't hit like a sedentary guy. His strike had been precise and powerful. If Val hadn't twisted at the last second, he would have crushed her windpipe.

Despite her reaction, the man had come close, and she struggled to draw breath through her bruised throat.

"I suppose it's safe to say he's not friendly," Mister E observed.

Val tried to croak out a response, but she could barely get enough air in her lungs to keep from passing out. The gambler pushed past her. She blinked back the tears as she watched him disappear into the crowd.

She lurched into pursuit. He wasn't going to get away that easily.

Val growled in frustration. There were too many people in the bar for her to use magic. She'd have to chase him down the old-fashioned way.

She fought her way through the crowd. The man was as slippery as a fish, darting between people with ease, leaving hardly a ripple in his wake. In contrast, Val felt like a water buffalo, pushing and shoving, her passage creating an expanding pool of outraged faces and raised voices.

She didn't care. She was focused on a single objective: catch the gambler.

"*On the bright side,*" Mister E said, "*this must mean we've got the right man.*"

"It's only a bright side if we catch him," Val wheezed. "How is he moving so fast?"

She'd lost sight of the man now. He'd been heading toward the door, and all she could do was push on in that direction and pray that he would be there when she reached the street.

"*At a glance, I'd say it must be the amulet. It's giving him strength and speed.*"

"Amulet?"

"*The thing around his neck.*"

"The magical thing beneath his shirt? How do you know it's an amulet?"

She stumbled into a businessman's arm, spilling his drink all over the front of his date's dress. The woman's outraged shriek joined the chorus of raised voices behind Val as she pushed on through the crowd.

Obi called out apologies behind her, but Val didn't slow or look back. If she ended up with a lynch mob after her, so be it. She would deal with that when the time came.

First she had to catch the gambler.

Val finally burst free from the crowd and shot onto the fog-shrouded street. It was empty. She cursed and turned to go back into the bar, thinking the gambler must have ducked out a side door. Then she paused as her ears caught the sound of running feet slapping against pavement.

She spun, trying to figure out which way the sound was coming from. Things echoed strangely in fog, bending and twisting, bouncing off unseen surfaces to come at you from unexpected directions.

"Give me your eyes again. Now!"

"*Your wish is my command,*" Mister E intoned, and the world burst into vibrant life around her.

There. Green light was jouncing through the fog off to her left. It was half a block away, at least.

Val sprinted after the light, cursing at how far ahead the gambler had gotten. She couldn't see the man's body at all, just a disembodied green light floating ahead of her like a will-o'-wisp.

She cursed as she chased him across block after block. The light wasn't getting any closer. If anything, it was slowly pulling away.

"Damn that amulet," she snarled. "With the shape he was in, that guy should have dropped dead from a heart attack by now."

"Be glad he hasn't." Mister E floated along just above her left shoulder, lounging on his back while making leisurely swimming motions. Val was sure he was mocking her. *"Dead bodies are notoriously difficult to get answers from."*

Val scowled at the green light in the fog. It wasn't her imagination; the gambler really was pulling away from her. She had to do something, or she'd lose him.

She examined her options. She couldn't see the man, and judging distance in the fog was impossible. So stopping him with a headwind the way she'd caught Obi was out of the question.

Well. If she couldn't slow the gambler down, Val would just have to speed herself up.

At her summons, a tailwind came gusting down the street and scooped her neatly off her feet. She could fly faster than she could run. Thanks to the fog, going airborne held minimal risk of being observed, as long as she got up at least twenty feet above eye level.

Unfortunately, this was a city, and flying in low visibility held other dangers.

Val was forcibly reminded of this as she was nearly beheaded by a black fiber-optic cable whistling out of the fog. She squawked and twisted her body at the last second, the cable snapping painfully against her ear.

"Flying toads," she cursed. "You don't know how lucky you are, being incorporeal. I need an air-traffic controller to fly in this city."

"Not having a body does have its advantages. Though the lack of privacy is a bit of a drawback."

"You're telling me."

Val swooped higher, getting above the dangerous maze of telephone poles and light posts and power cables before turning her gaze back down, searching for the green light in the fog once again.

31

V al caught a glimpse of the green light as it disappeared behind a
building.

"Not so fast," she growled, swooping around the corner in pursuit.

She flew over the light and landed on the sidewalk in front of the
man. He came running out of the fog and skidded to a halt, breathing
hard.

"You can answer my questions, or we can do this the hard way,"
Val snarled. The wind swirled around her, lifting her hair as if it were a
living thing. She clenched her fists. "Personally, I hope you choose the
hard way. I owe you for that sucker punch."

The man's eyes narrowed. They were cold and flat, the irises
shining with the green light of the amulet.

"What do you want, witch?"

"I want to know why you're going around shooting people with
arrows, for starters. A man is dead and Zoe Vasilevski is in the hospital
because of you. And that's only the people I know about. What are you
after? Who are you working for?"

The man sneered. "Why should I tell you anything?"

"Because if you don't, we're going to see how much you like
getting punched in the throat."

"The Brotherhood tells no tales. Besides, the information will do you no good. This is too big for you, little witch. Go back to your broomstick."

"Too big? Why don't you let me be the judge of that. Who are the Brotherhood? Who are you working for?"

Val pursed her lips as she considered the gambler. Something about the way the man was standing struck her as strange. His body weight was shifted oddly to one side, as if he were off-balance or uncomfortable.

"The Brotherhood are a bunch of self-important assholes who think they're better than everyone." Obi came sauntering out of the fog. "They're assassins for hire."

The man's flat eyes slid to the kid. "Careful, little fox. Those who tell tales get their tails cut off."

"By you, old man? I don't think so."

The assassin regarded the kitsune expressionlessly. Then, between one heartbeat and the next, he moved.

The man shifted his weight so fast that if Val hadn't been looking through Mister E's eyes, she might have missed it. Instead, everything seemed to happen in snapshots of slow motion. The assassin lunged toward Obi, a knife appearing in his hand. The kitsune's eyes widened as he started to twist away.

Too slow.

The knife sliced across the boy's belly, drawing a line of red.

Val stepped forward, gathering power in her fist.

The assassin turned his lunge into a dive and a roll, tumbling into the street, ending up on one knee. As Obi started to crumple, the man yanked the glowing green thing out from under his shirt, and Val got a good look at it for the first time.

It was a shining jade amulet on a leather cord, about three inches in diameter. Intricate carvings covered its surface. It blazed with power.

In one smooth movement, the assassin yanked the cord up over his head.

"Wait!" Val shouted. She punched out a fist of wind.

Again, she was too slow.

The assassin shoved the amulet down through the storm drain at his feet. The green light dropped away into the blackness.

Val's punch hit the man in the chest, the wind knocking him sprawling. She closed the distance in three strides and stood over him, ready to hit him again, this time with a real fist.

The man's mouth opened and closed as he looked up at her in confusion. His eyes blinked. The green light that had filled them was gone. So was the cold, flat look. He suddenly looked like exactly what he was: an old gambler, lying in the street beneath the drifting fog.

"Wha… where am I?" he stammered.

Val hesitated, her fist cocked back to strike. The man cringed away, raising a feeble hand to ward off the blow. He looked utterly transformed. The light in his eyes had fled, taking with it the confident sneer and the easy power of his movements. He looked old and slow and weak.

"Don't play games with me." Val hauled him up by the front of his shirt.

"Who are you? How did I get here?" The man clung to her arm, his eyes wide with fear.

"Stop acting. I'm not buying what you're selling."

"I don't think he's acting," Mister E said. *"His magical aura is gone."*

"What does that mean? The amulet was controlling him?"

"Possessing him, I'd wager."

Val considered the gambler. Aside from a superficial physical resemblance, everything about him had changed. His demeanor, his body language, even the look in his eye.

She swore.

"Where did you get the amulet?"

"Amulet?" the man stammered. "What amulet?"

But Val had seen his eyes widen slightly when she said the word amulet. She tightened her grip on his shirt.

"You were wearing a jade amulet. Where did you get it?"

"I don't know what you're talking about."

Val sighed and pulled out her knife. She held the gleaming blade in front of the man's face.

"I don't like it when people lie to me. It makes me feel stabby." She pressed the point to the gambler's neck. "Last chance. Where did you get the jade amulet?"

32

Malcolm groaned. Hillary crossed the room in two quick steps and knelt beside the couch where he lay. She could hear his heart beating. It was erratic, but stronger than it had been.

"Come on, Malcolm. You can do it," she urged.

Hillary had been pacing the room for almost an hour, waiting to see if Malcolm would wake up. Her blood seemed to have pulled him back from the brink of death, but his heartbeat was too weak. He was still teetering on the edge.

"Why don't you give him more blood?" Sandra asked. The gorgon sat in the window seat usually occupied by Val, her hands wrapped around a mug of coffee that had gone cold.

"It's too dangerous," Hillary replied. "I didn't want to give him any blood, but he was dying. It was the only way I could think to save him."

"You did the right thing," Sandra said.

Hillary didn't reply to that. She wasn't sure if she had done the right thing, but what was she supposed to do? Let him die? From blood loss that she'd caused?

No. Anything was better than that.

"Will he become a vampire now?" Sandra asked.

"No. I'm not a master vampire. I can't create other vampires." Hillary bit her lip. "At least, I don't think I can."

"Don't think? You aren't sure?"

"No, I'm not. I haven't been doing this vampire thing very long. I was told that only the master could create new vampires. But I was never sure if that was just a protocol thing or not. Like whether only the master is *allowed* to create vampires, or if only the master is *able to* create new vampires. I never bothered to clarify the question because I had no intention of making new vampires, so I figured it didn't matter either way." She bit her lip. "I think my blood will just give Malcolm strength."

"But you're not sure."

"I'm not sure."

"Wow, that's heavy." Sandra blew out a breath. "I'm glad I don't have that problem. Gorgons can't make other gorgons. At least I don't think they can." She suddenly looked alarmed. "They can't, can they?"

Hillary held up her hands.

"Don't look at me. I'm not the expert on monster lore around here."

"No, that would be me," Malcolm said weakly.

They turned to gape at him.

"You're awake!" Sandra said.

"You're alive!" Hillary added.

"Yes, I'm awake and alive." Malcolm looked amused, then his brow wrinkled. "Was there a chance I wouldn't be?"

"Well…" Hillary hedged.

"It was touch and go for a while there," Sandra said.

Malcolm's eyebrows scaled his forehead.

"Touch and go? I could have died?" He turned accusing eyes on Hillary. "You told me it was safe."

Hillary winced. "When I'm healthy, it is. But I was pretty heavily wounded. I didn't know what I was doing. I almost drained you dry. I'm sorry."

Malcolm's face paled.

"You almost drained me dry? Seriously?" He put his hands on his chest as if he was verifying that it was still there. "So why didn't you? What happened?"

"Sandra happened. She pulled me off you. Brought me back to my senses."

"Well, thank goodness you stopped feeding in time." He paused at the look on Hillary's face. "Didn't you?"

The silence stretched.

"Hillary, you're scaring me. What did you do?"

The vampire sighed.

"Sandra didn't stop me in time. You were in bad shape. Not dead, but I don't know if you would have survived. Things were looking pretty bad. So I did what I had to in order to save your life."

"What was that?"

"I gave you some of my blood."

"You what?" Malcolm's voice rose an octave.

"I gave you some of my blood. Just a little bit. You needed strength and that was the only way I had to give it to you."

"Does that mean I'm a vampire now?"

"No." Hillary grimaced. "At least, I don't think so."

"You don't think so?"

Hillary told Malcolm what she'd told Sandra. When she was done, she could hear his heart pounding. Smell the fear on him as he tried to keep his breathing under control.

"So, how do we find out?" he finally asked in a very small voice.

"There's nothing to find out," Hillary said. "Right now, I can assure you that you are a hundred percent human."

"Right now? What happens later?"

"That's the part I don't know," she admitted. "Hopefully nothing happens later."

"But something might."

"Something might. Hopefully it doesn't, but something might. I just don't know."

He was silent for a long minute, emotions scrolling across his face as clearly as text on a page.

Finally, he said, "Well if I become a creature of the night, at least I'll

be a sexy one. I mean, it's me, so I would have been a sexy one regardless. But vampires are sexy for longer."

Hillary gaped at him for a long moment. Then she snorted. Sandra
started to giggle. Malcolm joined in. In seconds, they were all on the
floor, howling and holding their sides.

Laughing while the tears rolled down their faces.

33

The gambler's eyes widened. His words tumbled out in a rush.

"I lost the amulet in a game."

"Lost it? Don't you mean you won it?"

"No. I lost it."

"That doesn't make any sense."

"It was the end of a long night. Big pot. I was all in. My opponent raised me. I didn't have anything to cover the bet, so he said if I lost I would have to wear this amulet. It seemed strange, but what could I do? I was out of money. Anyway, I was holding three kings. I was sure I would win."

"But you lost."

The gambler nodded sadly. "Bastard had a full house."

"Then he made you wear the amulet?"

"Yeah. I slipped the leather cord over my head… and the next thing I know, I'm out here in the street with you."

Obi let out a low whistle.

"Yeah," Val muttered in agreement. "That's a strong amulet."

She turned her attention back to the gambler.

"What did this guy look like?"

The gambler shrugged. "Nothing special. Asian guy. Middle-aged. Wore a suit."

"Do you know where I can find this guy?"

"No. I never saw him before."

Val cursed and released the gambler. Dead end.

"Now what?" she muttered.

"I have a suggestion," Obi said.

"What's that?"

"We retrieve the amulet." He gestured to the grate through which the gambler had dropped the jade.

The kitsune was right. The old gambler had told them everything he could. Which wasn't nearly enough. The amulet was their only lead.

Val cursed.

"Great. More sewers. Just what I didn't need."

They found a manhole cover in an alley. Together they managed to pry up the heavy metal cap and slide it aside. Val eyed the dark interior dubiously.

"Do you come here often?" she asked.

The kitsune laughed.

"I bring all my dates here. The smell really knocks them off their feet."

Val gestured to the hole. "After you."

"No, after you," Obi said. "Age before beauty."

"Gee, thanks."

Val kept Mister E's sight over her eyes as she descended into the underground darkness. She could see the iron rungs of the ladder beneath her hands as clear as day. Unfortunately, she could see the rest of the tunnel too.

It wasn't pretty.

Slime and mold grew thick along the arched brick ceiling, and the narrow walkway bordering the river of dark sludge was crumbling. The safety railing had been eaten away by rust.

The stench was awful, bringing tears to Val's eyes. They were deep in the heart of the city, far from the cleansing breezes of the Pacific Ocean or the bay. The air in the sewer tunnel was stagnant and stuffy, so thick Val could feel it coating her teeth with every inhale. As soon as her feet touched the walkway, she pressed a hand over her mouth and tried to take very shallow breaths.

"First time in the sewers?" Obi dropped next to her.

"I wish. I've been spending so much time in the sewer tunnels, I should build a summer home down here."

"I hear you can get a good deal on land. The neighborhood stinks, though."

Val rolled her eyes.

"Now that we've got that out of the way, let's find the amulet. I'm guessing it's this way."

They tiptoed along the slippery walkway, careful to stay far from the crumbling edge. Looking up, Val saw light seeping down through rectangular storm drains. She was relieved to see from the water stains that the flows from the drains ran down the walls of the tunnel instead of dumping into the center of the channel. Now they just needed to find the grate through which the amulet had fallen.

There was a green glow up ahead. Relief flooded Val as she rounded the bend and saw the jade amulet lying on the walkway beside a dark alcove.

"Thank Bob we won't have to go fishing for that thing."

As she bent down to pick it up, movement flashed in the corner of her eye. Something heavy connected with the back of her skull. Her face hit the walkway. Everything went black.

34

Val surfaced slowly, her thoughts as thick as oatmeal. The first thing she noticed was the darkness. The second was the stench.

"What?" she croaked.

There were hands on her back, helping her sit up. She turned her head to find Obi crouched down beside her, concern in his eyes.

"Take it easy," he said. "You've got quite a lump on your head."

She felt the back of her head with unsteady fingers. Sure enough, there was a fist-sized lump. It hurt when she probed it.

Images came floating to the surface. The amulet on the walkway. A movement in the corner of her eye. Pain. Falling. Blackness.

"What hit me?"

"*Who* hit me. Not what. Though I suppose some might consider him a what," Obi replied.

Val turned a grumpy glare on him.

"You can shove your semantics. Answer the question."

"Well, I have good news and bad news." Val's glare intensified and Obi hurried to elaborate. "The good news is, I know who hit you. And I know where the amulet is."

"The bad news?"

"The bad news is that the amulet is not here. And…" He gave her an apologetic smile. "The Dragon has the amulet."

"The Dragon? The same dragon whose dungeon we escaped from earlier tonight?"

"That's the one. It was the Oni who hit you."

"The one that chased us earlier?"

"Yeah, that Oni. I considered trying to fight him off, but then I remembered that I enjoy having all my arms and legs attached." Obi grimaced. "So he got the amulet and I got to keep my limbs."

Val buried her face in her hands. "So we're back to square one. We don't have the amulet and we still don't know who the assassin is."

"I thought the old gambler was the assassin?"

"The gambler is one assassin," Val corrected. "But he's probably not the only one. And he was only an assassin because he was wearing the amulet."

Obi made a face.

"That's as clear as the water in this sewer."

"The amulet was possessing him. Or the thing that lives inside it was. Which means he's not the assassin at all, the amulet is. Or whoever is controlling the amulet is."

"I'd just like to point out that the Dragon controls the amulet. Surely you don't mean mean the Dragon is the assassin?"

"Obviously not." Val shot him a withering look. "When the gambler stole the amulet, he killed one of the Dragon's guards. I doubt the Dragon is in the habit of killing his own people."

Obi screwed up his face. "Wait. That makes no sense. If the gambler was only the assassin because he was wearing the amulet, then how could he steal the amulet from the Dragon? I think there's a hole in your logic."

"Unless there is more than one amulet," Mister E added.

Val sat bolt upright.

"That's it!"

"What's it?" Obi asked.

"There is more than one amulet. The assassin is trying to collect them all. That's why the gambler stole that amulet from the Dragon, even though he was already wearing one."

"I'm afraid you've lost me again. He's trying to collect them all? Why? And how many are there?"

Val chewed her lip. "I don't know. But I feel like we've found the heart of the mystery. What I really want to know is: Is the assassin killing people in order to collect the amulets? Or are they collecting the amulets on order to kill people?"

"That sounds like a chicken-and-egg type of question."

"No, it's not. Depending on the answer, that would make their motivations very different."

"Let me get this straight." Obi started ticking off points on his fingers. "The assassin was wearing an amulet. He stole a second amulet from the Dragon. We caught up to the assassin, and he threw his amulet down the storm drain. Which the Dragon's Oni snatched away from us. So if all of that is true..." He held up a finger and waggled it at her. "Where is the second amulet?"

"Good question. I have no idea. But, returning to the question of whether the assassin is killing in order to collect amulets or vice versa, I think I might have a way to answer that question, at least."

"And that is?" Obi cocked an eyebrow at her.

"I need to ask a friend some questions."

35

"*Since when do you consider Zoe Vasilevski a friend?*" Mister E asked.

Val stood in the dark outside of San Francisco General Hospital. It was surprisingly busy, considering the time of night.

Or perhaps not so surprising. She'd heard somewhere that hospitals were usually busiest at night. Accidents happened when people were tired, or inebriated, or simply couldn't see what they were doing.

At the moment, the lobby of SF General seemed to confirm that. Through the lighted windows she could see at least a dozen people sitting in the waiting room. Four were bleeding. One looked like he had a broken arm.

"It's easier to just say 'friend' than to explain that I'm going to have a chat with a Russian mafia princess. Now be quiet, I need to figure out the best way to get up to her room."

Val had left Obi back in Japantown. He'd served his purpose for now and she wasn't going to drag the kitsune all over the city. Besides, it was late and she'd had a long day. After she talked with Zoe, Val was going to go home and collapse. She could figure out her next moves tomorrow.

"*You could always fly up to her room,*" Mister E suggested.

Val peered at the flat edifice.

"The hospital has a lot of windows, but it doesn't look like any of them are open. I don't even know if they can be opened. Why do they design buildings like that anyway? What's the point of a window that can't be opened?"

"Nothing promotes healing like good old recycled air."

Val chuckled. "No argument there. Unfortunately, that doesn't solve our problem."

"You could break a window."

"I don't think that's advisable." She took a deep breath and squared her shoulders. "We're just going to have to walk in the front door."

"It's not exactly visiting hours."

"No, but the hospital is pretty busy. Maybe no one will notice us."

Mister E gave her the side eye.

"I'm sure you'll blend right in. Especially with that lovely eau de sewer perfume you're wearing. No one will give you a second glance."

"The trick to blending in is to look like you belong."

Val squared her shoulders and lifted her chin. She pushed through the front door with a purposeful stride.

She avoided the cluster of people at the receptionist's desk and turned left toward the elevators.

The harried receptionist called out, "Excuse me, miss?" but Val pretended not to hear her. She kept her eyes locked on the elevator bank, as if she were on a mission and knew exactly where she was going. Her heart pounded while she waited for the elevator, but the receptionist didn't call out again, as a loud man at her desk monopolized her attention.

Val held her breath as the elevator doors slid open, but it was empty. Perfect. She stepped into the gleaming steel cube and pressed the button for the fifth floor.

She examined herself in the mirror as the elevator rose. There were bags under her eyes and a dirty smudge on her cheek. Her hair was a wild tangle. She licked a finger and rubbed off the smudge. Tried smoothing her hair with her fingers. There was nothing she could do about the bags, though. After this, she really needed to go get some sleep.

The elevator whirred to a halt and the doors slid open. Her luck held. No one was standing in the hall outside the elevator.

Val stepped out. There was a T-intersection to her left, while the hall stretched away to her right. The directory numbers on the wall told her 532 was to the left.

She'd only taken a few steps when she heard someone approaching the intersection. Panic surged through her. Breezing past the reception desk was one thing, but up here on the fifth floor she would stick out like a barrel cactus in Alaska.

Reacting on instinct, she reached for the handle of the nearest door. Relief surged through her as it opened, and she slipped inside what appeared to be a janitorial supply closet, quietly pulling the door closed behind her. Shelves stocked with cleaning supplies and toilet paper marched up the wall in front of her. To her left was an industrial sink with a mop and bucket parked beside it. A pair of blue jumpsuits hung on pegs. Beside them was a toolbox.

Val grinned.

"Just what the doctor ordered."

Three minutes later, Val emerged from the closet wearing a blue jumpsuit. She carried the red toolbox in her left hand. As had become her habit, she kept her right hand buried in her pocket. Most people didn't notice her petrified fingers, but when they did, it invariably caused a scene. Better to keep them out of sight as much as possible.

The lights were dim inside room 532. San Francisco's skyline sparkled through the window. The room's sole occupant was a motionless lump beneath the blankets on the bed. As she stepped into the room, a massive shadow shifted to Val's left. She whirled and locked eyes with a stone-faced member of the Vasilevski security team standing beside the door. He nodded at her ever so slightly.

Val hesitated, unsure if Zoe was awake. The girl's soft voice answered that question for her.

"Val Keri, are you moonlighting as janitorial staff now?"

"Something like that." Val crossed the room and stood next to the bed. "How are you feeling?"

Zoe put her hand over the spot where the arrow had pierced her chest. Bandages peeked out the top of her hospital gown.

"I've been better. The damn arrow missed my heart by about an inch. But they think I'm out of the woods. They're keeping me a couple days for observation." Zoe wrinkled her nose. "You stink. What have you been doing? Petting pigs?"

"Something like that."

"Sit." Zoe waved her toward a chair. "Tell me."

Val sat and told the mafia princess everything she'd discovered.

Zoe's china doll forehead creased as she listened, her mouth pressed into a pucker. When Val finished, she remained quiet for a long moment, her eyes narrowed in thought.

Finally, she pulled on a leather cord around her neck. A piece of jade emerged from beneath her hospital gown. Val's eyes widened as it caught the light, flashing between Zoe's fingers.

The injured girl sighed. "Those goddamn jade amulets. I told my uncle they were trouble, but he wouldn't listen. Now we're all fucked."

36

Val leaned forward in her chair, hands steepled over her knees. Mister E slid his magical sight over hers without being asked. The amulet shone with power.

"What do the amulets do?" she asked.

Zoe's mouth twisted. "It's complicated."

"I've got plenty of time."

The Russian princess leaned her head back against the pillows and fixed her eyes on the ceiling, gathering her thoughts. Her pink hair against the white linen made Val think of ice cream.

"In the days after the United States collapsed, people were panicking. There were riots. Food shortages. Things were chaotic, to say the least. The state of California was running around like a chicken with its head cut off, trying to put out a million fires at once, but unable to fully deal with any of them.

"The bay area was a mess, and the city of San Francisco didn't have the manpower or resources to help everyone. After a couple of weeks, it started to get really bad. People were starving and desperate.

"Some powerful people saw this as an opportunity. People who had organizations and manpower. Access to resources. My uncle Andrei was one of them. He used the Vasilevski network to bring in food and basic necessities. He didn't do it for money. Money was worthless at the time anyway. No, he handed things out for free to whoever needed them, cultivating goodwill and territory. He had faith that eventually things would stabilize, and by the time they did, all these people would have become dependent on the Vasilevski network. They would literally owe us their lives.

"My uncle wasn't the only one to seize this opportunity. Other organizations across the city did the same. The O'Ceallaighs, the Anands, the Wongs, the Yakuza; the list goes on. A handful of families expanded their power tenfold and seized control of different parts of the city. Like medieval kingdoms.

"Then things got ugly."

Val waited as Zoe paused to take a sip of water. Her head was spinning already. She hadn't known any of this. Of course, she'd only been in San Francisco for two years, and it had been over a decade since the collapse.

She'd been hardly more than a kid when it happened. Twelve years old. She still remembered that time like it was yesterday, though. Everyone did. They always had a ready answer when the conversation got around to, "Where were you when everything fell apart?"

Val had been in a foster home in Utica, New York. She remembered her foster parents, Tony and Gina, freaking out when the news hit. Tony had screamed and punched the wall. Gina had torn her hair out and cried.

She remembered living off bottled water and running out of toilet paper. Empty shelves at all the grocery stores, people fighting over cans of beans. She remembered the power going out and not coming back on for weeks.

But New York had been better off than a lot of the country. The state government had figured out pretty quickly that the federal government was gone and wasn't coming back. New York was a big state with a lot of resources. Within a month they had circled the wagons and become the first independent republic within the shattered shell of the United States.

California had plenty of resources too. But it was a lot bigger than New York. The cities were more widely scattered and the divide between urban and rural California was vast. California's state government had struggled to put things back together.

Then the big quake hit and blew all their efforts to pieces. The golden state had shattered into city-states and lawless territories.

Zoe cleared her throat and continued.

"Any student of history could guess what happened next. The city's new feudal lords started fighting over territory. There were turf wars and border skirmishes almost every day. Entire blocks became burnt out husks. No-man's land. It seemed as if the city was going to survive the collapse and the big quake only to get blown to pieces by internal strife.

"This went on for most of a year. Finally, a summit was arranged. All the leaders of the major families came together in one room.

"It went about the way you'd expect with all these family leaders with their egos and power and conflicting agendas. They argued for days. Sometimes they came to blows.

"Finally, the Dragon of Japantown proposed a radical solution. I don't know how he got the other families to agree to it, but he did. The Dragon produced a magical jade amulet, and a peace pact that bound the leaders of every family to it. Then the Dragon shattered the amulet, turning it into many amulets, and giving one piece to each family. But the Dragon secretly took it one step further. He also put a curse on the amulet. He tied their power to the amulet and made the families dependent on one another. Either they all prospered or none of them would."

"How does the amulet work?" Val interrupted for the first time.

Zoe gave her a tired smile.

"I don't know. I just know what my uncle told me. He said that if any of the families got too greedy, the curse would activate, bringing bad luck onto their organization."

"Bad luck? That doesn't sound like much of a threat."

"That's what I said too. Then my uncle told me about the Forti Family."

"Let me guess. They broke the pact."

Zoe nodded and took another sip of water. She was clearly exhausted, but she pushed on with the story.

"The Fortis were an old Italian mafia family. They controlled North Beach and the piers, from the edge of the Financial District all the way around to Ghirardelli Square. They agreed to the peace pact, but they never really stopped trying to expand their territory. They just became sneakier about it. Their closest rival was the Wongs, who controlled Chinatown and Nob Hill. The Wongs are led by my friend Shen's grandmother, Jing Wong, who is the toughest old woman you will ever meet. The Fortis didn't care about Chinatown, but having the Chinese in control of Nob Hill irritated them. It was like a scab they couldn't stop picking at.

"The Fortis started causing trouble in Nob Hill. Attacking Wong businesses and people. Trying to intimidate them and drive them out. The usual strong-arm tactics. But then bad things started happening to the Fortis. The thugs that were causing trouble in Nob Hill disappeared one by one. Then the head of the Forti family died. This was when the Dragon finally told us all about the curse. To say the Fortis were pissed would be an understatement. They declared war on the Yakuza and marched on Japantown en masse.

"On their way to war, a burnt-out building collapsed on the entire Forti gang at the corner of Geary and Gough. There were no survivors. The curse wiped them out. The last remnants of the Forti family fled the city, and the Wongs took control of North Beach. Nothing bad happened to them. Apparently, the curse lets you expand into empty territory; you just can't encroach on other members of the pact."

"If the curse is so effective, how was someone able to kill your uncle and attack you? Also, how could they steal pieces of the amulet? And why?"

"I don't know. I understand magic about as much as I do nuclear physics. That's why I hired you."

Val drummed her fingers and pursed her lips.

"How many families have amulets?"

"Five. The Wongs, the O'Ceallaighs, the Anands, the Yakuza, and us."

"And you have no idea which of these would want to kill you?"

Zoe laughed.

"All of them want to kill me. That's part of the game. But the amulets are supposed to make it impossible."

Val winced at the mention of the O'Ceallaighs. Their inclusion complicated things. She and Padraig O'Ceallaigh had worked together to defeat a plot initiated by Melinda Pearl's vampire coven and a visiting necromancer. He'd saved her life more than once.

Then she'd messed it all up by challenging him to a duel and taking Pandora's Box from his family as her prize. She'd shattered their relationship. Val would be the last person Padraig wanted to talk to.

She sighed and pushed her concern aside. She'd just have to find a way to deal with Padraig when the time came.

"Aren't Shen, Padraig, and Joumala your friends?"

"Friends is a pretty loose term. I'd say we are more friendly rivals than friends. We help each other when it suits our needs, but none of us would hesitate to stab the others in the back if we needed to. Our families come first."

"With friends like these, who needs enemies?"

"Exactly."

Zoe was struggling to keep her eyes open. Getting shot and pumped full of pain killers would do that to a person.

Val got to her feet.

"I'll let you get some rest. Thank you for the information. You've given me some important pieces of the puzzle. I'll talk to the other families and see what I can find out."

The witch turned and strode into the night.

37

As Val parked the Ural in front of her building, the old motorcycle coughed and died. The sudden silence was deafening. The city was deserted this time of night, the streets dark and empty except for the drifting fog.

A yawn nearly cracked her jaw in half as she reached up and rubbed at the tension in her neck. It had been a long day and night.

She used Mister E's sight to glance up at her wards as she stepped toward the entrance to the building.

Val froze. The wards were flaring bright. A threat was near.

She pretended to search her pockets for her keys, letting her eyes scan the street. She gathered power, ready to defend herself. One hand drifted to the hilt of her knife.

Silently, she cursed the fog. It was thick tonight, so dense she could hardly see the building across the street. If a monster was lurking, she might not see it until it was too late.

No glowing colors jumped out at her, which meant there was nothing magical in her immediate line of sight. Which was not particularly reassuring. Thanks to the fog, her line of sight was myopic.

A dark figure flashed out of the fog, moving fast. Val moved by instinct, tucking and rolling, putting the bulk of the Ural between her and them. Her knife slid free of its sheath as she came up onto one knee, pivoting to face the threat, preparing to punch out with a fist of wind.

A pair of black-clad shapes stood facing her, the streetlight glinting off their elongated incisors.

Vampires.

Val slashed out at them with an arc of wind. They were knocked away through the air but landed on their feet like cats. In an instant, they came bounding back, separating and coming at her from both sides.

She punched out at the one on her right, but this time the vampire dodged her strike. The one on her left flashed towards her, moving so fast his shape was a blur. His claws raked across her face, drawing blood.

Snarling, she spun a defensive cyclone, pushing the creature away. Her whirlwind scooped up dust and debris from the street, becoming opaque in seconds. She was safe, but she was also blind.

"The damn vamps are too fast. Can you float above the cyclone and lend me your eyes so I can see what's going on?" she asked Mister E.

"I could... Or you could just float up there yourself."

Val shook her head at her own stupidity. When pressed, why did she always revert to the simplest tactics? The demon cat had a point; she wasn't using her head. Why stay down here where the vamps could get her when she could fly out of reach?

A gust of wind flowed in, lifting her up above the whirling cyclone. The vampires stood just outside the circle of wind and snarled up at her.

Val took all the dirt and debris her cyclone had collected, all the rocks and glass and sharp bits of metal that accumulate on city streets, and flung it out toward the vampires in a glittering wave.

The grit chewed into her attackers, filling their nose, mouth and eyes, blinding them in an instant. It shredded their skin, exposing jagged chunks of red meat and bone.

A floodlight flared to life behind her, bathing the street in an intense light. Donna Summer's voice blared from a speaker.

The vampires hissed as their skin started to steam. They quickly retreated into the night.

Val stayed in the air for several seconds, maintaining the barrier until she was sure they were gone. Finally, she dropped to the ground and let the cyclone dissipate.

As she released her power, weakness swept in on its wake, buckling her knees. She'd been tired to begin with, and flying always took a lot out of her. Flying while sculpting a separate curtain of wind was like trying to carry two people up a flight of stairs at the same time.

She knelt there on the sidewalk for a long minute, wondering if she'd have the strength to stand or if she'd have to crawl up the stairs.

Then strong arms were lifting her. Hillary was there, wearing a big black hooded cloak to protect her from the light.

"Come on," the vampire said. "Let's get you inside. You know I can't leave a damsel in distress."

38

V al awoke with her face stuck to her pillow. A string of drool followed her as she peeled her skin away from the pillowcase. "Ugh. Gross."

As she sat up, she realized she was still wearing her clothes. She vaguely remembered Hillary carrying her to bed. After that fight with the vampires, Val hadn't even had the energy to climb the stairs. Apparently getting undressed had been a step too far.

The sore muscles in her back and legs protested as she yawned and stretched. Her head was stuffed with cotton. Her mouth felt like something had died in there.

She stumbled to the bathroom to pee and brush the foulness out of her mouth, then followed the scent of coffee to the kitchen.

"Good morning, sunshine." Malcolm was busy over the stove, the scent of frying potatoes and onions filling the small space. He was wearing a pink apron with fancy white scrolled letters which read, "Today's forecast: Cooking with a chance of drinking."

Val grunted and poured herself a cup of coffee, adding a generous dollop of both cream and butterscotch, beginning the process of becoming human again. She was basically non-verbal until after her first cup.

Malcolm chattered away at her as she sat at the kitchen table sipping her coffee, but most of his words bounced off Val's brain without sticking. As she finished her coffee and poured herself another cup, something he said finally registered.

"Wait, what did you just say?"

Malcolm gave her the side eye.

"I said, we're going to have to come up with some new security features now that the vampires have discovered where Hillary lives."

"Or Hillary could just move out like I asked her to. The vampires are after her, not us."

"Yes and no." Hillary came gliding in through the doorway. Unlike Val, she looked perfectly alert, with her black A-cut hair sleek and her makeup on point.

Val scowled at Hillary's perfection. Nobody should look that good first thing in the morning.

The vampire slid into the chair across from Val. She wore a black silk kimono adorned with white cranes in flight.

"Yes, the Coven is after me," she explained. "But no, I don't think they'll leave you alone after I leave. Melinda Pearl hates you, and she owes you payback for spoiling her schemes."

"What do we do then?" Val asked sourly. "Run away? Find somewhere else to live? Do you know how hard it is to find a decent apartment in this city?"

"As I was saying," Malcolm replied, "we need to install some new security features."

"You think your disco inferno isn't enough?"

"It's fine. But we could always use more pizazz."

He slid a plate filled with steaming eggs and potatoes onto the table in front of her, then filled one for himself and took a seat. Hillary simply sipped her coffee. The vampire never ate breakfast.

Val turned her gaze on Hillary and tried to gasp out words with her mouth full of scalding potatoes. "When are you leaving?"

"Val!" Malcolm protested.

Val ignored him and simply cocked an eyebrow at the vampire. "Well?"

Hillary held her gaze, refusing to be intimidated.

"I'm not sure. I need to figure some things out first. My rent is paid until the end of the month."

"That's fine, as long as you're out by then. In the meantime, I'd appreciate it if you could help Malcolm secure the apartment. I can freshen up my alarm wards but they won't do much more than slow the vamps down and give you some warning. I'm in the middle of trying to stop an assassin, so I don't have time to deal with this right now. It would be great if my roommates could be kept safe in the meantime."

"Maybe I can help with that." Sandra appeared in the doorway, the oversized hood of her fox onesie hanging down over her eyes.

"Flying toads," Val swore. "How did she get in here?"

"I gave her a key," Malcom said. In response to Val's glare, he added, "Just because she's sleeping in the basement doesn't mean she's not a part of the family. It felt awkward telling her she could come on up anytime but then making her knock."

Val scrubbed her hands over her face.

"Fine. We'll talk about this later."

"There's nothing to talk about," Malcolm said defiantly. "I live here too, and I want Sandra to have a key."

Val opened her mouth to retort, but Hillary spoke first.

"Sandra's right, her stone-gaze could be very helpful if the vamps attack. Also, as much as I'd love to watch the two of you go at it, maybe we could move this discussion to the living room? There isn't enough room in this tiny kitchen for all of us."

Val glared at Malcolm. Malcolm glared right back.

"Whatever." She snatched up her coffee cup and got to her feet. "But we will talk about this later."

Malcolm got to his feet as well, hands smoothing the front of his apron.

"Bring it on, sister."

39

"What's the latest on the ninja assassin? Have you tracked them down yet?" Malcolm asked.

Tempers had cooled as more food and coffee helped balance everyone's blood chemistry, and Malcolm was now ensconced on one end of the couch. Sandra had her feet tucked up under her at the other end, while Hillary sat in the old armchair on the gloomy side of the room, far from the windows. It was overcast outside, but a vampire can never be too careful.

Val groaned and tilted her head back in the window-seat nook.

"No. And the suspect list keeps growing."

"Oooo, do tell," Malcolm leaned forward expectantly.

Val filled them in on everything she'd discovered, adding what Zoe Vasilevski had told her at the hospital.

"So it's a gang war over a magical amulet?" Malcolm asked. "And there's an actual dragon in Japantown?"

"Yes, there's a dragon. As for the gang war..." Val threw up her hands. "It could be. Or it could be a lover's spat, or some outside party trying to get the pieces of the amulet together for their own agenda."

"Maybe it's Melinda Pearl," Hillary said. "She's never been shy about hunting power."

"Maybe," Val said. "But I think it's more likely to be one of the families. They have the most to gain if they can break free of the peace treaty the Dragon forced upon them."

"I thought you said they all agreed to the treaty," Malcolm said. "That doesn't sound forced."

"But they didn't agree to the amulet's curse," Val corrected. "They got more than they bargained for. If given the choice, I'm sure any one of them would break the treaty in a heartbeat."

"What does the amulet do?" Malcolm asked. "I mean if you put the pieces back together. It sounds like that might be what someone is trying to accomplish."

"I have no idea."

"So who do you think it is?" Hillary asked.

Val took a sip of coffee and shook her head.

"It's too soon to tell. I need to talk to the rest of the families first. Feel them out face to face. Hopefully I'll pick up some clues."

"What can we do to help?" Malcolm asked. "Do you need me to go to the Library?"

Val laughed at the eagerness on his face.

"If I didn't know better, I'd think you were having an affair with the Librarian."

Malcolm looked indignant.

"No. I am having an affair with the Library. Duh."

"The Librarian is cute, though," Sandra said softly. Everyone stared at her. She squirmed. "What?"

"Why Sandra, I never knew you had it in you. You go, girl." Malcolm patted her foot.

"I didn't mean... we aren't..." she stammered, the visible half of her face turning bright red.

"Never apologize for love," Malcolm said. "It's the only thing that makes life worth living. It doesn't matter if you love a man, a woman, or a non-binary librarian with godlike powers. Love is love."

Sandra's neck got so red Val thought she might melt. The gorgon shrank, pulling her hood all the way down over her chin.

"Leave her alone, Malcolm," Hillary said. "The poor thing's about to have a stroke."

"What did I say? I was being supportive."

"Anyway," Val tried to pull the conversation back on track. "Yes, Malcolm, it would be great if you took a trip to the Library. Research the amulet, the curse, the families, the Dragon, anything that can help me understand someone's motivation for stealing the pieces of the amulet. We also need to figure out how they're getting around the curse to be able to carry out the attacks in the first place."

"I'll take Sandra with me." Malcolm smirked. Sandra buried her head deeper inside her hood.

"But first we'll need to bolster security here." Val snatched up a pen and paper. "Let's talk it out. Get all of our ideas down and make a plan."

"We already discussed my floodlight and your wards," Malcolm said. "Hillary?"

The vampire steepled her fingers. "Yeah, I've got some other ideas."

They brainstormed for half an hour, debating and discarding dozens of possibilities. When they'd finished, they had a decent list of new security measures.

Val frowned as she ran her eyes over the page.

"Is this going to be enough?"

"It's a good start," Hillary said. "Those things will seriously inconvenience any vamps trying to get in here."

There was a loud knocking on the downstairs door. Val stuck her head out the window and peered down to find a teenage kid standing there, huffing like he'd just run up five flights of stairs.

"What is it?" she called.

"Zoe sent me to tell you Jing Wong has been killed," he gasped.

"When?"

"Last night. We just heard."

"Shit. Tell Zoe I'm on my way to Chinatown."

Val sprang to her feet.

"Hillary, you're in charge of installing new security. Malcolm and Sandra, you tackle the Library." She squared her shoulders as she headed out the door. "I've got to go question grieving Chinese family members."

40

Sandra trailed Val out the door. Left alone with Malcolm, Hillary finally let out the breath she didn't realize she'd been holding.

"Well, that was awkward. Thank you for not telling Val about... you know."

"About me becoming a vampire?" Malcolm asked.

"Yeah. That."

He waived a hand airily as he headed to the kitchen for more coffee. "I don't think it's going to happen. I feel completely normal. No cravings for blood at all."

"Well, I hope you're right. Still. Thank you."

"No, thank *you*. Without your blood, I'd probably be dead."

"Yes, but without me drinking your blood, you wouldn't have been on the brink of death to begin with," she reminded him.

"That's what friends are for, right? Helping us do things we can't do ourselves? They do say it takes a village."

"A village, right."

Hillary chewed on her lip. She wasn't sure about this next part. But she thought it needed to be done.

"On that note, I have another favor to ask you. It's kind of a big one."

"Of course, anything. Well, anything short of you draining me dry and turning me into a vampire." Malcom smiled as he breezed back into the living room, but the joke fell flat. "Sorry. That might have been too soon." He perched on the edge of the couch expectantly. "So, what's the favor?"

Hillary took a deep breath. She wasn't sure if she could do this. Trusting people was difficult. She'd always held her secrets close.

But Melinda Pearl's hunters had finally tracked her down. If anything happened to her... No. This needed to be done. Malcolm was her closest friend. And she had to trust someone.

"So, I have a little brother," she began, and slowly told him about Benji, finishing with, "If anything happens to me... Benji will need someone to take care of him. To at least help find him a good home somewhere. Could you...?"

Malcolm's eyes were as big as saucers.

"Could I become a parental figure to your brother?"

"No, you don't have to go that far. Just help him out. Maybe find someone else to look after him. A community he could join or another family, or..."

"I'd love to!"

Hillary stuttered to a halt. "You would?"

"Of course! I consider you family, so that makes your brother family too. And I've always wanted a little brother. What's he like? Tell me all about him."

How to explain Benji? About his oddities and peculiarities. His love for old video games and comics. His intelligence and hyper-focus. His difficulties socializing. Still, she did her best.

"He sounds like a girl I knew in the sixth grade. Emily Woo. She was always so shy and quiet; it was hard to get a word out of her. But one day I somehow got her talking about superheroes and, lo and behold, that little girl blossomed like a daisy. She talked my ear off for half an hour. I was flabbergasted. Of course, later I learned that type of behavior isn't unusual for people on the spectrum, which it sounds like your brother might be? To be clear, I'm not judging or trying to label. Whether he is or isn't makes no difference to me. He can be however he is. I mean, I live with a witch, a vampire, and a gorgon. Compared to that, your brother should be a piece of cake."

Hillary chuckled. "I guess when you put it that way."

"Can I meet him now? Or do I have to wait until you're dead? Because I'd really rather you didn't die, but your brother sounds great."

Hillary's head was spinning. Revealing her biggest secret had taken a big leap of faith. She'd expected hesitation from Malcolm. She'd been prepared for dismay and resistance. Never in a million years had she expected him to be excited about the prospect of meeting Benji. It was a one-hundred-and-eighty-degree shift, and it took a minute for her to wrap her brain around it.

Finally, she said, "I guess you could. If you really want to."

Malcolm clapped his hands.

"Huzzah! Of course I want to. Benji and I officially have a date."

41

Chinatown was the only place in the city more chaotic than the Mission District. As she walked down Grant Avenue, Val's senses were assaulted by a barrage of sounds, tastes, and smells. The shop displays overflowed onto the sidewalk, and the pedestrian traffic clogged and clotted, forcing her to step into the narrow street to make progress, where she had to dodge plunging rickshaws and rusty hand carts instead.

Vendors shouted out their wares, shoppers haggled, and children ran screaming. Roosters crowed and dogs barked. Meat sizzled, dumplings steamed, soup bubbled. Garlic and unfamiliar spices filled her nostrils, along with the less pleasant scents of sweat and urine.

A teenager knocked against her shoulder and she felt small hands slide into her pocket on the opposite side. She seized a dirty little girl by the wrist. The kid was skin and bones, her hair a tangled nest. She couldn't have been more than eight.

As soon as Val's fingers closed, the girl started to wail and struggle. Val held her long enough to make sure the girl's hands were empty, then let her go. The urchin disappeared back into the depths of the crowd like a fish returning to water. Catch and release.

The address on Zoe's list turned out to be a dim sum restaurant.

The place was packed. Six to ten people crowded around the big round tables, and a jumble of steaming dishes filled the center of each. Servers pushed carts piled high with a variety of dishes, weaving their way between chairs, stopping at the tables they passed to add more food to the pile.

Val double-checked the address. Yes, this was the place. The bustling restaurant looked nothing like what she would expect from the headquarters of the Wong family. Peering into the open door, she didn't even know where to begin.

Complicating matters was the fact that hers was the only non-Chinese face in the whole restaurant. The staff seemed to assume she was a lost tourist and ignored her inquisitive looks. Finally, she had to physically step in front of the hostess, stopping her in her path.

"I'm looking for Shen Wong," she said quietly.

"What?" the woman yelled to make herself heard over the hubbub.

"I'm looking for Shen Wong," Val repeated a bit louder.

"Speak up."

"I'm looking for Shen Wong," Val shouted. So much for being discreet.

The hostess looked her up and down dubiously.

"Nobody here by that name."

"I know he's here. Just tell him Val Keri is here to see him, OK?"

The woman sniffed and disappeared into the throng. Val hoped that meant she was going to get Shen.

She hovered just inside the door, trying her best to stay out of the way. The busy interior of the restaurant seemed like pure chaos, but as she watched, she slowly started to understand the rhythm of the place. There was a method to it. It was just that the method was different from every service industry job she'd ever worked.

Minutes passed. No sign of the hostess.

Val was about to flag down another server when the woman finally popped back out of the crowd.

"Come with me." She disappeared back into the crowd without waiting to see if Val was following her.

They threaded their way to the back of the restaurant, then through a swinging door into the kitchen. If the dining room had been chaotic, the kitchen was an absolute madhouse. A gang of white-jacketed cooks whirled around, chopping, flipping, sauteing, folding, and putting food on plates, all of them barking out rapid Chinese. Steam and smoke swirled across the ceiling. The heat was unbearable, and Val was instantly covered in sweat.

She assumed the office must be somewhere behind the kitchens and was surprised when the hostess instead shouted at one of the cooks. He handed his spatula to his neighbor and threaded his way across the room. As he reached them, she was shocked to recognize Shen beneath the white chef's hat.

"You work in the kitchen?" she asked.

"Family business. I do a little bit of everything."

Val blinked. This was a far cry from the limousines of the Vasilevskis, the opulent mansion of the O'Ceallaighs, or the high-end fashion of Joumala Anand. Definitely not what she'd been expecting.

"What are you doing here, Val?"

"Is there somewhere more private we can talk?"

He squinted up at her. "Sure. This way."

Shen led her to the back of the kitchen and up a flight of stairs. At the top of the stairs was a thick wooden door, its polished surface covered by an intricately carved garden scene.

She followed him through the door and into a cluttered office. A massive desk dominated the space, with stacks of invoices threatening to spill off every corner. Cardboard boxes were piled against the walls, full of sauces, spices, canned beans, and dried noodles.

Shen smiled at the look on her face.

"Restaurant supplies. You were expecting something else?"

"You could say that. I can't imagine Padraig O'Caellaigh working in an office like this."

He bobbed his head in understanding.

"My grandmother believed in hard work. She had nothing when she came to this country. No matter how successful our family became, she never stopped working."

"I'm sorry for your loss."

"Thank you. She was an amazing woman. A tiger. We will honor her memory. Is that what you wanted to talk about?"

"Yes. I understand that your grandmother was killed."

His eyes became hard.

"She was shot by a black arrow while she was out shopping."

"Did you catch the assassin?"

"No, he shot from a rooftop."

"Someone saw him, though?"

"Lots of people saw him. You've been outside. You can't sneeze in Chinatown without hitting ten people."

"Was he dressed the same as the other assassin?"

"All in black, yes. Black mask. Black bow and arrows. Just like the man that shot Zoe at her uncle's funeral."

"Did the assassin take your family's jade amulet?"

He narrowed his eyes and studied her. "Yes, the amulet is missing. How do you know about that?"

"I think the amulets might be the motivation behind the assassinations."

"Explain."

Val told Shen what she'd discovered. He listened quietly, saying nothing, his eyes intent. When she finished, he remained silent for a minute, fingers steepled before his lips.

Finally, he said, "How has someone broken the curse?"

"I don't know. I was hoping you might have some insight into that."

"No. I never paid much attention to that mystical stuff. I handle the mundane side of the business."

"Like running a restaurant?"

"Exactly."

"So, now that you've heard the whole story, do you have any idea who is behind these killings?"

Shen held her gaze, his eyes as hard and impenetrable as steel.

"I have more than a theory. I know who killed her. It was the Dragon."

42

The Ural roared beneath Val as she gunned the motor up the steep incline. She tensed as she neared the intersection. This was one of those San Francisco streets so steep it left you staring up into the sky as you drove up it. Val couldn't see the next intersection until her motorcycle entered it, which put her entirely at the mercy of the cross-traffic drivers. Every block was an exercise in trust. If one person didn't obey the traffic signs, someone else was likely to die.

It felt like an apt metaphor for the way the city's mafia families were all wound together. Any one of them could inflict a killing blow on a rival at any time without warning. The only thing keeping them in check had been the amulets.

Except apparently the amulets were no longer a deterrent. Which meant the body count was going to get a whole lot higher if Val didn't figure out who was behind the killings, and quickly.

She mulled over what Shen had told her. First he'd sent her after Joumala Anand. Now he seemed certain the Dragon was behind the attacks.

But the Dragon had been the one to give the families the amulets in the first place. Why would he send an assassin to retrieve them? Also, she'd seen someone steal the Dragon's amulet herself. It didn't make sense.

Well, there was one family left she needed to talk to. The one she'd been putting off and dreading.

The O'Ceallaighs.

Her relationship with Padraig O'Ceallaigh was complicated. Some weird mix of attraction and friendship. He had also saved her life more than once.

Or at least it used to be complicated.

Ever since they'd fought a duel for Pandora's Box, Padraig had wanted nothing to do with her. Full stop.

And now she had to go question him about the assassin and the amulet. Wonderful.

Preoccupied with her thoughts, Val almost didn't dodge in time.

If she'd been looking the other way—If it had been dark out—If she'd been unlucky, the arrow would have taken her right in the chest.

As it was, she leaned to swerve around a pothole just as the archer released the arrow. Instead of puncturing her heart, the shaft punched through her shoulder. It still hurt like hell, though.

The impact knocked her off the motorcycle and sent her skidding across the pavement to rest against the wheel of a rusty metal cart parked on the side of the road.

Her mind reeled. What just happened? One second she was riding along, mulling over the information she'd just learned, and the next there was pain and she was chewing asphalt.

A motorcycle revved and peeled out into the street, tires screeching. The black-clad rider clearly had no desire to stay and mix it up with Val. They'd taken their shot and missed, and now they were getting out of there so they could regroup and try again later.

Val ground her teeth against the pain as she retrieved the Ural from where it had come to rest against a telephone pole. The headlight and turn signals were smashed, but to Val's relief, the old bike started right up when she turned the key. She lurched off after her assailant.

"I wish I had one of those magnetic trackers you see in the movies. Then I could follow this guy back to his lair and find out who's behind this."

"Maybe you can," Mister E offered.

"Can you be more specific? And make it fast. That crotch-rocket he's riding has a lot more get-up-and-go than the Ural does."

"You can track the would-be-assassin with your blood."

"My blood?" Val grimaced as the bike crossed a set of tram tracks. Every jolt made the arrow in her shoulder bounce painfully up and down. "In case you haven't noticed, they're half a block ahead of me. How the hell am I supposed to get my blood on them?"

"That is your problem. Do you expect me to do everything for you?"

Val growled and throttled up, leaning forward over the handlebars. Acceleration was not the Ural's strong suit. The old bike had a lot of power and could move surprisingly fast once it built up momentum, but the stops and starts of city driving made getting up to speed almost impossible. Luckily, with the narrow city streets and traffic, the assassin was having a hard time pulling away.

Her mind churned. Who was the assassin? Why were they trying to kill her? She certainly didn't have one of the jade amulets. Were they just trying to cover their tracks?

Her train of thought was interrupted as the assassin pulled out onto Fell Street. Fell ran along the park blocks leading to Golden Gate Park, and her attacker would be able to accelerate without impediment here. If she was going to get some of her blood on them, it was now or never.

Access to her blood wasn't a problem. Thanks to the arrow in her shoulder, there was plenty of it running down the front of her leather jacket. It was even soaking through the pages of notes Zoe had given her that were stuffed into her inside pocket. She should probably be worried about that. If she passed out from blood loss in the middle of a motorcycle chase, the ensuing crash would not be pretty.

She shoved that thought aside. No time. Despite the Ural's best efforts, the assassin was pulling away. She only had seconds left to act.

Something tickled her mind. Something about her blood soaking through her jacket… Zoe's notes… Memories of being pelted with spit-balls made from wet paper flashed through her mind.

Wet paper! Spitballs!

She tore a blood-soaked corner from one of the pages, flipped up the visor of her helmet, and stuck the paper between her teeth. The metallic taste of blood filled her mouth as she chewed it into a gooey ball.

Ahead of her, the assassin slowed to weave around slow traffic. Still, they were almost a full block ahead of her now. She would only get one shot at this.

Val gathered her focus and waited until the assassin hit a clear patch of road. Their motorcycle straightened out, forming a stationary-ish target as the rider bent low over the handlebars. It was now or never.

Val put all her power into her breath as she spat the wad of paper at the assassin's back. The little puff of air came out of her mouth with hurricane force and the spitball shot forward like a rocket.

It hit the back of the assassin's jacket and stuck tight.

Val grinned as she braked the Ural to a wobbling halt.

"Got them."

"Do you really think it will remain stuck there?"

"It wouldn't surprise me. I remember spit ball wads drying like cement. Sometimes you had to scrape them off with a knife." A wave of dizziness hit her and Val leaned over the handlebars as she waited for it to pass. "It doesn't matter if it falls off, though. The blood will stain their jacket for sure. Wherever they go, I'll be able to track them."

"Clever," Mister E purred. *"I knew you had it in you."*

"Speaking of having things in me, I need to get this arrow out of me before I pass out."

She tried to swing her leg off the Ural, but her foot got lost somewhere between the seat and the ground. Val skipped the next step and went straight to passing out.

43

V al surfaced slowly, drifting up through thick layers of pain. She felt cool sheets beneath her back and a soft blanket pressing on her chest. Cracking her eyes open, she found herself staring up at a gauzy white canopy draped over the bed.

"What the funk?" she groaned.

The bed was familiar. Exactly like a certain bed she'd woken up in several times before, as a matter of fact. But that couldn't be right. That bed belonged to…

"Padraig?"

She turned her head to the side and found the expected table and chair sitting beside the bed. A pot of tea steamed upon the table. There was no question. She was in the guest bedroom in Padraig O'Ceallaigh's house.

But instead of Padraig sitting in the chair, there was an unfamiliar young woman.

The woman smiled, her canines gleaming and sharp, her hair all unruly tufts. She was wrapped in an orange silk dressing robe and sat curled in the chair like a cat, with her knees drawn up to her chest and feet tucked under her. Her bright blue eyes were predatory, though not in a hostile way. More as if she was slightly feral. The type of girl who would grab a boy by the front of his shirt and drag him into the bushes without warning.

"Who are you?" Val asked.

The young woman pouted.

"You don't recognize me, Val Keri? I've saved your life more than once now."

Val squinted at her. She realized what was missing from the bed and connections clicked into place in her mind.

"Fiona?"

The smile flashed again. "See. You do recognize me."

Fiona was Padraig's calico cat. Every other time Val had woken up in this bed, Fiona had been curled up by her side. As a cat.

Apparently, Fiona was more than your average cat.

"Where's Padraig?"

"Not here. He didn't approve of me bringing you home this time. He told me to take you somewhere else. I explained that this is my house too and that I can bring friends home if I want to." Her eyes sparked with mischief. "He saw things my way."

"I like this one," Mister E purred.

"Of course you do," Val muttered.

Fiona cocked her head. "What's that?"

"Nothing. You remind me of someone is all."

Mister E's laughter rang in her head. Val ignored him as she pushed herself up onto her elbows.

Or tried to, anyway.

Sharp pain stabbed through her shoulder and she groaned, sinking back down on the pillow. Turning her head, she found a thick bandage where the assassin's arrow had pierced her skin. She also realized she wasn't wearing a shirt.

"Where are my clothes?"

Fiona waved a negligent hand.

"Over there. You don't need them."

The young woman languidly stretched out her legs and Val realized Fiona was probably naked beneath the orange silk. Peering under the sheet, she saw that she was too.

"I'd like my clothes back."

"Not even a thank you for saving my life?" Fiona pouted. "Padraig was right. I should have left you bleeding on the street where I found you."

"Sorry. I'm not at my best when I first wake up. Thank you for saving my life. Now can I have my clothes back?"

Fiona rolled her eyes and scooped up Val's clothes from the floor, dropping them on the bed in an unceremonious pile.

"You might not want to put that shirt back on. It's crusty with blood. And I had to cut it off you." The cat shifter crossed to a wardrobe and pulled out a perfectly pressed men's dress shirt. She tossed it carelessly to Val. "You can wear this instead."

Val held the shirt up doubtfully.

"Does this belong to Padraig?"

"Don't worry, this is one of his backup wardrobes. He never wears the shirts in here. I don't think he even remembers he has them. Do you need help getting dressed?" Fiona grinned at her.

"No, I can handle it on my own."

"Are you sure?" The shifter shrugged one shoulder. "It's not as if I haven't seen you naked already."

Val felt heat creeping up her neck.

"No, thank you. I can handle it."

"Suit yourself." Fiona curled back into the chair, her bright eyes fixed on Val.

"Do you mind?"

"Do I mind what?"

"Giving me a little privacy?"

Fiona rolled her eyes.

"Humans are so weird. I'm the one who took the clothes off you. Watching you put them back on isn't a big deal."

"It is to me."

"Fine." Fiona huffed and spun around so her back was facing the bed.

"Thank you."

Val got up and gingerly pulled her pants on. She hesitated at Padraig's shirt, but one look at the mess of dried blood and torn cloth that used to be her shirt told her Fiona had been right in her assessment. It was completely unwearable.

Padraig's shirt was some sleek material, cool and smooth against her skin. As she fastened the buttons she said, "I need to speak to Padraig."

Fiona laughed.

"Good luck with that. He definitely does not want to speak with you."

Val sighed. "I know. I have to speak with him anyway."

"Suit yourself. It's your funeral." Fiona slunk across the room. "Follow me. We'll see if we can track his lordship down."

Val took a deep breath and stepped toward the door. Talking to Padraig was not going to be pleasant.

44

They found Padraig standing by the window in the library. He looked as beautiful as ever, with his hazel eyes and the light catching his artfully tousled hair. He wore a cream-colored silk shirt casually wrapped in a double-breasted vest with a paisley pattern.

Val's heart constricted with loss. Padraig had been a good friend, and maybe more. But that was all over now.

When he saw her, his face grew stormy.

"You are not welcome here, Valora Keri. Get out," he snapped as Val trailed Fiona into the room.

She held up her hands. "I know you don't want to see me. But this isn't a social call."

"It never is with you. In fact, you usually come here bleeding and unconscious. Or wanting to steal a priceless artifact from me. I didn't want you here in the first place." He shot a sharp look at Fiona.

The shifter ignored him, melting into her cat form and leaving her orange robe in a puddle of silk on the floor. She hopped up onto a velvet armchair in front of the hearth and nonchalantly started cleaning herself.

"I just need to ask you a few questions. Then I'll be out of your hair," Val said.

"What part of unwelcome do you not understand? Leave my home. Now, before I call security."

"If you'd just listen for a minute…"

Padraig stabbed a button on the house intercom system. "Security. Come remove an intruder from the library."

"I'm trying to catch an assassin," Val said. "Someone is killing your fellow heads of family. Maybe you could pull your head out of your ass long enough to help me do that."

"I am aware of the assassinations. In case you've forgotten, I was there when Zoe was shot. I saw her put you on the case. That doesn't make me any more inclined to help you." A burly security guard came striding in through the door and Padraig motioned toward Val. "Please escort Ms. Keri from the premises."

The man wrapped a meaty hand around Val's arm and steered her firmly toward the door.

"Are you aware the assassin is collecting the jade amulets from their targets?" she called back over her shoulder. "Did you know that someone has figured out a way to break the curse?"

"Hold on a moment, Seamus," Padraig called out. The big man dragging Val stopped in the doorway. "What do you mean, they've found a way to break the curse?"

Val yanked her arm from the security guard's grasp.

"Just what I said. Someone has figured out a way to break the curse. They're attacking the heads of the families and collecting the jade amulets."

Padraig's forehead creased. "How is that possible?"

"I don't know. I was hoping you might be able to help me out with that."

He glared at her for a long moment, clearly torn. Finally, he motioned to one of the chairs in front of the fire.

"Have a seat. You've got five minutes."

"How generous," she said, settling onto the chair beside the one occupied by Fiona. The cat ignored her, switching her attention to cleaning her other leg.

"Don't push it, Val," Padraig growled as he sank into a seat across from her. "You're lucky I'm giving you that much time. Now tell me what you know."

Val filled him in on what she'd discovered about the amulets, the families, and the assassinations. When she finished, he remained silent, staring into the fire, his beautiful eyes clouded.

"Do you know why someone would want to collect the pieces of the amulet?" Val asked.

"It was originally a single amulet. Presumably they want to put the pieces back together."

"But why? What would that accomplish?"

Padraig's frown deepened. "I don't know."

"Come on, you're the specialist in magical artifacts," she pressed. "Don't you know what the original amulet did?"

"I'm afraid I don't. That was all well before my time. And the jade amulet came from the Dragon's hoard, not my family's vaults. If you want to know what the amulet does, you'll have to ask the Dragon."

Val made a sour face.

"The last time I tried to ask the Dragon questions, he locked me in his dungeon. He's not very good at listening."

Padraig chuckled. "No, he's not. I guess when you're a magical being thousands of years old, you believe you already know all the answers."

They lapsed into a thoughtful silence, staring into the fire, orange flames dancing in their eyes. The mood in the room had changed. Val wouldn't call it companionable, but at least Padraig had stopped radiating hostility. Baby steps.

"Any theories on who could be behind this?" she finally asked.

"I wouldn't dignify my wild speculation with the word theory," Padraig began. "But simple logic can help us narrow it down. The Vasilevskis and Wongs are the two families that have been attacked, so we can probably rule them out."

"Which leaves the Anands, the Yakuza, and your family," Val finished.

Padraig nodded his head.

"Shen Wong told me to look into the Anands," Val said. "And that was before his grandmother was killed."

"Why the Anands?" Padraig asked.

"He wasn't very specific. He just told me I should talk to them."

"And did you?"

"Yes. Joumala was fairly belligerent. But she did shed some light on why Shen may have steered me in her direction."

Val filled Padraig in on what Joumala had told her about the love triangle between her, Shen, and Zoe.

Padraig made a face.

"That doesn't really help with the amulet question though, does it?"

"No."

Suddenly, Padraig sat up straight, like a cat catching sight of a bird on the ground. He cocked his head, eyes narrowed in concentration.

"What is it?" Val asked.

"I just remembered something about the amulet. Something my grandmother told me when I was a boy…"

"What?" she pressed.

"Hold on. I'm trying to remember…" He stared into the fire for a full minute while Val squirmed with impatience. "I can't be certain, but I think the amulet was originally commissioned by some Japanese emperor. His pet sorcerer created it to bind his empire together somehow. Maybe his vassal lords all had to swear some sort of blood oath on the amulet? I can't remember the story for sure, but I know it was supposed to make it so they couldn't betray him."

"Like the Dragon's curse."

"Yes, but there was more to it. I can't remember the whole story. There was something about binding. Making them all one." He shook his head in frustration. Then Padraig seemed to remember who he was talking to and his expression hardened. "And now your five minutes are up. Be on your way, Valora Keri."

Val's heart sank and a lump rose in her throat. For a moment, it had almost felt as if Padraig was her friend once again.

She swallowed the lump and got to her feet.

"Of course. Thank you for your time." Seamus reached for her arm again, but she froze the big security guard with a flat look. "I'll see myself out."

45

"It sounds to me as if the amulet is the key to the puzzle," Mister E said. The demon-cat was lounging in the sidecar of the Ural, leather goggles pulled down over his eyes, wind ruffling his fur.

"I agree," Val said. She was using a tracking spell to follow the trail of the spitball she'd stuck to the jacket of the person who had shot her. "Hopefully the assassin is still wearing the amulet."

"Are you sure the assassin was wearing an amulet this time? We never got a good look at them."

"No, but the last assassin we tracked was. If the pattern holds, this one will be as well."

"If the pattern holds. Don't you know we're living in a chaotic universe? Only fools put faith in patterns."

"Faith in patterns is all I have at this point. Don't piss on my parade."

The cat laughed.

Turning onto Divisadero, Val frowned. She'd expected the spell to lead her back to Japantown, where she'd found the previous assassin. Instead, the trail was heading south past Haight Street, curling around toward the Castro District. Which was problematic because...

She braked the Ural to a halt.

"Well, that's inconvenient."

They stared down at the west end of the Market Street chasm. During the big quake, what was once be Market Street got swallowed by an enormous crevice that divided the city. The chasm ended here, where Castro Street used to cross Market. Now the intersection was an impassable jumble of fallen rocks and debris where the hillside had tumbled down, filling the end of the crevice. The pull of the spitball was coming from somewhere on the far side of the rockfall.

"We can go all the way down to the Van Ness Bridge or we can detour through the hills." Val sighed, considering her options. Van Ness was pretty far out of their way. Winding through the hills was less distance, but going up into the hilly neighborhood contained its own challenges.

"If we have to take a detour either way, we might as well make it interesting. I say we take the scenic route."

"Your wish is my command. The scenic route it is." Val wheeled the Ural up the hill.

Twin Peaks loomed above the Castro and the ridge that ran from the peaks down to Haight Street was exceptionally steep even by San Francisco standards. The neighborhood clinging to these slopes had always been a quiet, affluent part of the city. Due to the topography, the streets up here couldn't follow the standard grid pattern and instead wound in haphazard loops and whorls, making them impractical for anyone who was trying to get anywhere. So, despite being bookended by the bustling Haight and Castro Districts, the homes on these hills were off the beaten path.

During the city's tech-boom years, the houses on these quiet streets had gotten bigger and bigger until they were isolated mansions locked behind iron gates and stone walls, peering down at the city like medieval lords. When the collapse came, many of these people had fled the city, leaving their empty castles to slowly rot.

And, as with many of the abandoned castles of old Europe, the barbarian hordes had come flooding in to occupy the fortresses.

These days the steep and winding streets were home to a motley collection of survivalists, cults, hippies, former tech billionaires, and refugees of every stripe who had fled to the hills and taken possession of the first empty house they found. The mansions were remote and easily defensible since most already had walls. Some also had that rarest of commodities in an urban environment: backyards. In a post-apocalyptic world, a backyard was perhaps the most precious treasure of all. Having earth meant the ability to have gardens. And in the first few years of post-collapse scarcity, being able to grow your own food was priceless.

All these factors made the winding streets an unpredictable place to pass through. They didn't get many visitors up here, and strangers were regarded with suspicion. The iron gates controlling access to the mansions remained closed and locked.

The loud rumble of the Ural announced Val's approach long before she arrived, and as she trundled past the estates, she saw more than one person peering through a gate at her and clutching a rifle. She nodded to them and kept moving. It was best not to engage the locals. Better to leave them to their isolation, where they couldn't hurt anyone but themselves.

Unfortunately, her plan to live and let live hit a snag. She rounded a corner to find the street completely blocked off by a pair of felled trees. As she painstakingly turned the Ural around, several people emerged from the bushes and blocked the road behind her. They were armed and did not look happy to see her.

"Oh good. Here comes the welcome wagon," she muttered. "You and your scenic route."

"Now we get to examine the natives too," Mister E replied. He barely lifted his head from his lounging position in the sidecar. *"Maybe we'll get a rich cultural exchange experience. Think of yourself as an anthropologist, researching long-isolated human tribes."*

A man clutching an assault rifle stepped forward. He had close cropped sandy hair and the muscle going to fat build of an ex-football player.

"This is private property," he said.

Val lifted an eyebrow. "This is a city street. I'm pretty sure that makes it public property by definition."

"You getting smart with me?"

"That would require intelligence on both sides," Mister E said. *"You could get dumb with him, but I don't think you could get smart."*

Val tried to contain her laugh, but a snort of amusement escaped.

"You think this is funny?" The man scowled and cocked his gun. "How about you leave that nice motorcycle with us. We'll see how funny you think that is." The other people spread out in a loose semi-circle behind him, blocking the road.

"I'm not looking for any trouble," Val said.

"Well, that's too bad. Cause trouble just found you."

46

"You really don't want to do this." Val held the leader's gaze and kept her voice calm and level, as if she was talking to a wild animal. Which in a way she was.

The people flanking the spokesman wore a lot of military surplus gear. Val guessed they were survivalists of some kind who probably had a compound nearby.

They all had guns, though other than the leader's assault rifle, they were held loosely and not pointed at Val. Clearly they didn't think she was a threat.

The spokesman laughed. "Oh, I assure you, I do. Now get off that pretty little bike and leave the keys in the ignition. Walk right back down the way you came and don't come up here again."

Val eyed her antagonists, weighing the odds. There were an awful lot of guns in the street. Could she get past them without getting shot?

Simply hitting them with a strong enough gust of wind might get her past them, but probably not before at least one squeezed off a few rounds in her direction. She needed a better option.

The downed trees had turned the street into a cul de sac. Judging by how fast this group had shown up, she guessed that wasn't an accident. To Val's right the hillside fell away sharply. She could see the orderly grid of the city spread out below and the sun sparkling on the bay in the distance. There was a driveway leading down and some bushes on that side, but the house was hidden from view. She wondered if that was where the survivalists' compound was.

To her left was a steep, rocky hillside. A row of pines and an evil-looking monkey puzzle tree guarded the edge of the road. The earth below them was covered in fallen branches and needles.

That was just the sort of thing she was looking for.

Closing her eyes, she reached her senses up into the sky. A cold river of wind whistled over the hills, breezes that had traveled across thousands of miles of open water before hitting the California coast. All that open space gave them a lot of room to build up momentum. Some of the gusts were moving at over a hundred miles an hour.

She felt the wind currents until she found the strong gust she was looking for. With a grim smile, she called to the air, bringing it down to brush the hillside to her left. The icy wind howled through the pines, scooping up loose needles and spiky branches before exploding across the street in a cloud, pelting the gunmen with stinging debris. Filling eyes, ears, and noses.

The gunman cursed and turned their backs to the wind, blinded and choking on dust, hands rising to protect their faces.

Val gunned the Ural. A couple of the survivalists heard the engine and blindly swung the barrels of their guns in her general direction, but their eyes were full of grit and there was nothing they could do. She knocked one of them down with her sidecar as she roared past to freedom.

"That was amateur hour," she muttered a couple of blocks later. "Pulling downed trees across the road? Really? That's on page one of the bandit's manual."

"Well, they did trap us with them. Sometimes the old ways work best," Mister E replied. *"I wish you hadn't let them off so easily. You had the chance to really teach those boys a lesson. Especially with those sharp monkey puzzle branches. You could have painted the street with their blood."*

"No, thanks. I've had enough blood today," Val said, fingering her still tender arrow wound.

"Spoilsport."

"You know me. I'm the life of the party." She turned the Ural back onto Castro Street.

"Now where are we going?"

"Screw those hills. I'm going down to the Van Ness Bridge."

"You're going to let those chumps change your route? I thought you said they were amateur hour."

"They are. And I've had all the amateur hour I can stand. Who knows what else is lurking in those hills? I'm going to Van Ness, where at least I know what type of freaks I'll be dealing with."

Val had no idea how much she would come to regret those words.

47

Hillary stalked the streets in a daze. The city around her felt different. Almost unrecognizable. Buildings she'd passed a hundred times stared at her with strange faces. She stopped at an intersection and peered down the street at a place she'd never seen before. She felt lost and adrift. Alone.

It wasn't the city that had changed. It was Hillary. She'd finally made up her mind. She was leaving San Francisco.

That mental shift had changed everything for her. Places that were once welcoming now hissed as she walked by. The city had its claws out. It did not like rejection.

Hillary was taken off guard by the change. Leaving was one of the most difficult decisions she'd ever had to make. She'd expected melancholy. Even outright sadness. But not hostility. Not the cold and sudden snarl of a rejected lover.

She'd broken the city's heart. And it, in return, was breaking hers.

As she wandered, she had to admit that, although it hurt, the city's rejection almost made things easier. With every hostile block she was less tempted to change her mind. Less tempted to abandon her decision and run back into the city's waiting arms.

She didn't know where she was going to go. Not yet. North or south seemed to be the best options. She definitely didn't want to take Benji inland. The central valley was a hellscape on the best of days.

It was better to stick to the coast. Head down to Los Angeles. Maybe up to Oregon. Find some small town to disappear into.

Though disappearing into a small town was difficult when you needed to drink human blood to survive. There was a reason vampires tended to live in big cities. The anonymity of crowds. Also, the abundance of feeding options. In a small town, it was much more likely to cause a stir if a corpse showed up drained of blood, or if the local apple farmer became pale and anemic. Suspicion would fall on the newcomer.

Still, there was something about small town life that sounded appealing at the moment. Especially when faced with the current animosity of the city. A smile played upon Hillary's lips as she imagined settling into some secluded farmhouse with Benji, surrounded by blueberry bushes and shade trees. Maybe they'd have a little pond and ducks and chickens in the yard. Goats for cheese and milk. Just the two of them in an island of peace and security. Safe from prying eyes.

She would miss San Francisco, though, with its colorful Victorians in their rows. The bustling street markets. The bracketing waters of the bay and the ocean. The curling fog and the rolling hills.

She might even miss Val, despite the witch's general prickliness.

Hillary would miss Malcolm most of all. Miss his enthusiasm and snark. His laughter. She'd miss him singing in the kitchen while he cooked, and the way he always had his things in the bathroom set out just so: soap parallel to his razor; toothbrush in the cup, bristles facing to the left; toothpaste tube carefully rolled up from the bottom. She'd miss the feel of his skin against her lips and the taste of his blood in her mouth.

She shuddered, hating that last thought as soon as it entered her mind. Hating herself.

Val was right: She had crossed the line with Malcolm. She never should have fed on him in the first place, but as soon as she stopped using the syringe, she should have known she was in trouble. Not only was she breaking her own rules, but she was putting Malcolm in danger. That was unacceptable.

And that was why she had to leave. She couldn't trust herself to do the right thing if she stayed.

The cough of a distant motorcycle interrupted her thoughts. She stopped, turning her head toward the sound. She'd know that distinctive chugging anywhere. That was Val's Ural.

The chugging stopped abruptly. She heard screams.

Hillary started to run.

48

Not for the first time, Val cursed the fact that the Van Ness Bridge was the only way across the Market Street chasm. Well, that wasn't entirely true. If you were on foot, you could climb down one side of the chasm, walk across, and hike back up the other side. But if you were driving, the bridge was the only way to go.

When she had been bartending at the Alley Cat, Val had driven the Ural across the bridge almost every day, commuting from her apartment in the Mission District to Polk Gulch. But since the Alley Cat had been closed by the SFPD following the murder of Andrei Vasilevski, she'd seen a lot less of the bridge.

Still, as the Ural's tires hummed across the rusty steel expanse, she was soothed by the familiar sound. Her mind started to wander. It was amazing how much her life had changed in a short time. She'd gone from being a fulltime bartender who occasionally dealt with weird shit to... what was she now? A private investigator? A hired gun? A monster hunter?

A little bit of all the above, she decided. For better or for worse, the supernatural activity in the city had been increasing lately, and Val's secret was out. A lot of people knew who she was and what she could do. A lot of people needed her help.

Not that her current employer was exactly an innocent victim. Val was not thrilled that working for Zoe Vasilevski was getting her tangled in a complex web of crime family politics. This whole mess with the assassinations and the amulets felt like wading through a swamp. It was sticky and it stank, and no matter which way direction she went, she ended up covered in muck.

But did the fact that Zoe's hands were dirty make her less deserving of help? Especially when the problem was supernatural?

No, it did not.

Val's own hands were far from clean. She had no right to cast stones at anyone.

She was so lost in thought that she didn't notice the arrow until it hit her.

The black shaft took her in the arm this time, piercing her forearm and shattering one of the big bones in there. The pain was so sharp it caused Val to yank the handlebars sideways. For a moment, all she could do was cradle her injured arm in shock, staring at the weird bulge of broken bone beneath her flesh.

By the time she wrestled her mind back into the present, the Ural was hurtling off the edge of the bridge. She reacted instinctively, pulling the breeze whistling through the canyon into an updraft, catching her falling body like a leaf.

The Ural was not so lucky. The old motorcycle was hundreds of pounds heavier than Val and much harder to stop. It nosedived into the depths of the chasm, tumbling end over end for several seconds before smashing onto the rocks below with a horrific crunch. Val stared at the wreckage in shock. She felt sick, her mind struggling to comprehend the depth of her loss. The old motorcycle had been much more than a simple means of transportation. They had been through so much together.

Another arrow whistled past her ear, pulling her back to the present moment.

She spun in the air to face her attacker. The assassin was standing near the end of the bridge, bow drawn, another arrow ready to loose. As the shaft shot toward her, Val flicked it away with a dismissive gesture. Her eyes burned with anger. The assassin had destroyed her motorcycle—and was going to pay for that.

The black-clad archer's eyes widened as she swooped toward them. They turned and ran.

"You can run, but you can't hide," Val called out. The triple adrenaline of shock, pain, and rage pounded through her veins. She was on the hunt now, and woe to anyone who got in her way.

The assassin ducked into an alley and Val followed, flying low above the pavement. Her knife was in her hand. Her eyes were fixed on her target.

Which was probably the reason she didn't see the net dropping down on her from above.

The weighted rope tumbled her to the ground, scraping her skin and sending fresh agony through her broken arm. The pain was so intense that for a long minute all she could do was grit her teeth and whimper.

When the alley finally came back into focus, she found herself looking up at the masked face of the assassin.

Then she frowned as she noticed another black-clad figure behind the first. And then a third.

The eyes of the first assassin narrowed with cold satisfaction.

"You are coming with us, Valora Keri."

49

The world was underwater. Val's eyes focused and unfocused. A camera zooming from near to far. Now she saw only the foreground. Now the background. Blobs of color moved in the periphery.

Something warm rested against the base of her throat, heat spreading outward through her body. Soothing like a hot bath. Relax and let the tension go.

Sounds swayed through her head. Strands of kelp in the tide. Coming together and moving apart.

The strands had different voices.

"Is she awake yet?"

"Soon. She's still coming out of it."

"Why is it taking so long?"

"She's fighting it."

"Should I be worried?"

"No. She's strong, but she's not that strong. Give it time."

Sometimes the voices were distant. Other times the voices were inside her own head.

It didn't matter either way. She was warm and floating.

Val sank beneath the waves and drifted.

An eternal moment later, she surfaced again. Things were sharper now, but still soft. The world in bubble wrap. All the sharp edges padded with foam. Toddler safe.

She heard voices again, and this time they had a direction.

Turning her head, she found she was sitting in an abandoned theater. Half the seats had been ripped out, leaving an expanse of bare, sloping floor pocked by empty anchor points. The faded remains of art deco murals covered the walls.

Val sat in a small island of seats that had been left behind, on the edge of this wasteland. Her thighs rested on worn velvet cushions. Booted feet stretched on the bare floor in front of her.

A trio of people stood talking a short distance away. These were the voices she had heard. They were all dressed in black, but their masks hung free, exposing their faces. To Val's surprise, she recognized one of them.

"Obi?" Her throat was dry, the word barely a whisper. She swallowed and tried again. "Obi?"

The young man smiled as he turned toward her.

"Welcome back to the land of the living."

Val blinked and rubbed grit from the corners of her eyes.

"Where am I?"

"There will be plenty of time for that," one of the others interjected. A woman with dark hair pulled back into a ponytail, exposing the shaved sides of her head. Val blinked as she recognized the Dragon's head of security, Aneka. "How do you feel?"

Val studied the woman, frowning at her black clothing.

"Are you the assassin?" Then she gasped as a memory surfaced. "My arm!" She clutched at her right forearm, the spot where the arrow had gone through, shattering the bone…

Her arm was smooth and whole.

Aneka smirked.

"I'm one of them. And as you can see, your arm is fine."

"But how?" Val asked, poking and prodding the flesh in disbelief.

"That would be my doing." The third member of the group spoke. A sun-bleached woman with a weathered voice. "You're welcome."

"Are you a healer?" Val studied her.

The woman's eyes were clear and bright, and Val was struck by her different-colored irises. One was sapphire blue, the other clay brown. The texture of the woman's face was like driftwood: contour lines sweeping over high cheekbones, gathering in deep crevices at the corners of her eyes and mouth.

"Yes."

"But you're an assassin? Isn't that a contradiction?"

"No contradiction." She smiled, exposing yellow teeth. "Everything will become clear."

Val frowned at her, something tickling at the back of her mind.

"Do I know you? You look familiar."

"We met at my settlement. Under the Golden Gate Bridge."

Val eyes widened. This was the woman who had approached her when she came to the shantytown tracking Sandra. The settlement that had swirled and shone with magic. Val remembered the power she'd seen in this woman. She was strong. And a healer, apparently.

"You're the woman with the dandelion in her hat."

The woman smiled. "I'm Lucy. Nice to see you again."

"But how did you end up here?" Val frowned, her eyes turning to Obi, including him in the question.

"I brought her here." A new figure stepped into the light. A middle-aged man in a well-tailored suit. Olive skin. Black hair and a black mustache.

"And you are?"

He bared his teeth in a shark's smile.

"My name is Sandro. Sandro Forti."

50

Val narrowed her eyes at the man in the suit.

"Forti? Where have I heard that name before?"

"They were the Italian family Zoe told us was wiped out by the curse," Mister E said.

"Right. The Wongs took over their territory."

"Yes, they stole my family's birthright." The man's lip curled in disgust. "I am going to take it back."

"I thought the Fortis were all killed by the curse?"

"Not all. Just the men. The women and children were left to fend for themselves. They had to flee the city."

"Let me guess. Your mother was one of those women."

"I was just a boy when my mother was forced from her home. Driven from the city like a rat. I had to grow up in Oakland." He shuddered.

"Oh, you poor thing. The horror."

"You scoff at my mother?" Anger flared in his eyes as he approached Val with three quick steps. His hand lashed out, stinging her cheek, snapping her head to the side.

Val glared at him, her hands clenching into fists.

"Mister, you just made a big mistake." She cocked her fist back, ready to take the asshole down.

"Violence won't be necessary."

The woman with the ponytail spoke softly, but her words echoed in Val's head. Something pulsed at the base of her throat. A green amulet. Warmth washed over her, spreading out from the amulet, soothing away her anger.

No. Of course violence wasn't necessary.

Val's fists relaxed, her hands dropping back to her side.

Sandro Forti smiled.

"Now you see how it is."

"What are you doing? Rip his head off." Mister E's outrage didn't touch Val. He was no more than an annoying voice in the back of her head. She ignored him.

"You are mine," Forti continued. "And you will do what I say. Yes?"

"Yes," she agreed.

His smile widened.

"Good. Now we are on the same page. There are two more amulets. Two more families to bring down. The Anands and the O'Ceallaighs. You will kill the heads of these families and bring me the amulets. Once I have them, nothing will stand in my way. The other families will be forced to kneel before me, and the Forti family will take their rightful place."

"Wake up, Val. Take this guy out now," Mister E snapped.

But she didn't. She simply nodded her head.

"It will be done."

Joumala Anand sparkled. The elegant young woman wore a sleek white dress with a green shawl draped across her bare shoulders. Her hair was swept up in an elaborate twist, revealing strings of pearls dangling from her ears. Gold embroidery laced the edges of the shawl, and the green fabric was the same shade as the jade amulet that rested against her throat.

"We have eyes on the prize," Aneka said quietly.

They were squatting behind some bushes in the center of a small park. Fog raced across the starry sky. Houses with lit windows surrounded the park, rectangular-eyed owls peering into the darkness.

The flat-faced security woman was the leader of their little quartet. As far as Val could tell, Aneka must have been the original assassin in black. As she'd collected the amulets, she had used them to recruit magic users into the group one by one. The same way she'd now recruited Val.

She wasn't sure what that meant about Aneka's loyalties. She was the Dragon's head of security. Did that mean the Dragon was working with Sandro Forti? Or was Aneka a double agent?

Val shook her head, her forehead creasing as she worried at the problem. Too many questions.

The warmth of the amulet spread through her, and she relaxed. Her forehead smoothed.

None of that mattered. She was one of the team now. All she had to do was follow orders.

Joumala was at a cocktail party inside one of the grand old Victorians bordering the park. They could see half a dozen people through the front window, all dressed impeccably, drinking cocktails and smiling too-white smiles.

"Obi, you go around to the back. Get inside. Make sure she doesn't escape through the kitchen," Aneka said.

Get inside? How was he going to do that?

Val turned her eyes toward the young thief and gasped. Shen Wong stood beside her, dressed in his sharp red jacket. Obi's voice came out of his mouth.

"Don't look so shocked. I told you I'm kitsune. Wearing other people's faces is as easy as changing my underwear."

"That's a handy talent," Val said.

He winked and gave her a rakish smile. "You don't know the half of it. I'm a very talented guy."

He jogged away across the darkened park. Val watched him slip through a small gate next to the house and disappear.

She turned to Aneka. "What's the rest of the plan?"

"Once Obi is in place, I'll cut the power. While I do that, you are going to walk in the front door, kill Joumala Anand, and grab the amulet."

"All right."

"All right?" Mister E repeated incredulously. *"Nothing about that plan strikes you as off?"*

The amulet pulsed softly against her throat. Soothing waves of certainty rolled through her.

"No. It seems pretty straightforward."

"Straightforward, yes. All right, no."

"What's your problem? I thought you liked killing people."

"As a general rule, I do. But I don't think you're in your right mind right now."

"In my right mind? I haven't been in my right mind since I was six years old. This is a job. We do the job and get the amulet. That's all it is."

"I just don't think you've ever killed anyone on purpose before."

"An accidental body count is still a body count. Killing someone on purpose is no different. They're just as dead."

"I suppose you've got a point," Mister E conceded. He grinned. *"And you're right. I do love a good killing."*

51

Obi had made it into the party. Val could see his red coat flashing through the crowd inside. Aneka was poised to cut the power. Lucy would stay hidden in the bushes. The healer was there for support, not action. She'd patch up whoever needed it when the job was finished.

Val took a deep breath. She could see Joumala Anand through the windows, laughing and smiling her elegant smile. Unaware this would be her last night on earth.

If Joumala had known, would she have done anything differently? Or would the socialite choose to spend her last hours at a cocktail party?

If given the choice, Val decided she would personally rather not know it was her last night. If she knew in advance, there would be too much pressure to spend her final hours in the best possible way. Get everything exactly right. All that anxiety would ruin any chance she had of being content.

"In position," Aneka's voice was soft in her ear. A neat little bit of magic, that. Val thought Lucy must be doing it.

"In position," Obi echoed.

"In position," Val confirmed.

She crouched just across the street from the house, gripping the hilt of her knife. She kept her eyes fixed on Joumala's position. Once the lights went out, she'd use Mister E's night vision to make a beeline toward the heiress.

Her stomach fluttered and she blew out a breath, trying to shake off the jitters.

"We are a go in 5, 4, 3…" Aneka's countdown was cool and professional. No nerves in her.

Val's breath hissed between clenched teeth. The world came alive with color as she switched over to Mister E's vision. This was it. Go time.

As she prepared to dash out of the bushes, Aneka's voice stopped counting.

"Hold. The situation has changed."

Changed? What did she mean changed?

Then Val saw him. Padraig O'Ceallaigh, strolling down the sidewalk.

He was immaculately dressed, as always. A long wool coat and a silk scarf hanging loose over his dark suit. Hair artfully tousled above his handsome jawline.

But the most important detail was the green glow visible beneath the neckline of his shirt. He was wearing his family's amulet.

Val watched him stroll up the steps and enter the party. Grab a cocktail and kiss the hostess on the cheek. Completely in his element.

Aneka's voice was smug.

"Looks like we have two birds in the nest. That's a nice stroke of luck. Saves us time later."

"You want to get them both?" Val whispered.

Horror clawed its way up her throat. The amulet pulsed, soothing her anxiety back down.

Don't worry. Everything is fine.

"Of course," Aneka said. "We'll have to strike fast, though, and get them both at the same time. New plan. Obi, you will take care of Joumala. Val, your target is now Padraig O'Ceallaigh."

Adrenaline surged through Val. Every muscle in her body tensed.

This was wrong. She might be at odds with Padraig, but she still considered him a friend.

Her lips started to form the words: *No. I won't do this.*

The amulet flared. Waves of soothing heat inundated her body. She was a child, comforted in her mother's arms. Warm and safe. Everything was going to be all right.

Her clenched muscles relaxed. Her mind cleared.

"Understood," she said. "I have eyes on the target."

Aneka began her count again. "… 3 … 2 … 1 … Go." She cut the power to the entire block, plunging the party into darkness.

Val was already up the stairs, pushing the front door open. Surprised voices rose all around her. With Mister E's night vision, she could see heads turning in dismay. Blind eyes searching for light that wasn't there.

Their eyes would adjust soon, but for a precious few seconds it was as if someone had dropped a black curtain over their faces. She would never have a better chance to strike.

Val slid through the crowd toward Padraig. She knew the man was at least part fae and a dangerous adversary. She had to do this quickly and surgically. She wouldn't get a second chance.

She closed the last two steps, drew her knife back, and plunged it toward his throat.

A scream pierced the air. Joumala.

Padraig jerked in surprise and Val's knife missed the mark. Instead of severing his jugular vein, the blade only grazed his collarbone.

Val cursed as he fell back with a cry.

Then she saw the glow of his amulet tumble to the floor. She grinned and snatched it up. Her blade had hit the mark after all. Just not the mark she'd intended.

Amulet clutched in her fist, Val turned to slip back out the door.

Padraig's hand closed around her wrist.

"Not so fast, Keri."

Val cursed. If Padraig knew who she was, that meant he could see. Which eliminated all her advantages.

She relaxed her wrist, twisted it toward his thumb, and jerked it free. At the same time, she elbowed him in the face.

Or at least, that was her intention.

Padraig slipped past her elbow, his hazel eyes shining in the darkness.

"You've bit off more than you can chew this time, Val."

His hand flashed toward her face. In the weird light of Mister E's vision, his movements looked strangely stop-motion. Stuttering and jerking as if the world were under a strobe light.

Flash: Padraig stepping toward her.

Flash: His hand raised.

Flash: The sting as it connected with her cheekbone.

Val collided with someone's glass and champagne splashed down the back of her neck. She swore but didn't have time to do more than that as Padraig came at her again. He was all bright eyes and dark limbs, his fae blood making his skin shine with a faint golden glow.

Trying to dodge his next strike, Val collided with someone else. Voices were raised in alarm.

She growled. It was too crowded in the party; she needed room to move, or better yet, open space so she could use her magic. In here, there were too many innocent people. Too much collateral damage for her to cut loose.

Padraig's kick caught her in the stomach and she tumbled to the floor. He stood over her, a thin blade appearing in his hand. He pointed it at her face.

"Give me the amulet, Keri." He slashed her cheek with a flick of his wrist. "Now."

Val swallowed, frantically looking for a way out. She could feel blood running down her face.

The situation was not good.

She was on her back on the floor. She couldn't use her magic in the crowd. Padraig stood over her with a blade. He was faster than her to begin with. Starting from these positions, she didn't have a prayer.

His lips peeled back into a snarl.

"Last chance, Val. Hand it over or I swear I'll leave you bleeding on the floor and take it from your corpse."

Val gaped at him. Things were rocky between them, but he wouldn't actually kill her. Would he?

The grim look on his face said he would.

Then Padraig jerked and his eyes rolled into the back of his head. He slumped bonelessly to the floor.

Padriag's fall revealed Obi standing behind him, a marble bust in his hands. The thief grinned at Val.

"Lying down on the job, are we?"

52

"Did you get the other amulet?" Val asked.

They were several blocks away from the party already. The driver, Jorge, had scooped them up, and now they all sat in the back of the van, moving quickly through the darkened streets.

What Val really wanted to ask Obi was: *Did you kill Joumala?*

But she couldn't force the words past her lips. She didn't want to know the answer. She might not like Joumala Anand very much, but that didn't mean she wanted her dead.

"Was there ever any doubt?" Obi grinned and held the glowing jade up for all to see. Like the amulet Val snatched from Padraig, Joumala's jade fragment dangled at the end of a simple leather thong.

Aneka motioned impatiently. "Hand them over."

They did as they were bid and the assassin slid the fragments into a black pouch, which she tucked into an inner pocket.

"What are you going to do with them?" Val asked.

"Deliver them to Mr. Forti, as promised."

"Then what happens?"

Aneka's smile was evasive. "You'll see."

"It's all about dragon power," Obi said, grinning at her. Val cocked an eyebrow at the kitsune, inviting him to elaborate. He leaned forward, gesturing enthusiastically as he spoke. "The Dragon put a lot of his power into the amulets. That's how he was able to maintain the curse. Putting all the fragments back together will release the stored power."

Val frowned. "So the Dragon will get his power back? How does that help Sandro Forti?"

Obi laughed.

"No. Forti has figured out a way to capture the released power and pull it into his own body."

"So he'll get some of the Dragon's power?"

"Not just some. All of it. In order to force his peace onto the city, the Dragon had to spread his power pretty thin. There's more power in the combined amulets than there is left in the Dragon himself."

Val thought back to her brief audience with the Dragon in his lair beneath Japantown. The old man had seemed anything but frail. His power had been so thick in the air, it was nearly suffocating.

She shuddered. If the amulets held more power than that, Sandra Forti was about to become a very big problem.

The van parked in the loading dock behind the abandoned theater, and they all filed inside. Entering the giant hall, they found the decorative alcoves lining the walls aglow with candles, with dozens of waxen tapers flickering over the boards of the worn stage. A huge pentagram had been painted on the center of the stage.

"Forti isn't wasting any time," Mister E observed.

Aneka gave one of the amulets to Jorge and directed them to each stand on one of the five points of the pentagram. Sandro Forti put the sixth fragment around his neck and moved into the center of the formation.

Lucy began a chant, slow and repetitive. The words were fairly simple, and after a couple of repetitions, the rest of them joined in.

Val could feel the magic building in the air. It began as a pressure in her ears. Then a tingling on her skin. She smelled smoke, and tasted metal, copper and iron. Colored light began to swirl in the air, green and silver and gold, tendrils of power rising from the five amulets at the corners, gathering above them in a swirling storm.

All the hairs on her arms stood on end. The pressure in her ears thickened, pushing the sounds of the chant far away. The tingling grew until it felt like a swarm of ants were biting her skin.

The storm of magic began to funnel down into Sandro Forti. His eyes became lanterns. He screamed as his skin swelled like ripe sausage, his mortal shell unable to contain the immense power. Cracks split his flesh. Blood ran down his face.

Val started to scream as well, the swirling power searing her bones. Aneka joined her. Then Lucy, Obi, and Jorge.

The light grew so intense she had to close her eyes, and it hurt even through her eyelids. The pressure on her ears sharpened until it felt like someone was stabbing her eardrums with an ice pick. Her skin burned. Dimly, she was aware that she had fallen to her knees.

A massive force punched Val in the chest, hurling her back across the stage, sliding and tumbling across the boards as the ceremony burst out in a wave. All the candles in the theater were extinguished in a whoosh, plunging the cavernous space into darkness. Val came to rest against a wall, bruised and aching, the skin on her hands torn.

The sudden silence was deafening.

A deep voice began to laugh.

53

Laughter rang through the darkness. The sound was heavy with power, so thick it made Val's bones ache.

At least the pressure in her ears was gone. Another second of that and her skull would have split wide open.

She levered herself onto her elbows, cautiously taking stock of her body. Her skin was scraped and raw from sliding across the floor. She was bruised and tender, but it didn't feel like anything was broken. A small win, anyway.

The laughter came again, and a jade green light grew on the other side of the stage. Squinting into the sudden glare, Val could just make out a silhouette against the illumination.

She choked as it came into focus. The form wasn't remotely human.

Sandro Forti stood, his now serpentine body rising high above the stage. Green scales covered his skin. His enormous eyes shone silver.

He had become a dragon.

Someone screamed on the other side of the stage and his head whipped toward the sound. He struck like a snake, dagger-sharp teeth glinting in his gaping maw.

The scream cut off abruptly and Forti's head reared up into the air. A pair of kicking legs protruded from his mouth, and the rest of the body was impaled on his teeth. Val thought it might be Jorge, but she didn't have time to see for certain before Forti tossed his head back and swallowed the legs in one quick gulp.

More screams sounded and Forti turned his monstrous head toward them. Lucy and Aneka cowered across the stage. Forti reared back to strike.

"Hey!" She hit him with a fist of wind. "Leave them alone!"

The dragon paused, his lambent eyes snapping toward Val. The weight of that gaze hit her like an anvil, the power so heavy she could barely breathe.

"A brilliant strategy," Mister E observed. *"Let's call the monster to us like some stray dog. What could possibly go wrong?"*

"It got his attention away from the others, didn't it?"

"Ah, the standard hero's ploy. Sacrifice yourself to save the innocent. Not very imaginative, Val."

"I'm not sacrificing myself. Nobody else has to die here."

"Tell that to the dragon."

Forti stalked across the stage toward her, his ponderous steps shaking the boards. His teeth gleamed. A mouthful of knives.

"Sandro," she called out. "Are you still in there? Think. You are a human being, not a monster. You don't have to kill anyone."

Forti laughed, the sound deep and echoing.

"I am not a monster? Do you not have eyes? Of course I'm a monster. I'm exactly the monster I've always wanted to be." His shining silver eyes fixed on her, enormous pupils dilated like those of a cat stalking its prey. He smiled, baring all his deadly teeth. "As for killing people, I've barely gotten started with that."

In a blink, he struck, his neck whipping forward, maw gaping. Val's eyes widened, her muscles locking up with primal fear. She couldn't think, couldn't move. The dragon was going to tear her to pieces.

Something hit her from the side, knocking her out of the path of the dragon's strike. His teeth snapped shut on empty air, so close she felt the wind of their passage. As Val tumbled to a stop, her eyes focused on the familiar bloodless face of her rescuer.

"Hillary? What are you doing here?"

Her vampire housemate gave her a tight-lipped smile.

"We can talk later. Right now, we need to get you out of here."

The dragon roared, the sound so loud it shook the old theater. Dust fell from the rafters like snow.

"Not just me," Val said. "We have to get the others as well."

"That might be a problem."

Val followed the vampire's gaze to find Lucy sprawled on the stage, the dragon's deadly maw swaying above her, poised to strike. The old healer had her hands raised, her magic swirling helplessly. Val scowled. Lucy was an extremely strong witch, but her magic was only healing magic. She was helpless before the monster.

Forti struck.

So did Val.

As the dragon's teeth plunged toward Lucy, Val summoned a howling wind, yanking it across the stage. The air spun Lucy across the boards like a leaf, delivering her to the spot where Val and Hillary stood.

Forti roared in rage.

Val helped Lucy to her feet, casting her eyes around the stage. There was no sign of Obi. Hopefully that meant the young thief had scampered away. Aneka stood near the dragon, but she didn't look afraid, and he showed no sign of attacking her. Apparently, the assassin had been helping Forti even before the mind control of the amulets.

Which made Val realize something else. The mind control was gone. The ritual that had sucked the magic out of the amulets had also freed her.

Despite the desperate situation, a grin curled her lips. It was good to be the master of her own ship again. Being under the amulet's control had been creepy.

Hillary pulled her out of her thoughts.

"Val, we have to go. Now."

"Right. What about Lucy?" The old witch wasn't putting weight on one leg. Val thought she probably had a sprained ankle.

"You worry about yourself," Lucy snapped. "I'm fine."

As Val watched, Lucy bent and circled her ankle with both hands, closing her eyes and whispering. Val could see the healing power flow into the injured area.

The dragon roared and lumbered across the stage toward them.

"We don't have time for this," Hillary snapped. "Follow me."

Without another word, the vampire scooped Lucy up and threw the old witch over her shoulder. Lucy yipped, but shut her mouth and hung on, recognizing that she didn't have time to heal her leg properly with a dragon bearing down on them.

Hillary moved like the wind. Even carrying someone, she still possessed all her preternatural strength and speed. She disappeared into the wings of the theater with Val running hot on her heels.

Behind them, the dragon howled in frustration.

54

They were several blocks away before Hillary finally slowed to a halt. Val sucked air as she pulled up behind her.

"I think we're safe," Hillary said as she set Lucy down on her feet.

"Yeah," Val agreed. "For now."

There was no sign of pursuit. Hopefully the dragon was still in the theater, plotting his next move.

"Let's not do that again," the old woman groaned. Hillary set her down and watched her sink to the ground, wincing as she put her hands around her ankle. "Being carried like a sack of potatoes is not fun."

"Sorry. It was the fastest way to get you out. I'm Hillary, by the way."

"Lucy," the old woman said. The healer's eyes were clear and bright, and Hillary was struck by her different-colored irises. One blue, the other brown. There was power in her gaze. "And thank you. I'm not complaining; I'd probably be dead if you hadn't scooped me up like that. I'd just rather not have to do it again."

"Agreed." Hillary looked at Val. "So, what's the plan?"

"Give me a minute," Val wheezed. "Not everyone can run like you can."

"Don't you work out all the time?"

"Martial arts training is not the same as running for your life. Different muscle groups."

"Uh-huh." Hillary smirked.

Val put her hands behind her head, taking deep breaths and working to get her breathing under control.

"What are you doing here, anyway?" she asked. "I don't believe you randomly happened upon that theater."

"I've been following you," Hillary admitted. "I was trying to figure out how to free you from Forti's mind control. Then he turned into a dragon and started killing people, so I figured my time to decide was up. I did the first thing that came to mind."

"What you did saved us all. Thank you."

Hillary's face fell. "Not all of you. Forti ate the driver."

"If it weren't for you, he would have eaten us all," Val reminded her. "Don't beat yourself up. You can't save everyone."

"I guess you can't."

Hillary felt sick. Though she'd just saved several lives, she kept seeing the one she hadn't been able to save over and over in her mind. Hearing the man's screams as the dragon's teeth pierced his body.

"Did anyone see what happened to Obi?" Val asked.

"You mean the exceptionally handsome kitsune?" Obi's voice came floating down the alley. He grinned as he sauntered up to them. "I'm pretty sure he made it out in one piece."

"Saved your own ass, did you?" Val scowled at him. "Thanks for all your help."

"It looked like your vampire friend had everything under control. Besides, one has to protect their ass-ets." He leaned against the wall of the alley, unconcerned.

Val rolled her eyes. "Anyway, I guess I'm glad to see you made it out."

"It's OK to admit it. Just because I love me, doesn't mean you can't love me too."

"Where did you find this guy?" Hillary asked.

"I caught him trying to steal my motorcycle," Val said.

"Of course you did." Hillary narrowed her eyes at Obi. "Why are you here, exactly?"

"Well, you see," the thief explained, "when a man and a woman love each other very much…"

"Can I rip his throat out? Or do you want to do it yourself?" Hillary asked Val.

"He's insufferable, but he can also be useful." Val turned to Obi. "I assume that's why you're here? To make yourself useful?"

"Indeed. I am here to once again offer my services, such as they are. Judging from what I saw in that theater, you're going to need all the help you can get."

"Not me," Lucy said. "I'm going back to my people. All this running and fighting is a game for younger bones."

"All right," Val said. "Stay safe out there."

"You too." Lucy winked her blue eye and shuffled off down the alley.

Hillary turned to Obi. "Do you know how to slay a dragon?"

"I believe the traditional method involves a great deal of heavy armor and a very sharp sword."

"We seem to be short on those," Val put in. "Any other suggestions?"

Obi shrugged apologetically. "Not at the moment, no."

"Malcolm might have some ideas," Hillary said. "He and Sandra went to the Library to research the amulets."

Val scrunched up her face, then nodded.

"OK. Let's go see what Malcolm has to say. At the very least, we can get some coffee and regroup."

55

Their living room had never been so crowded. Val sat in her designated spot in the window seat. Hillary slouched in the armchair across the room. Malcolm and Sandra shared the couch, leaving Obi to sit on the carpeted floor, his back against the wall, shoeless feet stretched out before him. He wore turquoise socks with a pattern of icebergs and polar bears on them.

They all held steaming mugs of coffee and assorted teas. Malcolm had delighted in playing host and getting everyone exactly what they wanted. Now he sat on the edge of the couch and beamed at the group.

"Well, isn't this cozy!"

"That's one word for it," Val muttered.

"You know, Val, you can bring company over anytime you like. It doesn't always have to be an emergency," Malcolm continued. "It's nice to have people over when there's no dragons to slay." He eyed Obi's socks enviously. The kitsune wiggled his toes and grinned.

"Any insight on how exactly we're going to do that?" Val asked.

Malcolm frowned at her. "Can we not enjoy having company before we get down to saving the city? Is five minutes too much to ask?"

"That depends on how many dead people you're OK with having

on your conscience," Val shot back. "The more time we waste here, the more bodies Forti is going to leave in his wake. But by all means, let's drink tea and make small talk."

Malcolm huffed. "Fine. But when all this is over, we are going to have some guests over for a proper dinner party." He glared a challenge at Val. She kept her mouth shut and circled her finger in a get-to-the-point gesture.

"OK. Here's what we learned at the Library: From what we could gather, the jade amulet is a family heirloom from long before the Dragon crossed the Pacific. It has been a symbol of his family's power for generations. The organization now known as the Yakuza has existed in one form or another for over a thousand years. According to legend, there has always been a dragon leading it. Whether the current dragon came to power in modern times, or whether the leader has been the same dragon throughout history is unclear."

"It's also irrelevant," Val snapped impatiently. "What does the amulet do? More importantly, how can we stop Forti now that he has become a dragon himself?"

"I'm getting to all of that." Malcolm shot Val a baleful look at the interruption. She growled and leaned back against the window, folding her arms over her chest.

"Also, I think it's pretty relevant if the Dragon is a thousand years old or not," Hillary said. "Anyone who has managed to live that long is no joke."

"Thank you." Malcolm beamed.

Val grudgingly acknowledged the point with a scowl.

Malcolm continued, "The amulet and a dragon have been together for a thousand years. From what I read, it sounds like the amulet and the Dragon have become synonymous. Like the Dragon's power and the amulet's power are part of one another. So when the Dragon broke the amulet into pieces, he literally broke his own power into pieces and scattered it around the city."

"Wouldn't that weaken him?" Obi asked.

"Yes. But it also put parts of his power in other areas of the city, extending his influence by proxy."

"Which is how he was able to maintain the curse."

"Exactly," Malcolm winked at Obi. "Give the man a prize."

"But that's the bad part too," Sandra added. She shrank a little as everyone's eyes turned to her, but gamely continued. "We think he might have put most of his power into the amulet over the centuries. Which means if Forti has absorbed that power…"

"He is now more powerful than the original Dragon," Val finished. "That's just wonderful."

"I think it's pretty clear Forti is going to go after the Dragon next," Hillary said. "He's got the biggest bone to pick with him, and if he has become more powerful than the Dragon…"

"It makes sense that he would try to kill him," Obi put in. "I doubt he'll waste any time either. I wouldn't."

"So how do we stop him?" Val asked.

"That's the billion-credit question, isn't it?" Obi said.

Everyone's eyes turned back to Malcolm. For once, he didn't look happy to be the center of attention.

"Well," he said hesitantly, "none of the ways I read about to kill a dragon sounded particularly promising. Dragons are supposed to be insanely powerful. But, if I had to do it, I'd probably try one of these ways…"

They all listened, rapt, while Malcolm tried to teach them how to slay a dragon.

When he finished, they looked at each other, with nobody speaking for several seconds.

'Well, that's not exactly sunshine and rainbows, is it?" Obi said.

"No, it's not." Val sighed. "But it's the best chance we're going to get."

Glass shards filled the air as the window behind her exploded.

56

S hattered glass covered Val's hair as a ball of flame expanded in the center of the living room. Chaos erupted. Cries of alarm and screams of pain. Smoke rolled across the ceiling.

It took Val's brain a few seconds to catch up. When it did, hot rage filled her body.

Someone had thrown a firebomb through the window.

She caught Hillary's eye. "Get everyone outside!"

The vampire nodded, and Val turned her attention to more pressing matters. Namely, the fire spreading across the carpet. The coffee table was already black, and flames were licking up the side of the couch.

She had to get the fire under control, and she had to do it now.

Val used her power to reach out through the window. It was a typically misty San Francisco evening, and the air was heavy and moist. She pulled the fog into the burning room, willing it to become thicker, sucking in more and more moisture.

Her skin and hair became damp. The fire started to steam but showed no signs of abating. The firebomb must have contained gasoline or some other accelerant. It would take more than a heavy fog to put it out.

Bodies headed for the door. Hillary was herding people like a sheepdog, getting them moving on their own or bodily hauling those who were too terrified or startled.

Val didn't have time to focus on that. She needed to get the fire out. Now.

She sucked more mist in through the window, thick white clouds swirling across the ceiling. Finally, they became too dense to hold water and it began to rain inside the living room. The fire hissed and the steam thickened, combining with the smoke and mist to obscure everything. It rushed out the open window, the heat scalding Val's face.

As tears streamed down her cheeks, she coughed. She couldn't see anything. She had to keep pulling in the mist, keep the rain falling in the living room, and hope it would be enough to extinguish the fire.

Something whistled past her head and the room exploded again.

The force shoved Val backwards. More glass shattered over her body. In an instant, she was through the window and falling.

Only her training saved her from splattering all over the sidewalk.

Mister E had spent hours drilling her in flying. Forcing her to fly and fall and catch herself over and over, in all kinds of situations, until flying had become as instinctual and natural to her as walking.

Still, she almost didn't have enough time. Their apartment was on the third floor. The hard surface of the street was only seconds away.

Val curled the wind up beneath her, trying to achieve maximum lift. The air whistled and howled. She felt her body start to slow… then impact knocked the air from her lungs as she bounced off the roof of car and tumbled to the asphalt.

The air had helped to slow her fall, so it didn't feel like she'd fallen three stories. Maybe only one.

It still hurt.

She lay there for a long moment, trying to remember how to breathe.

Smoke and steam poured from the living room window high above. She didn't know if the rain she'd created would be enough to extinguish the flames.

As she reached up to draw more mist into the apartment, a dark silhouette stepped in front of her. Shiny shoes and sharp creased slacks filled her field of vision.

"Nice of you to drop in, Valora Keri."

She raised her head to find a familiar face staring down at her. Dark eyes and black hair slicked back from a sharp widow's peak

"Rodrigo," she croaked.

The second-in-command of the vampire cabal bared his fangs.

"You were warned, Val. You chose to shelter the traitor anyway. Now you will pay the price."

Screams pulled her attention to the side. Her housemates and guests were pouring out the entrance to the building, only to be met by more vampires. Lucy and Malcolm were pressed back against the wall, terror in their eyes. Sandra stood protectively before them, reaching for her sunglasses, ready to turn their attackers to stone with a glance. But the vampires were too fast, dropping a black sack over her head in a flash, cinching it tight. Hillary tried to fight, transforming into a whirl-wind of rage that was quickly smothered beneath a trio of vamp muscle. Val recognized the enormous bulk of Jonathan Gray.

"What do you want?" she snarled.

"We want what is ours," Rodrigo said calmly. "And we shall have it."

Val started to push herself to her feet, but Rodrigo clamped her neck with an iron grip, pressing her cheek down against gritty street. He wrenched her arms behind her back and cold metal clicked around her wrists. She saw Malcolm, Lucy, and Sandra get similarly handcuffed.

Hillary's limp form was slung over Jonathan Gray's massive shoulder.

Rodrigo smiled.

"Now. My queen would like a word."

57

The vampires covered Val's eyes and carried her for what felt like forever. When they finally removed the blindfold, she found herself in the dark. The smell of damp rock told her she was underground. A cave. She wondered if it was the same cavern beneath the Presidio where she had met Melinda Pearl before.

She stood in the darkness, waiting for her eyes to adjust. They did not. The natural dark was thicker than the blindfold had ever been.

Shuffling sounds and indistinct whispers came to her ears.

"Hello?" Her voice was startlingly loud in the silence, echoing back to her.

"Val?" Malcolm's voice came from somewhere off to her left. "Is that you?"

"Malcolm, are you all right? Is anyone else with you?"

"I'm fine." His voice shook, but it sounded like fear, not pain. "I don't know about anyone else."

"I'm here," someone said in a soft voice. Sandra.

Val cursed silently. The gorgon's power would be useless in the darkness. She wouldn't be able to turn anyone to stone if they couldn't see her eyes.

"Hillary?" Val asked. "Ooi?"

"Yeah," Obi said.

"I'm alive," Hillary's voice was filled with pain.

A new voice hissed in the dark. A cold, ancient sound that made the hairs on the back of Val's neck stand on end.

Melinda Pearl.

"Valora Keri. I told you what would happen if you continued to defy me."

Val stiffened. She couldn't tell where Pearl's voice was coming from. The vampire queen seemed to be everywhere at once. She could be on the other side of the cavern, or she could be standing right behind Val. She had no way to know.

Val set her jaw and tried not to let her fear show.

"Where's Hillary?" she growled. "If you've hurt her…"

Melinda Pearl's laughter echoed in the darkness.

"Save your empty threats. My spawn belongs to me. She is mine to do with as I wish." Pearl's voice was suddenly right in Val's ear. "As are you, Valora Keri. The only question now is whether I allow you to live or not."

Val flinched, terror shivering down her spine. She drove her fingernails into her palms, stopping herself from whirling around in a panic with an effort of will.

"Let the others go," she said. "They have nothing to do with this."

"Don't they?" Pearl's voice sounded amused. "Did they not know that you had stolen my spawn? That you were hiding her from me? Anyone in your orbit is guilty by association."

"What do you want?" Val asked. "Or are you just going to make us stand here in the dark forever? Make us shake so you can stroke your ego?"

Something struck Val across the face and she fell hard onto the stone floor, unable to catch herself with her hands bound behind her back.

"Be careful, Valora Keri," the vampire queen hissed. "I can snuff your life in an instant."

"Yet you haven't done it," Val said. "So I ask again. What do you want?"

There was no answer. The silence stretched so long she suspected the vampire queen had left the chamber. Val was opening her mouth to repeat her question when Pearl's voice finally came out of the darkness.

"We both have a problem. The Dragon is dead."

"The Dragon is dead?" Val echoed dumbly.

She remembered what it had felt like to be in the presence of that ancient being. The suffocating, overwhelming power.

"Forti," she whispered.

"Yes," the vampire queen confirmed. "Sandro Forti's power has grown. He is swatting the heads of the great families like flies."

"You're afraid that you are next on the list," Val said.

"It is not a fear; it is a certainty. Forti will come for me. And all the power of my coven will not be enough to stop him."

"Are you saying you need my help?" Val laughed. "I appreciate the faith, but you've got an oversized opinion of my power. If the Dragon of Japantown couldn't stop him, I don't see what I can do."

"Forti took the Dragon's power. He was unable to defend himself against his own stolen might. You have powers I do not, Valora Keri. Magic gave Forti his new form. Only magic can take it away."

"Kidnapping me and my friends is a funny way of asking for help. Why should I care what happens to you? Why shouldn't I just let Forti take you out and save myself the trouble?"

"Because Forti will not stop with me. How long will Zoe Vasilevski cling to life? Do you think Shen Wong will get to enjoy his newfound status as the head of his family? Or Padraig O'Ceallaigh?" Val must have flinched at Padraig's name, because she could hear the smile in Pearl's voice as she continued. "Forti will not rest until all the great families have been wiped from the face of the city and every last member has been exterminated. If you want to save your little friends, you'll have to save me as well."

"Maybe I should let Forti eliminate you first," Val snarled. "Then I can protect my friends afterward."

"You could do that." The vampire's breath was suddenly cold on her neck. "But only I know the ritual that will undo Forti's power. If I die, you sign your friends' death warrant."

Val scowled. Pearl had her right where she wanted her.

"Let Hillary go."

"No. All vampires in this city belong to me. My spawn are mine to do with as I wish."

"Let her go, or I won't help you."

"You would let all of your other friends die for her sake?"

"That's right. We'll all burn together."

A tense silence fell. Even in the utter blackness, Val could feel the vampire queen's eyes burning into her.

"No, Val. I'm not worth it." Hillary's voice came from somewhere off to the side. She sounded like she was in pain.

"That's bullshit," Val snapped. "We didn't fight for your freedom just to give you back now."

"My life isn't worth all of those others." Hillary's voice was flat, as if she'd lost all hope. "I'll give myself up, if that's what it takes."

The misery in Hillary's voice broke Val's heart.

"No," she said. "There has to be another way." Val turned to where she thought Pearl was. "You said all the vampires in this city belong to you. What if Hillary leaves the city? For good this time. Then you won't have to worry about her disturbing your precious control."

"Why would I let her go when she has said herself that she will stay?"

"Because you need my help." Val crossed her arms over her chest. "That's the deal. I'll help you defeat Forti, but you have to let Hillary leave the city."

The silence that followed this pronouncement felt dangerous, like a naked blade held inches from Val's throat. She knew she was pushing her luck and half expected Pearl to kill them all and have done with it.

When she spoke, Pearl's voice was flat and cold.

"I will consider it. But if she ever steps foot near the bay again, her life will be forfeit. She will be killed on sight."

"Agreed." Val felt a great weight lift off her. Hillary was going to get her freedom.

"But first you will help me undo this new dragon. Until Forti is vanquished, Hillary will remain my guest."

Val scowled, but she really hadn't expected anything less. The second Pearl let Hillary go, she lost all her leverage.

"Unharmed," Val clarified.

"She will come to no further harm," the vampire queen agreed.

Val noticed Pearls' use if the word "further" but didn't remark on it. It was obvious the vampires had already hurt Hillary. What was done was done. All she could do was try to prevent her from getting hurt more.

She took a deep breath, squared her shoulders, and stuck her hand out into the darkness.

"It's a deal."

After a moment of hesitation, she felt an icy hand clasp hers. Melinda Pearl's hand was bony and cold but filled with an immense strength. Val knew the woman could crush all the bones in her hand in a heartbeat if she wanted to.

She could hear the cruel smile on Pearls' lips.

"A compact has been struck." Pearl's voice lowered to a whisper meant for Val's ears alone. "If you break the compact, know that your friend will die."

58

"It looks like a bomb went off in this place," Val whispered.

She stared at the wreckage of the Japantown arcade. The entire building had caved in, the roof collapsed, leaving broken walls reaching up toward the overcast sky. Yellow police tape fluttered in the breeze. They surrounded a rubble-strewn graveyard of broken video game cabinets: circuit boards and disemboweled wires curling like intestines around the jagged, shattered faces of screens.

"It looks like Godzilla stomped through the building," Obi said.

The young thief searched the rubble, picking up and discarding things seemingly at random. Sandra meandered through the wreckage in a different direction, squatting to see things from odd angles, pencil scratching across the sketch pad in her hand, a smile playing on her lips. Malcolm shifted from foot to foot, unusually pale and quiet.

Val had wanted to send Malcolm home, but Melinda Pearl had insisted she bring all her housemates along. No doubt the vampire queen thought of them as a weakness that could be exploited. A chink in Val's armor.

"Godzilla is not far from the truth," Rodrigo said.

Val flinched at the voice of the vampire lieutenant. She didn't like having Rodrigo along, or the hulking shape of Jonathan Gray. But, again, Melinda Pearl had insisted.

If Val were being honest, part of her was grateful for the extra muscle, even if she knew they were really there to keep an eye on her. Despite insisting she was fine, Hillary was still walking tenderly, and Val caught her grimacing in pain more than once. Whatever Pearl had done to her had hurt more than she wanted to admit. Hillary was far from at her best.

Also, Forti had killed the Dragon. He was a literal monster. If she was going to take him on, she needed all the help she could get.

The ritual Melinda Pearl had given her seemed pretty straightforward, but it would take time. While she was casting the spell, Forti would need to be confined to a certain area for the magic to work on him.

That was where the problem lay.

In his new form, Forti was above Val's power level. She would need the vampires to keep him occupied and distracted. Ritual magic required concentration and she would be unable to defend herself while casting the spell.

So Melinda Pearl had sent Rodrigo and Jonathan Gray to help. Val kept sneaking sideways glances at the vampires. She had fought them several times; it felt weird to be standing next to them as allies.

"Necessity makes strange bedfellows," Mister E observed. The demon cat floated in the air on his back, blowing smoke rings at the sky with his candy cigarette.

"But can we trust them?" Val muttered.

"Definitely not."

"So I should get rid of them?"

"No, you're going to need their help."

Val ground her teeth.

"You're infuriating."

The corners of the cat's smile stretched past his face.

"Thank you. I try not to be boring."

Val changed the subject. "Will the ritual Pearl gave us work?"

"How would I know?"

"You're the magical expert around here. Thousands of years old and all that. I thought it was your job to know things like this."

"My job?" Mister E laughed. *"Darling, I'm a cat. We don't have jobs."*

"You know what I mean. Aren't you supposed to be teaching me magic? So teach me something. Will the ritual work or not?"

The cat gave a long-suffering sigh.

"Oh, all right. Since you insist on being pedantic. As far as I can tell, the ritual seems to be genuine. I can't vouch for its effectiveness, but it's definitely a legitimate ritual. I'd say it's got at least a fifty percent chance of working."

Val sighed. "That's better than nothing, I suppose."

"Hey! I found something!" Obi's cry drew everyone's attention. He was crouched in the rubble, digging at the debris.

They all converged on the thief. Val got there first.

"What is it?"

"I'm not sure yet," Obi grunted. "But it definitely wasn't part of the arcade."

"How do you know that?"

"Because." He made a triumphant sound as the thing he was digging at came loose. The kitsune held up an iridescent green thing as large as his palm. "This did not come from a video-game cabinet."

The light glinted on the surface of the thing like oil on water, while also somehow sinking into it, like a tiny pond. Rainbows and glitter sparkled in the depths.

"Is that what I think it is?" Val breathed.

"A dragon scale," Mister E confirmed.

Obi held it out to her, and she took it with reverent hands. The scale was hard, but flexible, almost like sheet metal, though it felt a lot stronger than that. It also contained a strange warmth, like it had been sitting in the sun for hours. Which was impossible, since it was overcast and she'd watched Obi dig it out from under the rubble just now.

"Do you think it belonged to Forti? Or the Dragon?" Obi asked.

Val shook her head. "I don't…"

"It was Forti," Mister E interrupted. *"That's the scale of a young dragon."*

"How do you know that?" Val muttered.

The cat smirked. *"I've picked up a thing or two over the centuries."*

She glared at him, but he simply turned his back and started cleaning his whiskers. Infuriating.

Val looked up to find everyone staring at her.

'Uh. It belongs to Forti," she stammered.

"How do you know that?" Rodrigo asked.

"Because it's the scale of a young dragon."

"Meaning?"

Val gave him the same smirk Mister E had given her.

"Meaning I've picked up a thing or two over the years."

Mister E snorted Val ignored him.

"So what do we do now?" Obi asked.

Val held the dragon scale up to the light. Despite the overcast sky, it flashed and glistened and glowed.

"Now," she said, "I can use this to track him down."

59

The tranquil exterior of San Francisco General Hospital was indifferent to the rushing of the people inside. From her spot crouched behind a car in the parking lot, Val could see into the waiting room through the large front windows. Doctors and nurses rushed about, and nervous patients squirmed in padded chairs. There was no sign of Forti, or anything else out of the ordinary.

"Are you sure this new dragon is here?" Rodrigo asked.

"Yes, I'm sure," Val growled. The tracking spell was one of her most reliable. Forti was here somewhere. It just wasn't obvious where, exactly.

"You would think a dragon would be hard to miss," Obi added unhelpfully.

"You said the Japantown Dragon was in human form. Could Forti do that?" Hillary asked.

"I have no idea. What's the learning curve for a newly made dragon? How long does it take them to figure out how to shape shift?"

"He's figured it out," Obi said.

"How do you know?"

"Because he's right there." The kitsune pointed through the windows of the hospital.

Val followed his gesture and saw Sandro Forti standing in front of an elevator. She cursed as he stepped inside and the metal doors slid closed behind him.

"He's going after Zoe." Val broke into a run.

"Where is she?" Hillary jogged along beside her.

"Fifth floor. Room 532."

"I'll take the stairs," Hillary shot forward, her vampiric speed easily leaving Val behind. Rodrigo and Jonathan Gray went with her.

Val careened through the lobby and slammed her hand on the elevator call button. She, Obi, and Sandra watched the bank of elevators impatiently until one of them dinged. They piled inside.

At the fifth floor, the doors opened onto chaos. Val flinched as the deafening roars of a dragon shook the building. People in hospital gowns and scrubs were screaming and pushing into the elevator. The three of them had to fight their way out as if they were swimming against a subway tide at rush hour.

The noise was coming from her left, the direction of Zoe's room. Val could hear gunshots and see flashes of light and smoke down the hall.

Unfortunately, that was the direction the tide of people was coming from as well. She tried to push through them, but it felt like for every step forward she took, she was forced back another two.

In desperation, she slammed a hurricane-force wind down the hall in front of her, forcing people to cover their faces and duck away from the blast. She picked her way through the cringing people as fast as she could, with Obi and Sandra right on her heels.

When they were ten feet from Zoe's room, Jonathan Gray flew out of the doorway, flung by some incredible force. He hit the opposite wall so hard his torso went through it, leaving his legs protruding awkwardly from the drywall. Curses, growls, and crashes attested to an ongoing battle inside the room.

"Stay behind me." Val gathered her power and spun into the room.

The first thing she noticed was that the exterior wall of the hospital was missing. Where the windows should have been, a massive hole gaped instead. Outside and below, white houses in neat rows marched down toward the bay.

The second thing she saw was the dragon. Forti was impossible to miss, his green reptilian bulk dominating the room. His scales shimmered with a watery depth, just like the one Obi had found in the arcade.

The dragon seemed smaller than he had in the theater when he'd first transformed, and Val guessed he must be able to manipulate his size. Which made sense. Obviously, his human form was much smaller than his dragon one.

Hillary and Rodrigo were fighting him, darting in and out, striking at him like gnats while dodging the heavy blows Forti returned. Unfortunately, their attacks didn't seem to be having much effect.

Scanning the room, Val found Zoe's bed shoved into the far corner, nearly hidden behind Forti's bulk. Zoe lay motionless beneath the twisted blankets, and from Val's angle it was impossible to tell if she was all right.

With a snarl, Val punched a fist of wind at the dragon's eyes, hoping to blind him. To her dismay, he barely flinched. Forti blinked a translucent set of inner eyelids shut over his silver eyes, which protected his eyes but still allowed him to see.

The new dragon turned his baleful gaze on Val and the power behind that glare made her blood run cold. This creature had killed the Japantown Dragon. He could squash her like a bug. His neck snapped out, dagger-sharp teeth flashing toward her.

Val flung herself to the side, but she wasn't fast enough to dodge the strike entirely. The dragon's jaw clipped her, and the force spun her into the wall. Her face met plaster and the world exploded behind her eyes. Her vision went black as she fell. The noise of the fight squeezed down to a distant whisper. The cool tiles of the hospital floor pressed against her cheek.

She lay there for an eternal moment, awake but not, her head thick and stuffed with wool. Eventually, she resurfaced to the sound of immense wings.

As the world came back into focus, she saw that Forti was outside now, moving away from the hospital, his body borne aloft by leathery wings.

"He flies too?" she muttered. "That's not good."

"Are you all right?" Hillary knelt beside her. "How many fingers am I holding up?"

"Don't worry about me," Val pushed the vampire aside and struggled to her feet. "How's Zoe?"

As if no one had thought to ask that question yet, they turned as one toward the bed in the corner. Two steps were enough to tell Val what she would find, but she continued across the rest of the room anyway. She latched onto the side of Zoe's bed as much to keep from falling as anything else.

Zoe lay still beneath the twisted sheets. It was clear she had struggled. A pistol was gripped in her right hand.

It was just as clear that her struggle had been in vain.

The girl's eyes were wide and staring. Her head lay at a frightening angle. Forti had snapped her neck like a twig.

A moaning sound rose and filled the room. It wasn't until Hillary grabbed her that Val realized she was the one making the sound.

"She was just a kid. Zoe didn't deserve this." Her cheeks were wet. Val scrubbed the tears away with the back of her hand and turned toward the door. Her expression was grim. "I have to stop that asshole before he kills anyone else."

60

As they followed Forti's trail across the city, Val felt worse with each passing block. Her head was pounding and her center of gravity kept veering to the side. She was pretty sure the impact with the wall had given her a concussion.

It was hard to stay focused on the tracking spell, but she gritted her teeth and grimly held on to the trail, like a wounded hunting dog that refuses to let go of its quarry.

But worse than that was the cold ball of guilt in her gut.

Zoe Vasilevski was dead. The young heiress had asked for Val's help, and Val had failed to protect her.

She should have stopped Forti in the theater when she had the chance. He had been at his most vulnerable then, right after his transformation. Still coming into his dragon powers. If she had been smarter or faster, none of this would have happened.

Val was so wrapped up in her own misery that it took her a while to realize which part of town Forti's trail was leading toward. And who lived there.

"Padraig," she gasped. "Go faster."

The vampires were carrying the humans on their backs, like some kind of undead older siblings. Rodrigo carried Sandra while Val clung to Hillary's back. Jonathan Gray carried both Malcolm and Obi, one in each arm, like overgrown toddlers. It wasn't the most dignified way to travel, but it was undeniably the fastest. The vampires dashed through the streets with more speed than the Ural had ever had, and Val was grateful for the cold wind that numbed her aching head.

As Padraig's mansion came into view at last, her worst fears were realized. The front doors had been torn from their hinges and now lay in the hedges to either side of the entrance.

"We need to contain him this time," she shouted. "Keep him busy long enough for me to perform the ritual."

Hillary nodded grimly.

They rushed inside, following the roars of the dragon and the sounds of battle.

"At least he's not hard to find," Mister E observed.

"Apparently stealth isn't one of a dragon's talents," Val said.

Padraig's immaculate living room was in shambles. The expensive furniture had been flung aside and smashed against the walls. One of the big windows that showed off Padraig's expansive view of the bay had been smashed, and cold wind whistled in through the shards of glass still clinging to the frame. There was no sign of Padriag, or the dragon. Fiona lay at the end of a long smear of blood across the marble tiled floor.

"Downstairs," the cat shifter hissed as Val knelt beside her. A roar sounded deeper in the mansion. At Val's hesitation, Fiona snarled, "I'll be fine. Go!"

Val nodded and got to her feet. "This way."

She dashed down the stairs, following the sounds into the subterranean maze beneath the house. Like most of the dwellings in this area, the O'Ceallaigh mansion had been built during a time when it was common to have a staff of servants, and the architects had built the grand house with that in mind. A labyrinth of discrete passages honeycombed the bedrock beneath the entire area so that the servants could go about their business and even travel between houses without disturbing their wealthy employers.

Val had discovered these passages on her first visit to Padraig's house, when she had tracked the necromancer, Baron Blood, down to an underground cavern — where he was siphoning years of life into his wealthy patrons, incidentally turning them into vampires in the process. More recently, she'd been down here to fight a duel in Padraig's training room over Pandora's Box.

The sounds of battle led her to neither of those places.

As she dashed through the twisting passageways, smears of blood on the stone walls told her the battle was not going well for someone. She hoped that someone wasn't Padraig.

She rounded a corner and discovered a towering set of green doors. The door handles were made of gold, and matching filagree scrolled along the wood. The doors were massive and heavy — a set of vault doors meant to lock out the world.

Like the front doors of the mansion, the massive doors had been torn open. One of them had a jagged crack running down its length, while the other listed drunkenly on a single hinge.

Inside was what looked like a vast storage cavern. Row upon row of tall shelving units marched away into the gloomy interior. Some of them had been knocked over, spilling their contents across the rough stone floor. Even without the aid of Mister E's sight, some of the items glowed in the dim light.

"The O'Ceallaigh family vault. Where they store their hoard of magical items," Val breathed.

"Padraig must have retreated here, thinking the doors would be enough to keep the dragon out," Hillary added.

"It looks like he was wrong," a new voice said from behind them. They turned to find Melinda Pearl gliding down the passage.

"What are you doing here?" Val snapped.

"I couldn't miss the big showdown, could I?" Pearl purred. "And it's a good thing I didn't. The legendary O'Ceallaigh vault, cracked like an egg. I never thought I'd see the day."

Val stood glaring at her, until Pearl finally made a little shooing motion with her fingers.

"Don't let me hold you up. Go on and do what you came here to do. Pretend I'm not even here."

Val ground her teeth, but a crash and a scream of pain from the interior of the vault told her the vampire queen was right. Padraig needed her.

"Fine," she said. "But make sure you stay out of my way."

Val spun on her heel, clenched her fists, and strode into the O'Ceallaigh vault.

61

The first challenge was navigating the collapsed shelving units. Several of the aisles had been completely blocked, and those that weren't were strewn with magical items. They picked their way carefully around the debris.

"Don't touch anything," Val said. "We don't know what these items do."

"How else are we supposed to find out?" Melinda Pearl asked, brazenly snatching up a golden scepter set with a ring of sapphires. The gems sparkled in the light. "This looks like it should suit me just fine."

Val winced, but nothing happened.

The vampire frowned and shook the scepter a little, then tossed it over her shoulder with a shrug. "It must be a dud."

Val exhaled a breath she didn't know she'd been holding. Picking up unidentified magic items was like playing Russian roulette. Literally anything could happen.

The dragon bellowed as a crash sounded in the depths of the cavern. It was dark back there. The silhouette of a vast bulk was moving. She picked up her pace, jogging in that direction.

She was interrupted by a whoosh of flame behind her, accompanied by a triumphant shriek.

"This one works!"

She whirled to find Hillary holding a long metal staff. Flames shot out the end, and the vampire laughed, spraying fire into the air.

"That's a terrifying sight," Mister E said.

"Yeah," Val said. "I liked the world just fine without vampires having magical flamethrowers."

"I want magic." Jonathan Gray stepped over to a shelf full of knives and picked one up. He swung it experimentally. When nothing happened, he tossed it aside and grabbed another.

Everyone started snatching up random objects.

"That's really not"—Val ducked as a trio of metal discs shot down the aisle—"a good idea."

Melinda Pearl opened a small wooden box, releasing a cloud of translucent butterflies. Rodrigo found a spear that immediately turned into a python and started curling around his torso. Malcolm placed a silver tiara on his head and stood poised, head cocked to the side as if trying to identify a strange taste. His mouth dropped open when his body started to fade into a cloud of mist.

"Hey, kids?" Val felt like she'd suddenly become a kindergarten teacher. "Can we not play with the magic items?"

Even Sandra couldn't resist the temptation, plucking up an oval palette board and paintbrush. She started creating streaks of color that floated and stayed in the air. As Val watched, she sketched a small red bird with sure strokes. The bird left the brush and started singing as it winged away into the darkness.

"OK, that was pretty cool," Val admitted. "But still. Magic is not a toy."

She was saved from having to intervene when a shelf came crashing down across the aisle behind her. Val whirled to find the dragon and Padraig facing each other less than fifty feet away.

Padraig was breathing heavily, his fine clothing singed and torn. Blood soaked the cloth in several places. He held a sword at a defensive angle, the blade gleaming with a pale internal light.

Sandro Forti looked unscathed. The dragon's oily green scales shimmered as his serpentine head rose above the level of the shelves, weaving back and forth hypnotically, wicked fangs gleaming. His silver eyes smoldered.

As Val watched, that head whipped forward like a snake's. Once. Twice. So fast she almost couldn't follow the movement. Padraig slipped away from the first strike, his fae reflexes nearly a match for the serpent's. But he couldn't avoid the second strike, and Forti's teeth snapped shut on his sword arm.

Padraig cried out, and in a blink the dragon had yanked him off his feet. Forti shook Padraig like a dog with a bone. The fae's sword fell from his grip and went clattering across the floor.

"Padraig!" Val rushed forward, though she had no idea what she could do to help. Dragon slaying was not listed under the special skills section of her resume.

She hit the dragon with a howling gust of wind. "Let him go!"

Forti ignored her and continued to shake Padraig. Her friend's cries were growing weak. She had to do something fast.

"Let me help." Hillary stepped up beside her. With a wicked grin, the vampire leveled her new staff. Flames erupted from the end.

The dragon roared as fire engulfed it.

Screams joined the roars as the fire also crackled around Padraig.

62

"**S**top!" Val shoved Hillary, knocking the jet of flame away from the dragon.

Forti's green scales were charred in places, blackened with soot.

But that wasn't the reason Val had shoved the vampire.

Padraig's arm was still locked in the dragon's jaws. His fine clothing was now ablaze, and his screams redoubled as the flames licked his body.

Val needed water or a way to smother the flames. But she didn't have either of those things.

"Pretend he's the world's biggest birthday candle," Mister E suggested.

Val saved her snarky reply and focused. She would only get one shot at this. If she didn't hit Padraig just right, the wind wouldn't extinguish the flames — the air would instead fan the flames to even greater heights.

She summoned all her power and tried to condense it down to a single focal point. She pictured all the howling winds of Twin Peaks funneling through a drainpipe.

With a cry, she released all the stored energy. A torrent of air roared past her, shrieking like all the souls of the damned.

Just before the gust reached Padraig, the dragon flicked his head, tossing his prey away. The fae's body went spinning through the air like a rag doll, tracing a flaming arc across the darkened cavern.

All of Val's effort slammed into the space Padraig had just vacated, missing the flying fae completely.

"Padraig!" She dashed to where his burning body had come to rest.

Malcolm got there first. His insubstantial body settled over Padraig, the flames hissing and spitting as the cool mist came down. A great pillar of steam rose into the air. In seconds, the flames were gone.

"Stop wasting time. Begin the ritual," Melinda Pearl snapped. She had discarded the box of butterflies and now held a long whip. She cracked it in the dragon's direction and bolts of lightning shot from the end.

Val scowled, but the vampire queen had a point. They wouldn't be able to contain the dragon for long. The longer she delayed, the greater the chance someone would die.

"Keep him in the center of the room," Val shouted.

The others spread out, surrounding Forti in a loose circle, clutching the magical objects they'd picked up as if they were lifelines. Melinda Pearl stood poised like a coiled snake. Rodrigo and Jonathan Gray were grim and deadly. Hillary and Sandra looked scared but determined.

Val stood frozen for a long moment, watching them contain the giant lizard. She was used to fighting on the front lines. Facing the danger head on. Leaving others to contain the dragon while she worked in the shadows felt wrong. Cowardly.

"Move, you idiot," Melinda Pearl barked. "We won't be able to keep him here for long."

Val clenched her fists and turned away. The vampire queen was right. She had to let the others face Forti. Her job was elsewhere.

Pulling a piece of chalk from her pocket, Val marked one corner of the pentagram and placed a candle on the ground. Then she scampered off and did it again a couple of aisles over.

Her palms were sweating. This would be the biggest ritual she'd ever attempted. Obviously, she couldn't draw a pentagram within a chalk circle the way she normally would; there were too many obstacles in the way. The best she could do was to create a gigantic pentagram by marking only the points of the star, and trust that the others would keep Forti in the center.

It was dangerous. Without a circle, it would be almost impossible to keep the ritual magic contained. It would be like painting around a window without taping the edges first. She would do her best to keep her magic within the lines, but there was bound to be some spillover, with unpredictable consequences.

She just had to hope that the ritual would still be successful, despite the unorthodox setup.

Val lit the final candle and tried to settle her mind. Taking a deep breath, she began to chant.

63

Hillary felt the staff grow hot in her hands. Her skin was starting to sizzle. Whoever decided that turning a metal staff into a magical flamethrower was a good idea clearly hadn't considered how well metal conducts heat.

On the one hand, she was a vampire, which meant she didn't really feel pain in the same way that regular humans did. So if her hands burned, she could grit her teeth and endure it.

For a little while, at least. Hopefully long enough for Val to complete the ritual and strip Sandro Forti of the dragon's power, transforming him back into a human.

On the other hand, flames and heat were a vampire's Achilles' heel. Everyone knew their skin couldn't stand up to sunlight, but what most people didn't know was that fire was just as bad. Hillary's skin was dry and papery. Under direct flame, it would blaze up like old parchment.

So it was ironic that the magical staff she'd found doubled as a flamethrower. The staff was perhaps the single most dangerous object she could have picked up. If the flames hit her, she'd go up like a Roman candle.

At least Forti seemed to fear the fire as well. The dragon shied away from her blasts, shielding his eyes with one massive wing. He tried to retreat, but Melinda Pearl had found a whip that made lightning, and she cracked bolts out at his other side, making Forti flinch back in Hillary's direction.

The dragon lunged forward, but Jonathan Gray blocked its path. The enormous vampire now held an equally enormous sword. Blue runes shone down its length as he swung it. Forti clearly wanted no piece of that, so the dragon whirled away again.

This time he found himself facing Sandra, and the dragon's toothy mouth curled into a smile. A girl holding a palette and paintbrush was no threat. He lumbered toward her.

Sandra flinched but held her ground. She drew the brush across the air in swift, sure strokes. A flock of tiny birds appeared, sketched so quickly they were little more than abstract suggestions of birds. They darted toward the dragon's face.

The giant lizard didn't even slow down. The birds were no bigger than his toenails. They were nothing to him.

Until, one by one, the birds burst into flame.

"Phoenixes!" Hillary breathed.

Noting Forti's aversion to fire, Sandra had created a flock of tiny phoenixes to oppose him. As Hillary watched, the girl created more birds with every swift stroke of her brush. Five little phoenixes became ten. Ten became twenty.

The dragon roared his frustration and shied away from the burning flock. He whirled toward Hillary again.

She let loose another blast from her flame staff.

"Hey! Be careful with that thing," Melinda Pearl snarled. The vampire queen had to dodge as the spillover from the jet of flame almost hit her as well.

Hillary paused, a wild idea taking shape in her mind. Melinda Pearl was as vulnerable to flames as she was. She held the means in her hands to end the vampire queen's life.

The downside was that, if the stories were true, she would be ending her own life as well. Legend held that if the master vampire was killed, all the vampires they had created died with them.

For herself, she was more than willing to die if it meant taking Melinda Pearl and all the other vampires down with her.

But it wasn't just about her. She hadn't made this cursed bargain for her own benefit. If she died, who would take care of Benji? Yes, she had asked Malcolm to take care of him if anything ever happened to her. But that was more of a last-resort type of arrangement. She couldn't voluntarily drop Benji into Malcolm's lap. Could she?

The thoughts went round and round as she continued to spray flames at the dragon. Forti darted from one side of the circle to the other, his movements growing increasingly desperate. He made a strong effort to break through, charging directly at Jonathan Gray. Hillary and Sandra both moved in that direction, lending the big vampire support until the dragon finally broke off his attack.

Their shifting of positions left another section of the circle undefended, and Forti lunged toward that gap instead.

Melinda Pearl and Rodrigo moved with inhuman speed, putting themselves in front of him. Forti snapped at them with his dagger-sharp teeth, catching Rodrigo and flinging him into the darkness the same way he had flung Padraig earlier.

Hillary cursed. Their defensive formation was growing ragged. Forti was eliminating defenders, and the gaps were growing as the rest of them were forced to shift positions to close them. It was only a matter of time before the dragon broke free.

"Come on, Val," she muttered. "We can't hold him much longer. You've got to do your thing."

64

Val was trying to complete the ritual as quickly as she could. The spell Pearl had given her was an exceptionally complex one, requiring her to chant several long Latin phrases over and over. Latin had never been Val's strong suit and she stumbled over the unfamiliar words, which interrupted the spell and forced her to start over.

"If I'd known you were so bad at Latin, I would have given you more homework," Mister E said as she mangled the chant for a third time.

For once, the demon cat wasn't floating in the air with insufferable calm. He was pacing back and forth, his tail twitching in agitation. Val thought that was a bad sign.

"I guess we know what to work on next week." Val swore and started from the beginning again. The sounds of battle were becoming more frantic. She had to get this right. And she had to do it now.

"Focus. Don't worry about reading the entire scroll. Simply take the words one at a time."

"Easy for you to say." She grumbled but tried to follow his advice, focusing on only the word in front of her, instead of worrying about the entire text of the ritual.

To her surprise, it helped. Grappling with one weird Latin word was a lot easier than attempting to tackle a whole scroll full of them. So she simply worried about pronouncing each word on the scroll individually, one at a time. Then she moved on and repeated the action with the next word. And the word after that.

Halfway down the scroll, she could feel the magic building. The sounds of battle grew distant. Her hands started to tingle. The ritual became her whole world as magic filled her like a sponge.

She allowed her eyes to stray down the scroll. Only a few lines left. The ritual was almost complete.

Then a dark shape flew through the air, crashing into Val and sending her sprawling. The chant was broken, the power evaporating in an instant.

"What the…" Val shook her head in the darkness.

Somebody groaned beside her. She turned her head to find Obi on the ground next to her.

"Sorry, Val," he whispered. "I got a little too close to the dragon. Forti flung me like a frisbee."

"Are you all right?"

"I've been better," he sat up slowly, poking at his ribs with his fingertips. "But I don't think anything's broken."

"Nothing but the spell I was casting." She sighed and got back to her feet, smoothing the crumpled scroll. She glared at the Latin. "Now I've got to read this whole thing all over again."

Obi winced. "Sorry. Anything I can do to help?"

A roar sounded, followed by a crash as the dragon flung someone else into a shelving unit. Forti's silver eyes focused on Val as he started to move in her direction.

"Yes. You can keep that dragon away from me," she snapped. "I have to get through this chant uninterrupted or the spell won't work."

Obi turned wide eyes toward the dragon bearing down on them. Hillary flanked it, trying to get its attention with her flaming staff. The dragon ignored her efforts, intent on reaching Val.

Obi swallowed. "I'll do what I can."

He got to his feet, clutching a short sword that had fallen from the shelf beside him. In a blink, he was gone.

"What the?" Val wondered.

"*Kitsune magic,*" Mister E informed her. "*I think he has a limited form of teleportation.*"

True to the demon cat's prediction, Obi appeared right behind the dragon's head. The short sword flashed, slicing into the back of the monster's neck. The dragon roared and whipped its head around, sharp teeth snapping at the boy. But Obi was already gone, blinking away to appear behind the dragon's back leg, slashing at the tendons. The dragon's scales were too thick for the sword to do any real damage, but the thin line it drew must have been painful, because the dragon whirled, snapping again at the annoying thief.

Val let out a sigh of relief. Obi had done his job. The dragon had forgotten about her for the moment.

"Now I just have to read all of this Latin," she groaned. "Again."

"*Take it one word at a time,*" Mister E reminded her.

Val sighed and started the spell over.

65

Obi dove and rolled, barely avoiding the dragon's snapping jaws. He gulped. Those teeth were long and sharp. If the beast got ahold of him, he'd become shredded thief in no time flat.

Still, he was glad to see that he'd gotten Forti's attention. That was his job. Annoy the beast and get it to focus on him. Give Val time to complete the ritual that would strip away Forti's power.

Part one accomplished. Which, he had to admit, wasn't all that difficult for him. He'd always had a talent for getting under people's skin. He'd been born to annoy dragons.

As he blinked away from the dragon's swiping tail, reappearing on Forti's other side, he knew that part two would be more challenging. Getting the dragon's attention was one thing. Keeping its attention long enough for Val to complete her spell — without getting mauled — would be a lot more difficult.

The sound of boiling air was his only warning as a wash of flame came rushing at his back. He blinked away again, narrowly avoiding the fire shooting from the end Hillary's staff.

He cursed.

That was one of the problems with popping around like a jack-in-the-box. Sure, the dragon didn't know where he would appear next, but neither did his allies. If he happened to appear in front of them at the instant they were shooting flames at the dragon, for example, he'd be barbecued in short order.

Still, their motley crew seemed to be doing all right. They were keeping the dragon busy, and no one had been killed or seriously injured yet. That was a definite win in Obi's book.

Off to the side, he could hear Val chanting her spell. A glance in that direction showed him that she was starting to glow with power. Definitely a good sign.

His next dodge was a beat slow, and the dragon's claw ripped through his shirt, tracing a line of fire along his ribs. He blinked away, cursing, pressing his hand to his side. His fingers came away wet with blood.

"Less thinking, more dodging, Obi," he told himself. "Don't forget rule number one: No Dying."

Hillary's hands were on fire. She'd been shooting flames through the metal staff nonstop, and the metal glowed a fiery orange. The pain was excruciating. She could smell her skin sizzling. Every instinct she had was screaming at her to drop the burning staff.

She hung on and grimly fired another blast of flame. The dragon bellowed with pain and rage.

Across the circle from her, Sandra was painting wave after wave of tiny phoenixes. Melinda Pearl shot lightning bolts while the other vampires darted in and out, slashing at the dragon with their speed and strength.

Though sometimes even vampire speed wasn't enough.

Forti's jaws snapped forward, closing on Jonathan Gray like a steel trap. The big vampire screamed as long sharp teeth pierced his chest.

Hillary winced. Even being undead, that had to hurt.

Out of the corner of her eye, she saw Val growing brighter as her spell neared completion.

Come on Val, she silently urged, *we need you to take this asshole out.*

Val struggled to contain the tide of power as it swelled higher and higher. The ritual magic had her bursting at the seams. This wasn't her normal gather-and-instantly-release type of magic. This was a slow, methodical cultivation of power. Each word of the chant stacked on itself, building layer upon layer until the entire spell formed a grand construction.

Val groaned. She felt like an overripe sausage. The power was too much. One more drop and she would burst.

She intoned the last three words on the scroll.

The entire world paused.

She could see everything in the room in exquisite detail. Every scale on the dragon's hide. Every flicker of the candles' flames. Every drop of blood on the stone.

Then power burst from her in a rush.

The wave of magic extinguishing every candle as it went. The flames from Hillary and Sandra's magic items went out.

Val collapsed as the entire room was plunged into darkness.

66

For a moment, there was no light. No movement. No sound.

Then Melinda Pearl's laughter filled the air. The vampire queen lit up like a star, illuminating them all with a sinister red light.

Forti had collapsed to the floor of the cavern, surrounded by his tormentors. He'd reverted to his human form and now lay pale, naked and still. To Val's magic-sensitive eyes, he looked inert. Not even a glimmer of power shone through his skin. The ritual had worked. It had stripped him of his stolen power.

"But I don't think it worked the way it was meant to," Val muttered.

"It worked exactly the way it was meant to," Melinda Pearl countered. In contrast to the drained form of Forti, Val's sight showed the vampire queen bursting with magical energy.

"You lied to me," Val snarled. "The ritual didn't just strip Forti of his power. It transferred the power to you."

"Yes, it did." Pearl smiled, her fangs gleaming long and white. "Forti was very useful, killing all those heads of families for me. Especially that troublesome Dragon. Now I only need to remove one more, and this city will be mine."

She turned a predatory gaze to where Padraig lay unconscious and bleeding.

"Over my dead body." The room swam around Val as she pushed herself to her feet.

She felt like she had been wrung out and pounded flat. She could barely stand. She was pretty sure she couldn't do magic if her life depended on it.

Still, she had to try.

She had let herself be duped by the vampire queen. This was all her fault.

Val clenched her teeth and reached deep, summoning all the power she could find. She gathered her magic and hurled it at the vampire queen, falling to one knee with the effort.

The breeze she summoned barely tousled Melinda Pearl's hair.

"Fret not. Your turn is coming." The vampire queen backhanded Val with a casual motion that hit like a bag of bricks.

Val sprawled, her cheek slamming into cold stone. Her ears rang. Spots swam before her eyes.

Melinda Pearl turned her attention to Padraig.

Hillary watched Sandro Forti's power flow into Melinda Pearl. The vampire queen swelled with it, puffing up like a balloon.

Despair filled her as Pearl swept Val aside like a paper doll, leaving the witch crumpled upon the floor.

The vampire queen had won. After she killed Padraig O'Ceallaigh, there would be no one left who could stand against her. Melinda Pearl would rule the city with her bloodless fist.

Hillary couldn't let that happen. If she did, there would be nowhere she could run. Nowhere that would be beyond the vampire queen's reach. Nowhere Benji would be safe.

She knew what she had to do. Her life didn't matter. She had squandered her days, then sold her soul for more time and squandered that too.

She didn't care what happened to her. She'd been tired of living for a long time now.

She'd miss Benji. And Malcolm. Her heart ached at the thought of leaving them behind.

But they'd be better off without her.

If she could take Melinda Pearl down with her, the entire world would be better off.

She couldn't give herself time to think about it. If she did, she'd chicken out. Just like she had the last time she'd died. The day she'd sold her soul to Melinda Pearl.

She had to act now.

Hillary turned her staff on the vampire queen of San Francisco. A jet of flame roared from the end.

Melinda Pearl screamed.

Pearl might have stolen Forti's magic, but she hadn't stolen the dragon's hide. She was still a vampire, and her skin was paper thin. Vulnerable to sunlight and fire.

Pearl's screams rose as a pillar of hungry flame engulfed her. Rodrigo and Jonathan Gray started to scream too. The vampires writhed as if they, too, were burning up.

Hillary joined in the chorus. It felt like she was being cooked from the inside out. Her internal organs were white-hot coals. Her blood was molten lava.

But she kept the end of her staff trained on Melinda Pearl and grimly continued to pour on more fire.

Her skin started to crack and char. Her flesh withered and collapsed, like fruit left in the sun. The room dimmed as the life was cooked from her body.

The pain was indescribable, but still she held on to the staff. Still poured fire from its end.

By the time the metal shaft finally fell from Hillary's nerveless fingers and rolled slowly across the floor, there was nothing left of Melinda Pearl but charcoal.

But Hillary didn't hear the sound of the metal on stone. Her eyes weren't there to see it. They stared sightless at the ceiling. All that was left of Hillary was a dried-out husk.

67

Despite the pain in her head, Val struggled to where Hillary lay. Her roommate wasn't moving. Her skin had sunk over her bones and now clung to them in stark relief, as if every scrap of fat and muscle had melted away. As if someone had left her drying in the sun for weeks.

"No," Val whispered.

She cradled Hillary's body in her hands. Her bones were as light and hollow as a bird's.

"Why did you do that? You didn't have to do that."

Sandra's hand fell on her shoulder, and it wasn't until Val turned and saw herself in the gorgon's mirrored sunglasses that she realized she was crying. Tears ran down Sandra's cheeks as well, carving little wet tracks before dripping off the end of her chin.

Obi stood awkwardly to one side. Val caught his eye.

"I guess that's one way to take down a dragon," she said.

The thief nodded. "A dragon and a city full of vampires at once. That's pretty badass."

Val smiled sadly. "Yeah. Hillary was pretty badass."

"No. She can't be dead," Malcolm flung himself onto Hillary's body, sobs wracking his frame.

Val's heart constricted. Malcolm and Hillary had been close. Her loss would hit him especially hard.

"This can't happen. I won't let it."

Before Val could stop him, Malcolm slashed a long knife across his wrist. Blood gushed from the wound. He pressed it to Hillary's desiccated lips.

"Malcolm, that won't bring her back." Val stepped toward him, but Sandra stopped her.

"Let him try," Sandra said softly. "He needs to try."

Val tensed. Her first instinct was to argue.

Then she sighed and nodded. She understood. Malcolm had loved Hillary. He'd never forgive himself if he didn't do everything he could to save her. Even if his efforts were in vain, she had to let him try. He deserved that much.

Val got Padraig upstairs and into bed. Fiona helped clean him up, then brought them tea. The cat shifter walked with a slight limp, but otherwise seemed completely healed from her run-in with the dragon. Val tried to help with the tea, but Fiona just hissed at her.

"We cats are proud and independent," Mister E told her.

Val rolled her eyes. "Tell me something I don't know."

She helped Padraig sit up, stacking pillows behind him to make him comfortable. His face was paler than usual and he moved like an old man, but she thought he would be fine. He just needed rest. He had fae blood, after all, and fae were very hard to kill.

"Don't think this makes us even, Valora Keri," he said weakly. "You still owe me."

She eyed him curiously.

"I owe you? Does that mean we can be friends again?"

He scowled.

"Don't push your luck. This may balance the scales a bit, but it doesn't erase all the harm you've done. We aren't friends." His hazel eyes held hers for a moment, considering. Finally, he grunted. "We can be cordial, though. You've earned that courtesy. Just see to it that you don't come around too often. It's better if we stay out of each other's hair."

Val nodded.

"Yeah, OK. Cordial it is."

68

The first thing Hillary knew was blood. Warm, life-giving blood. It flowed down her throat and spread into her veins, bringing life back to her thirsty limbs

She sucked at it greedily, overwhelmed by a hunger as vast as the sky. Her body was a husk on the verge of the final death. It would take a lot of blood to bring it back.

Dimly, she became aware of voices. Hands pulling at her body. She ignored them. Only one thing mattered. Blood. More blood.

After what felt like a long time, her mind finally resurfaced. She had downed enough blood to become a thinking being once again. More than just blind starving-animal hunger.

She was still weak. Lucky to be alive, really. It would take several feedings to overcome such profound injuries.

But at least she knew who she was again. Now she just had to figure out where she was and try to remember how she got here.

Hillary opened her eyes. She lay on a cold stone floor. A dark cavern arched high above her. Someone's wrist was clamped tight between her fangs. A body lay slumped on top of her.

Malcolm.

She released his wrist in horror.

Sandra, who Hillary hadn't noticed until now, pulled his body away from her. The girl was saying something, but her words were no more than a jumble of noise in Hillary's ears.

Her focus was on Malcolm. Pale and limp. He wasn't breathing.

It only took a second for her to realize what had happened. Malcolm had given her his blood to save her. And she, in her mindless hunger, had drained him dry. She had killed him.

There was only one thing she could do.

Sandra tried to fight her, to keep her away from his body, but Hillary flung the girl aside as if she weighed nothing. There was no time to waste.

She slit her wrist with a sharp nail and pressed it to Malcolm's open mouth.

For long seconds, nothing happened. Ice gripped her heart. She was too late. She'd taken too much from him. He'd been dead for too long.

Then she felt his lips move against her flesh. He started to drink.

She let him drink for a few seconds, then forcibly pulled her wrist from his mouth. It only took a little blood to begin the transformation, and she was too weak to spare any more.

Malcom mewed like a hungry kitten, but he didn't have the strength to fight her. He curled forward like a newborn. Which he was, in a way, his eyes still tightly shut. It would take time for the transformation to change him. Time before he gained his vampire strength.

"What did you do?" Sandra was back, standing beside her, mouth hanging open in shock.

"The only thing I could," Hillary replied. "To save his life, I had to turn him into a vampire."

Red tears ran down her cheeks as she stroked Malcolm's face.

"I'm sorry," she whispered.

69

Val sipped her butterscotch latte and breathed in the scent of fresh baked bread. She leaned her head back against the wall and sighed. It was good to be home. Even if home was a bit… rustic at the moment.

The living room was a burned-out shell. The shattered bay windows had been boarded up. The carpet had all been torn out, leaving scorched hardwood in its place. The couch, coffee table, and recliner were gone. They had all been consumed by the fire.

Val, Hillary, and Sandra were sitting on throw pillows on the floor. Sandra had brought a couple of boxes up from the basement to function as makeshift tables.

"This is all very bohemian," Hillary said.

Val shrugged. "I've lived in worse. I spent a lot of time on the streets and sleeping in squats growing up. At least this is private."

"Me too," Sandra said. "Even all burned up, this is still cleaner than that punk-rock squat I was living in after Val kicked me out of the apartment."

"Yeah, that place was gross." Val winced. "There was mold growing on the walls. Sorry about that."

"It's water under the bridge. If there's one thing life has taught me, it's how to be adaptable. I certainly never expected to end up having snakes for hair."

"At least you're still breathing." Malcolm swept into the room carrying a plate of fresh sliced bread. "I've had 'Bela Lugosi's Dead' playing on repeat in my head all day. If I don't find another song soon, I may have to kill myself all over again."

Val watched her roommate carefully. Malcolm was doing what he did best — putting on a brave face. Hiding behind wise cracks and sarcasm.

But Val saw through his facade. Behind the smile, Malcolm was terrified.

Of course he was. Hillary had nearly killed him; then, in order to save him, she'd turned him into a vampire. Fortunately, he was in good company. Everyone in the room knew what it felt like to be a monster.

"You're a saint, Malcolm." Val took a slice of the still-steaming bread. "Don't worry. I've got your back."

"Someone better have it. It'd be a crime to let an ass this good go to waste." Malcolm turned around and wiggled his hips at her. His ass was indeed firm and round inside his tight red pants.

Val tried not to choke on the bite of bread she'd just taken as she laughed. Malcolm was deflecting, but she'd seen the flash of gratitude in his eyes and knew her message had been received. He was family, and nothing was going to change that. Not even him becoming a bloodsucker.

"I still can't figure out how it worked," Hillary said. "I should have died when Melinda Pearl did. Vampires aren't supposed to outlive their masters."

"You were saved by the strongest force known to the universe: The power of friendship," Malcolm said.

Hillary snorted. "I suppose you're going to say that's what allowed me to save you too? You know, a power of friendship that turns you into a vampire is pretty fucked up."

"Friendships don't have to be perfect to be powerful," Malcolm retorted. "In fact, I think it's the flaws that give the best ones their power. Anyone can be a friend when things are perfect. It takes a true friend to embrace you fangs and all."

"Have you had any problems finding people to ... um ... feed off of?" Sandra asked.

"Are you kidding me? Did you not just see my ass? The boys are lining up to let me suck on their necks," Malcolm replied. "Though it's a good thing I can still eat regular food. If I had to give up baking bread, immortality would not be worth it."

"So, is Hillary going to stay now?" Sandra asked.

Everyone looked at Val. She scowled.

"I kicked Hillary out for endangering Malcolm's life with her reckless feeding behavior. My concerns turned out to be valid, and now Malcolm is a vampire. This is supposed to get Hillary off the hook?"

"Well, my life isn't in danger anymore," Malcolm pointed out.

"Because you're dead," Val shot back.

"Undead, technically," he said, before singing, *"Undead undead undead."*

"That doesn't make it any better."

"It kind of does," Sandra said. "You're always saying we need to love ourselves no matter what we look like on the outside."

"That doesn't sound like something I would say," Val grumbled.

"Malcolm has a different kind of life now, and he's going to need a lot of support as he goes through this difficult transition period," Sandra insisted. "Hillary is the only one of us who really knows what he's going through, which means she's the only one who can give him the support he needs. Also, Melinda Pearl is dead and her coven is dead with her, so the other vampires won't be hunting her anymore. It should be safe to let Hillary stay here now."

Val sighed. Sandra made sense. But that didn't mean she had to like it.

"Fine. Hillary can stay. But only because rent is due in a week and we don't have time to find another roommate before then."

Malcolm and Sandra cheered.

Hillary looked relieved. "Thank you, Val. I really appreciate it."

"Speaking of rent, Val," Malcolm smoothly changed the subject, "Did you get paid for stopping Forti?"

"Paid by who? Zoe Vasilevski is dead." Val grimaced.

"Valid point. That does throw a wrench in the works."

"Any word on when the Alley Cat might open back up?" Hillary asked.

"I don't think it's going to." Val sighed. "Tommy Walker took the insurance money and skipped town. So it looks like I'll need to find another job."

Hillary shuddered. "In this economy? Good luck."

"Yeah."

They all sat sipping their coffee for a few minutes, unpleasant economic realities sucking all the air out of the room.

Finally, Malcolm cleared his throat.

"I've got an idea. Why don't you become a detective?"

"A detective?" Val snorted. "Don't you have to have some kind of training for that? I don't know how to solve mysteries."

"I disagree," Hillary said. "You've been doing a pretty good job of it so far."

"Did you miss the part where my last client ended up dead?" Val asked.

"That's true, but you still solved the case and stopped Sandro Forti."

"Just like you did with Ruby and Stephen's killers," Malcolm said.

"And don't forget about the Puca and the Harbinger of Winter," Sandra added.

"Woah, slow down, everyone." Val held her hands out in front of her. "I did those things because my friends were hurt or in danger. Because those monsters needed to be stopped. Not for money."

"What's the difference?" Malcolm asked. "There will be more monsters that need to be stopped. We all know you're going to try to stop them regardless. I think you should get paid for the service."

"Val Keri, P.I.," Sandra said.

"Val Keri, Witch for Hire," Hillary mused.

"Val Keri, Monster Hunter." Malcom grinned.

Val grimaced again. "Give me some time to think about it, OK?"

"*Don't think too long.*" Mister E floated on his back near the ceiling. "*Your bank account won't make it through another month.*"

"Don't you start, too," she grumbled.

They were interrupted by a knock at the door. They all looked at each other.

"Is anyone expecting a visitor?" Malcom asked.

No one was. He cautiously pulled open the door.

"Can I help you?"

A familiar voice came through the open door.

"I need to speak to Val Keri."

"Rosa?" Val called out. "Is that you?"

"Val." Rosa pushed past Malcolm into the living room.

"Rosa, what's wrong?" Val was taken aback by the change in her friend's appearance. Her hair was tangled and there were dark circles under her eyes. She looked gaunt and pale, the skin of her face drawn taut against her cheekbones.

"Val, you have to help me. Something terrible is about to happen."

Mister E smirked at Val. "*If that's not a sign, I don't know what is.*"

She shot him a glare but didn't bother arguing. She sat Rosa on a cushion and Malcolm put a mug of hot coffee in her hands.

"OK," Val said. "I'll help you. Start from the beginning. I need you to tell me everything."

<<<<>>>>

Thank you so much for reading Jade Secrets. I hope you enjoyed reading it as much as I enjoyed writing it.

Before you go, please take a moment to leave a review. Even just some stars or a few words can make a huge difference in helping other readers discover the world of The Keri Chronicles.

Thank you very much.

Yours,
A.C. Arquin

P.S. I'll see you in the next Keri Chronicles Adventure: BLACK RAIN.
Coming Soon!

GET YOUR FREE STORY!

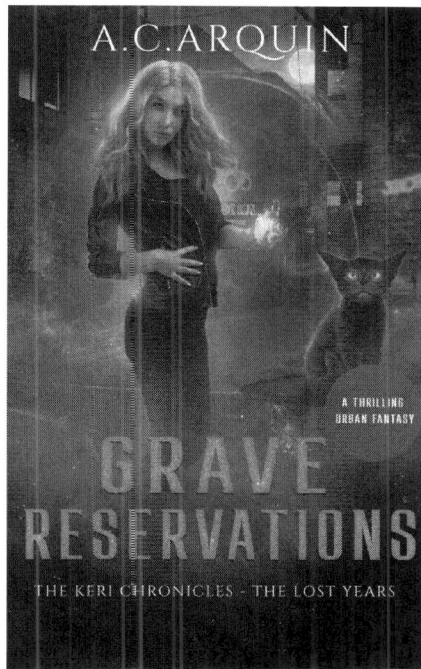

ABOUT THE AUTHOR

A.C. Arquin lives in his own worlds. At least, that's what his teachers always told him when they caught him reading a book in class instead of paying attention to the lesson.

Now all grown up, he still prefers realms of imagination to reality. The only difference is that nowadays, he writes down his adventures and shares them with the world.

When not writing, he is also a very busy audiobook narrator, under the name J.S. Arquin.

He is hard at work on the next book in The Keri Chronicles.

Get a FREE KERI CHRONICLES PREQUEL STORY as well, as all the latest news and deals, by joining his Reader's Group at www.arquinworlds.com/

f 𝕏 ⓘ

BOOKS BY A.C. ARQUIN

THE KERI CHRONICLES

Dead Wrong

Pale Midnight

Twilight Storm

Jade Secrets

Black Rain - Coming Soon!

Grave Reservations (Val Keri, The Lost Years)

THE CRIMSON DUST CYCLE (A Dystopian Space Adventure. Published as J.S. Arquin)

Ascent (Book 1)

Slide (Book 2)

Peak (Book 3)

Twist (A Crimson Dust Prequel)

The Crimson Dust Cycle Box Set

OTHER BOOKS

The Itch (A Stand-Alone Gaslamp Fantasy Thriller)